W. J. Burley is a Cornishman born and bred, going back five generations. He started life as an engineer, and later went to Balliol to read zoology as a mature student. On leaving Oxford he went into teaching and, until his recent retirement was senior biology master in a large mixed grammar school in Newquay. He created Inspector (now Chief Superintendent) Wycliffe in 1966 and has featured him in Cornish detective novels ever since.

D1144041

Also by W. J. Burley

WYCLIFFE AND THE SCHOOLGIRLS
WYCLIFFE AND THE SCAPEGOAT
WYCLIFFE AND THE PEA-GREEN BOAT
WYCLIFFE AND THE BEALES

and published by Corgi Books

WYCLIFFE AND THE FOUR JACKS

W. J. Burley

CORGI BOOKS

WYCLIFFE AND THE FOUR JACKS

A CORGI BOOK   0 552 13231 4

Originally published in Great Britain by Victor Gollancz Ltd.

PRINTING HISTORY

Victor Gollancz edition published 1985
Corgi edition published 1988

This book is set in 10/11pt Mallard.

Corgi Books are published by Transworld Publishers Ltd.,
61-63 Uxbridge Road, Ealing, London W5 5SA, in Australia by
Transworld Publishers (Australia) Pty. Ltd., 15-23 Helles
Avenue, Moorebank, NSW 2170, and in New Zealand by Transworld
Publishers (N.Z.) Ltd., Cnr. Moselle and Waipareira Avenues,
Henderson, Auckland.

Reproduced, printed and bound in Great Britain by
Hazell Watson & Viney Limited
Member of BPCC plc
Aylesbury Bucks

People who know Roseland will recognize the places described, and they may be irritated by inaccuracies in the topography. These are deliberate in order to reduce any risk, through an accidental resemblance, that a real person might be identified with one of the characters in this book – all of whom are imaginary.

W. J. B.

CHAPTER ONE

Thursday June 16th

As usual Cleeve was in his library study by nine-thirty. He stood by the window gazing out over his own garden and the clustered rooftops of the village below, across the creek to the headland where a line of pine trees descended with the profile of the promontory in a perfect curve, almost to the fringe of white water and the sea. Grey slate roofs, the glittering surface of the creek, rising green fields, and the arc of the pines against a misty-blue windy sky. Rain in the offing.

Seven or eight years ago, when he first came to live at Roscrowgy, there had been twenty pines, now there were thirteen; gales and old age had taken an erratic toll. It was absurd, but each morning he counted them in a ritual act, not that he needed to, for any fresh gap would have been immediately obvious.

June 16th; on June 16th, 28 years ago . . .

He heard his secretary moving about in the next room; in a few minutes she would bring in his mail and then he would know.

He watched a fly, a large grey fly with a chequered pattern on its abdomen, crawling up the window pane; it reached the top without finding a way out and went back to the bottom again. He watched while the performance was repeated twice more, then he opened the window and let the creature out, to be whisked away on the wind. As a small boy he had often sought to appease a hostile fate by such little acts of grace.

There was a tap at the door and Milli came in with the mail. She had opened and vetted most of it – everything from his publishers and his agent, everything addressed to him as Peter Stride; she was not permitted to open his Cleeve mail.

He did not turn round, determined to be casual, ordinary.

'Good morning, Mr Cleeve.' Milli bright and brittle.

He said, 'Good morning!' with just the right degree of preoccupation.

Milli was small, with black hair and dusky skin; lithe and agile as a monkey; he sometimes thought she might be capable of all 30 classical positions, but not with him; athletic sex was diversion for the young.

'Anything in the post?'

'Nothing I can't deal with.'

'Then take it away. I want to get on with the *Setebos* revision, so Milli – no telephone.' She was already moving to the door having left the Cleeve mail on his desk. Normally he would have added something facetious. 'Tell 'em I'm suffering from premenstrual tension.'

It seemed all right but at the door she looked back and he fancied she had sensed his unease; not that it mattered.

Childlike, he counted to a hundred before he would allow himself to look at the few items of mail on his desk: four buff-coloured envelopes, probably bills; two white ones with typewritten superscriptions and a third, addressed in bold, well-formed capitals. That was it! He held the envelope for a time without opening it. When he did, he drew out a single playing card – the Jack of Diamonds. Along the top margin of the card someone had written: Thursday June 16th and the number four.

He sat at his desk and with a key from his pocket unlocked the bottom left-hand drawer. It was here that he kept his automatic pistol, the current volume of his journal, and certain lists which might be of use to his executors. There was also a cardboard box which had once held a hundred cigarettes. From the box he removed three envelopes similar to the one he had just received. From each of the envelopes he extracted a playing card, three Jacks of Diamonds identical with the fourth he now had, but each carrying a different date and number. He arranged them on his desk, from left to right: Saturday September 4th – 1, Tuesday March 8th – 2, Friday May 13th – 3, and Thursday June 16th – 4.

He stared at the cards for some time, then with a grimace gathered them up. He put them back in their envelopes and returned the envelopes to the box and the drawer.

Still seated at his desk he reached for the fat wad of typescript which was *Setebos*, picked up a ballpoint and set to work. He had thought the opening chapter good, now it had the impact of a wet sponge, but he persevered, making deletions and insertions, knowing they would come out again in a later revision.

Writers come in all shapes and sizes but Cleeve was a surprise to the few people who penetrated his privacy. They found it hard to accept that David Cleeve, who looked and sometimes spoke like a prosperous farmer, must be reconciled with Peter Stride, the sophisticated creator of the terrifying Manipulators in *Xanadu* and the sadistic Preceptors in *Medicus*. A generous build, an open countenance, a fresh schoolboy complexion and guileless blue eyes – these, with an exuberant moustache, sandy hair and freckles, must surely mean innocence and simplicity of soul.

The room darkened as clouds crept up the sky and the first flurry of raindrops spattered against the window. At eleven o' clock Milli came in with a cup of black coffee and when she had gone he laced it with whisky.

He existed in two worlds; in this comfortable room

with his books and the paraphernalia of his work about him; defined, secure and purposeful; and in that other world of more than a quarter of a century ago through which he had prowled like some feral young animal. That world was no longer real, even his memories of it were vague, like the recollections of a dream, yet it acquired fresh substance through those four cards.

He drank his coffee and when it was gone he went to the drinks cupboard again and poured himself a whisky. He took it to the window and stood there, looking out. A vestige of sunlight silvered the edge of the blue-black clouds and miniature white horses reared on the dark water of the creek, sending the sailing dinghies scurrying for shelter like a flock of frightened geese. During the next hour or so he made other visits to the drinks cupboard and between times sat at his desk brooding over the typescript.

Patricia would diagnose one of his Occasionals – her word for episodes which occurred without warning and at longish intervals, but always with the same scenario. He would start drinking in the morning, contrive some sort of scene over lunch, then continue drinking through the afternoon. In the evening he would go to sleep in a small bedroom near his study and stay there until morning.

The buzzer sounded for lunch and he got to his feet; he was not yet drunk, for his step was firm. In the corridor outside his study he paused by the open door of his secretary's office where she was working, oblivious.

'Milli!' A bellow.

She looked up, startled and annoyed.

'Lunch!'

Roscrowgy sprawled across the flank of a hill, two storeys at each end, single-storeyed between, built on split levels and accommodating to vagaries of contour like a Tibetan monastery. Cleeve had his working suite of rooms on the upper floor at one end, while the dining and reception rooms were at the other. He went down an oak staircase and along the length of a broad passage which had occasional steps both up and down; the floors were of polished wood with Afghan rugs, and the white walls were relieved by a series of large uniform pictures of a Graham Sutherland genre. Patricia's taste; it reminded him of a well-endowed nunnery and he was accustomed to refer to the pictures as Stations of the Cross.

'Bloody hell!' An inarticulate protest.

The dining-room continued the monastic theme; oak floor with rugs, white walls, furniture in natural beech. The table was laid for five but the room was empty. He went to the sideboard and poured himself a whisky.

His wife came in silently and he did not see her at once. Cleeve might have been mistaken for a farmer but there was no mistaking Patricia Cleeve for a farmer's wife. She was a Tull of the Oxfordshire Tulls and God had thoughtfully endowed her with features admirably suited to half-tone reproduction in *The Tatler*. Patricia was forty-three, nine years younger than her husband; an English rose, not yet faded; a blonde, with a pink and white complexion, but with large limpid eyes whose steady gaze could unsettle the most hardened conscience.

Cleeve saw his wife and turned away, but not before she had recognized the symptoms.

Carrie Byrne wheeled in a trolley of food; bowls of salad and other vegetables and a platter of sliced chicken-breast. Carrie, a Tull cousin of thirty-eight, occupied an ambivalent position in the household; somewhere between a member of the family and a housekeeper. In colouring, personality and opinions Carrie was neutral, a congenital 'don't know'. In Cleeve's words, 'Clay which had waited too long for the potter.'

11

They took their places at table; Milli joined them with a muttered apology. Patricia said, 'There's chilled fruit juice if anybody wants it.'

Cleeve mumbled unintelligibly. It was a relief to take refuge in the established routine of an Occasional. No one would question it. 'Are we not to have the twins' company at lunch?' Ponderously aggressive.

'I told you. Andrew is at the School of Mines today. Some vacation work he has to do for his course at the university. Christine is changing; she came back wet from the dig.'

Cleeve looked out of the window at the rain sweeping in from the sea. 'What does she want to spend her time up there for? Surely at her age she's got better things to do.'

Nobody spoke. Plates and bowls passed from hand to hand. With an imperious gesture Cleeve refused the salad but speared several large slices of chicken breast with his fork. Seated at the head of the table he munched the chicken with pieces of bread roll, scattering crumbs and eyeing the three women with sullen aggression. The syndrome was complete.

Christine came in; a slim girl of nineteen with her mother's looks and her father's colouring. She wore skin-tight jeans and a denim shirt; the bloom was intact. She sat in her place, glanced at her father, then at her mother – questioning; her mother answered with the faintest shrug.

At the age of three Christine had dubbed her father 'daddy bear', and it had never been improved upon. It spanned the whole repertoire of his moods, from playful, affectionate whimsicality to the aggressive unpredictability of his Occasionals.

They ate in silence; when it seemed that someone might speak the tension rose, only to subside again when nothing happened. It was Patricia who finally took the plunge: 'How is the dig going, Christie?'

Christie responded with self-conscious enthusiasm.

'Oh, very well. Of course, we spent most of this morning in the shed sorting out pottery sherds; there was nothing we could do outside, but Gervaise says that with any luck we should finish excavating the third hut by Tuesday or Wednesday. Of course, it all depends on the weather. . .'

Christine was a lively, kindly girl with boundless enthusiasm, searching for a cause; the present candidate was archaeology and she had given up her vacation to an Iron-Age dig in Henry's Field, a site adjoining Roscrowgy. The enemy was philistinism in the shape of developers, farmers, tourist boards and planners of every ilk.

Cleeve made a sound which could only be described as a deep growl and turned to Carrie Byrne. 'Did you hear that, Carrie? I don't suppose you've been up to the dig this morning?'

Carrie, realizing that she was to be the focus of today's scene, seemed to shrink into her thin frame like a snail into its shell. She said, 'No, David, I've been doing the shopping.'

'Pity!' He mimicked his daughter's enthusiasm with grotesque cruelty: ' "Gervaise says that with any luck we shall finish excavating the third hut by Tuesday or Wednesday." Think of that now, Carrie! Of course it all depends on the weather.' After a pause he said, 'Gervaise . . .! Bloody pouf!'

Christie flushed but she said nothing. Cleeve glared round the table as though challenging a response and when none came he went on: 'Who cares about the sodding huts anyway? Or the squalid little savages who lived in 'em? If it hadn't been for their screwing we wouldn't be here now and the world would be a better place.'

Patricia turned her steady, disquieting gaze on her husband. 'You are being quite disgusting, David.'

'Me?' He feigned surprise. 'Oh, I forgot! We don't screw in the Shires, we "make love" or we "have sex".'

13

Patricia said nothing but she persisted in her gaze until he lowered his eyes. The meal continued in silence; only Milli seemed quite unaffected by the exchanges; she behaved as though the others did not exist.

When there was no more chicken on the platter Cleeve got to his feet, pushing back his chair so that the legs scraped over the floor.

'Aren't you staying for dessert?'

He glared at his wife and turned away without a word. For an instant he seemed to stagger, but recovered his balance and walked to the door which he left open behind him. They listened to his footsteps down the corridor.

Carrie got up and closed the door. 'David isn't himself today.' Carrie had an unchallenged mastery of the banal. Before sitting down again she went to the kitchen and returned with a bowl of fruit.

They helped themselves except for Christie; she got up from her chair: 'If you will excuse me . . .'

'Aren't you having any, Christie? You mustn't let father upset you like that.'

The girl was near to tears. 'It's so unfair. I mean, it's his land; he gave permission for the dig and he's even paying for it. It doesn't make sense!'

Patricia looked uneasily at Milli, but she was busy dissecting an orange. 'You must know your father's moods by now, darling; he'll be up there as usual tomorrow, telling you all what a good job you're doing.'

'Will he!' Christie went out and her mother watched her go.

'Don't get up again, Carrie; I'll make the coffee.'

While Patricia was in the kitchen the telephone rang; there was a phone in the short passage between kitchen and dining-room and she answered it there.

'Roscrowgy, Mrs Cleeve speaking.'

A man's voice: 'It's me. . . . Is it all right to talk?'

14

'I suppose so; what is it?' She had lowered her voice, so that she would not be overheard in the dining-room.

'I must talk to you, can you come down?'

'If I must.' She was in no mood for her brother's problems.

'It really is important, Tricia.'

'It usually is; I'll be there in about an hour.'

'Can't you make it sooner? I'm really worried.'

'All right, I'll come as soon as I can.'

'Thanks, darling! I know you think—'

'I'll be there as soon as I can, Geoffrey.' And she replaced the receiver. She finished preparing the coffee tray and carried it into the dining-room. 'Where's Milli?'

Carrie said, 'She's gone back to work; she didn't want any coffee. Was that Geoffrey?'

Patricia nodded. 'He's really upset. Of course, it's money. I'm going down there. If anybody asks, I'm taking Biddy for a run.'

A few minutes later Patricia, followed by her English setter, walked down the drive and through the white gates. The rain had eased to a fine mist blown landward by the wind. The estuary and the bay beyond were a waste of grey waters under a grey sky; only the tower of the little lighthouse, like a stumpy candle, stood out white in the gloom. June in Cornwall; but tomorrow, or the next day, or the next, could be gloriously fine.

Down the steep hill, past expensive villas, hidden in their own grounds, to the fringes of the old village. Mount Zion Chapel, then Mount Zion Steps, leading down to the waterfront and the harbour – really a steep, narrow, cobbled street with steps at intervals to ease the slope. Several of the little granite cottages had been tarted up and three or four had been turned into shops.

Patricia made her way down the Steps among tourists,

15

disconsolate in the rain. They turned to look at her and her dog, an unselfconsciously elegant pair. Near the bottom of the Steps a shop with a bow window exhibited a neat sign, gold-on-green: 'Geoffrey Tull, Herbalist and Naturopath.'

There was a 'closed' sign on the door, but Patricia tapped on the glass and a man in his middle thirties came to open it. Geoffrey was fair and good-looking, a blond moustache glistened in the light. But his features were too soft and he was slightly overweight. He wore a green silk shirt and fawn trousers.

Patricia angrily evaded a kiss. 'Don't be so foolish, Geoffrey!'

He was immediately contrite. 'Sorry, darling! But bless you for coming. I would have phoned before but I wanted to make sure that secretary of David's wasn't listening-in at the other end.'

Patricia snapped. 'You know perfectly well that the house phone is a separate line.'

Inside, the shop was laid out like a small Edwardian pharmacy with gilded glass jars on the shelves and a battery of little polished wooden drawers behind the counter, each labelled with its white-enamelled plaque: *Arctium lappa, Laurus nobilis, Spiraea ulmaria* . . .

'Come through to the back where we can talk.'

Biddy settled complacently on the doormat.

The back room was a laboratory-cum-kitchen where the herbal decoctions, extracts and tinctures were prepared.

They sat on stools. 'Now, what is this about?'

He put on an absurdly guilty look, like a small boy confessing to naughtiness. 'It's about money, Tricia, dear.'

'So I imagined.'

'But this is worse than anything . . . Connors from the bank rang this morning and asked me to come and see him.'

'Well?'

'He's stopping my cheques unless I can find a guarantor or pay off my overdraft.'

'You must have seen this coming.'

Geoffrey squirmed. 'Actually, Tricia, I didn't. The money has been coming in pretty well lately; business is brisk, and I just didn't do my sums.'

Patricia sighed. 'Will you never learn?' She shifted impatiently on her stool. 'What exactly are you asking me to do? I'm not made of money, Geoffrey: I only have what David gives me and he likes to have some idea where it goes.'

Saturday July 16th
In a rented cottage on the waterfront Wycliffe stood at the window and looked across to that same headland and those same pine trees which Cleeve contemplated ritually each morning. Only the narrow road to the castle and the low sea wall separated the cottage from the water. In the creek, sailing dinghies formed a fixed pattern on the surface of an unrippled sea. A boy in a rowing-boat, oars shipped, trailed a fishing line; children idled in the shallows. There was a raft moored off-shore for swimmers and on it a girl in a bikini stood motionless. It seemed to Wycliffe that the scene had been frozen in an instant of time, as though a ciné-film had suddenly cut to a single frame. Then, into this static world, came a bustling ferry boat, pushing a moustache of white water ahead of blue bows; another cargo of trippers from Falmouth, and more to come. They would spill out on to the quay and spread through the village spending their money in the shops and cafés, helping to sustain the inhabitants through the long close season.

The Wycliffes had arrived that morning for a fortnight's holiday walking in the Roseland peninsula. It was no more than 50 miles from home, and part of his police territory, yet they had never explored the area, never visited the places with those evocative names

17

which sprinkled the map: St Just, St Mawes, St Anthony, St Gerrans, Percuil. . .

They had lunched at a wine bar a few doors away; crab salad with a carafe of white wine. Since then Helen had made up their bed in the little upstairs room which had a timbered ceiling and a latticed window. It was beginning to feel like a holiday.

Helen was taking off her apron. 'I thought we could look round the village this afternoon – perhaps go over the castle, then tomorrow we could start our real walking. . .'

They joined the drifting movement of visitors and trippers along the waterfront in the direction of the quay. There were shops and pubs, toytown banks with original opening hours, and some elegant little houses that had metamorphosed from fishermen's cottages. Most of them had their pots of geraniums, begonias or mesembryanthemums outside.

The beach was a strip of grey shingle. White and pink flesh was exposed there within the limits of decency; there were no deckchairs, no life-guards (only a leaden soldier could drown there) no radios – in fact, no anything but the rather grubby-looking shingle and the well-mannered sea.

The shops seemed unexciting, at least resistible, but Helen dawdled and Wycliffe said, 'I'll wait for you by the harbour.'

He rejoined the meandering groups; all ages and both sexes clad in shorts, T-shirts and bikinis, sometimes with startling effect. Alone among them an elderly man made his dignified way, immaculate in a pale-grey suit and a white straw hat; he carried two library books; a relic. To Wycliffe he seemed like a gentle dinosaur loose among baboons.

Arrived at the harbour, Wycliffe lit his pipe and rested his arms on the sea wall to watch three youngsters – two girls and a boy, putting off in a tiny drop-keel sailing boat. Orange lifejackets and blue shorts.

He had been brought up on Arthur Ransome long before he had even seen the sea. Did these children lead story-book lives? After 30 years in the police he was still looking for the kinds of people he had read about as a child. The man in the white straw hat, these children . . .

Helen joined him and they continued their walk but almost at once she was diverted again.

'Look!'

A narrow cobbled street, little more than an alley, rose steeply away from the waterfront, the knobbly spine of the old village. A blue-and-white-enamelled sign read: Mount Zion Steps – and there were steps at intervals to ease the slope and a tubular iron handrail to assist the weary. The granite-fronted houses were stacked against each other like steps themselves; one had a 'Police' sign over the front door. There were a few shops, rather twee: a herbalist's with a bow-fronted window, a vegetarian restaurant all varnished pine ('We must eat there sometime'). Further up a shop sold silver brooches and buckles of Celtic design, and next to that was a photographer's which looked as though it had been left behind by the 'twenties.

Helen was attracted by the brooches displayed on simple velvet cushions in the little window of the jewellery shop; they were oddly interspersed with books bearing esoteric titles: *Earth Magic, Leys and Power Centres, The Psi Connection* . . . There was also a hand-written poster headed, 'The Celtic Society of Roseland' and announcing, 'There is still time to halt the desecration of Henry's Field! Details inside.'

The shop was so small that they had just room to stand between the counter and the door. Jewellery was displayed in the glass-topped counter-case, and on shelves behind the counter were more books of pseudo-science for the lunatic fringe.

A woman came from somewhere at the back: middle forties, big-boned, strong features, with blonde, shoulder-length hair, a striking woman. She wore an emerald-green frock that was almost a gown, a silver torque round her neck and silver bangles on her arms which were bare to the elbows. Theatrical but effective.

Her manner was crisp. 'As you see, the showcase is divided into three: hallmarked silver pieces to authentic Celtic designs on your right; modern enamel-on-copper pieces in the middle; and a selection of similar enamel-on-silver designs to your left.'

She stood, monumentally immobile, an operatic princess awaiting her cue. Helen asked to see a particular tray of the Celtic designs and it was lifted out on to the counter without a word.

Helen pointed to a brooch of intricate pattern, 'I think this one is very beautiful, don't you, Charles?'

The princess volunteered, 'That is late-Irish – the triskele design is based on an eighth-century medallion in the National Museum, Dublin.'

A Siamese cat came from somewhere and leapt on to the counter, examining the customers with green-eyed suspicion. Wycliffe reached out to stroke it.

'I shouldn't touch her! She can be quite aggressive with strangers.'

Helen, concentrating on the brooches, said, 'Do you make these lovely things yourself?'

'I do.'

They bought the brooch and while it was being packed in its box with a certificate of provenance Wycliffe said, 'What's this about Henry's Field?'

The blue eyes sized him up. 'Henry's Field is on the hill above the village. With the Stone Field next to it, it is one of the sacred places of the Celtic people and the ground should never be broken or ploughed. It is situated at the convergence of ley-lines from early Celtic settlement sites over the whole Roseland peninsula and is a centre of power.'

'So, what are they doing with it, building council houses?'

She suspected him of levity and became more severe. 'If you are genuinely interested you should read the Society's leaflet.' She handed over a couple of pages of duplicated typescript, clipped together. 'You will see that after remaining undisturbed for close on two thousand years the site is now being excavated by archaeologists who should know better.'

They escaped. Outside, with her brooch, Helen said, 'It cost a lot of money, Charles.'

'Never mind, call it an unbirthday present.'

At the top of the Steps they were brought face to face with the non-conformist Gothic of Mount Zion Chapel; they had reached the boundary of the old village. Further up the hill, nineteen-twentyish villas peeped out from behind their thickets of laurel and bamboo, escallonia and hebe, and there was a larger building which looked like an hotel. A black-on-yellow AA sign pointed still further up the hill: *To the Excavations.*

Wycliffe said, 'This must be what Boadicea was talking about; shall we take a look?'

The hill was steep and the sun was hot but the climb was short and, looking back, they could see the creek, the Fal estuary, and the bay spread out like a sixteenth-century map, with Henry VIII's two castles facing each other across the narrows, and the lighthouse at the bottom of its grassy promontory, its feet almost in the water. A container ship in ballast, putting out from the harbour, churned up a foamy wake.

They passed an estate with Roscrowgy on the white drive-gate, and immediately beyond there was open land covered with gorse and heather. At a considerable distance from the road they could see, well spread out, a large wooden shed, two bell-tents which looked like army surplus from the Boer war, and a caravan. Another AA sign directed them down a narrow, stony lane and brought them to the shed. Over a large area, where gorse and heather had been cleared, the ground was

21

marked out with surveying poles and ribbons and a number of young people, minimally clad, were working in trenches.

A notice on the shed read: 'Henry's Field Iron-Age Site. Visitors welcome. Please report here.' Field archaeologists are usually polite, probably because they are territorial intruders.

The wooden hut was part office, part museum and part laboratory, all in a space less than 20 feet square. A pretty, auburn-haired girl was scrubbing something in a sink and a minute or two went by before she became aware of the Wycliffes and came over, wiping her reddened hands on a towel.

'My name is Christine. If you know anything about archaeology please say so; there's no point in me nattering on about things you know already.'

They were shown aerial photographs of the site before excavation began.

'These were taken in winter when the vegetation had died down. You see the outlines of the hut-circles? They seem to be cut off abruptly at the Roscrowgy boundary, that's because the settlement extended into what is now part of the garden of the house . . . We'll look at the actual dig first, then we'll come back here and you can see some of our finds. . .'

They followed her out of the hut to where the work was going on and she dutifully kept up the flow of information. 'Henry's Field is most likely a corruption of an old Cornish name for the place, *Henros* – *hen* means old and *rōs* means heath . . . the field bit has been added. This is the hut numbered "one" in the photograph—'

'Mr Wycliffe! A surprise to see you here!' Gervaise Prout, whom Wycliffe had met in connection with security arrangements for a touring exhibition of archaeological goodies from the Far East. A man in his early fifties, with a mass of white curly hair, a long thin face with a healthy outdoor tan and slightly

22

protruding teeth. His voice was high-pitched and there were occasional disconcerting ascents into actual falsetto.

The girl looked disappointed at losing her audience and Prout apologized handsomely: 'I really am sorry, Christie, but Mr Wycliffe and I are already acquainted.'

This disposed of, he turned to Helen and greeted her with nervous cordiality. 'A pleasure, Mrs Wycliffe! I hope you and your husband will allow me to show you round.'

So they were shown round the site by Prout instead of the girl. 'Actually it's a very promising dig. Plenty of "B" pottery as we expected, but I'm fairly sure some of the fragments are from the "A" period which would put us in the same league with Bodrifty . . .'

They had reached the highest point of the field where they were able to overlook the house and part of the garden next door.

Helen said, 'How extraordinary! It's like a ranch house – who lives there?'

'Don't you know?' Prout seemed surprised. 'That's Roscrowgy – David Cleeve's place. He owns this field and the Stone Field next to it. As a matter of fact he's our patron. He put up most of the money for this dig.'

Wycliffe asked, 'Should we know him?'

Prout laughed. 'Perhaps not as Cleeve but you will have heard of Peter Stride. You must have seen his books in the shops even if you haven't read them. I must confess, I'm no addict.'

But Helen was, with a row of Stride's fat masterpieces on her shelves. She was impressed. 'You mean he lives there? Is he there now?'

Prout seemed pleased to display his intimacy with a celebrity. He glanced at his watch. 'Half-past three. You may see him while you are here. He often takes a stroll round the site about this time. Incidentally, Christine, the auburn-haired girl who brought you over, is his daughter. Charming girl!'

23

Wycliffe had read Stride's books and seen three or four of them serialized on TV, though with less enthusiasm than Helen. The man had a remarkable ability to create an atmosphere of brooding dread, a chilling awareness of violence.

Wycliffe said, 'I gather you've had some opposition to your dig.'

A short laugh. 'Madam Laura and her ley-lines! There's an old superstition about this having been an ancient Celtic burial ground for the whole Roseland peninsula, so anyone who disturbs the dead et cetera et cetera . . . It seems that the tale got a fresh lease of life some years back when the previous owner of Roscrowgy took part of Henry's Field into his garden and was dead within the year. Nobody mentions that the poor man was a cardiac case.' Prout made a dismissive gesture. 'In any case this has never been a burial place nor was it a sacred enclosure. It is an ordinary settlement site which seems to have enjoyed an unusually long period of occupation, making it more interesting than most.'

They completed their tour and Prout led them back to the wooden hut. He pushed open the door and they were confronted by two men in earnest conversation; one was large and pleasant-looking with a luxuriant reddish moustache. There was something expansively Edwardian about him and he carried a polished cherry-wood stick with a silver mount that was almost a staff. The other was very tall, of a skeletal leanness, with a completely bald head; he was terribly disfigured down the left side of his head, face and neck, as if by burns.

Prout, for no obvious reason, was clearly displeased by the encounter, but with contrived affability he performed the introductions – 'Mr and Mrs Wycliffe, Mr David Cleeve, of whom you have heard, and Mr Kitson, a neighbour who takes a great interest in our work here.'

A mild surprise for Wycliffe to discover that the amiable-looking one with the reddish moustache was Cleeve.

A shaking of hands and murmured exchanges without meaning. Kitson immediately excused himself and left. Wycliffe noticed that the disablement extended down the whole left side of his body, for he limped badly and held the arm on that side at a curious angle.

Cleeve had been formally polite, then his manner changed to sudden interest: 'Wycliffe? Not Superintendent Wycliffe?'

'I'm afraid so.'

Cleeve laughed. 'This is my lucky day! I've always wanted to meet a real live detective. I cut my literary teeth on what French call *le roman policier* and criminal investigation fascinates me still.'

Hard to believe that this pleasant man, apparently anxious to be agreeable, was the author of a dozen books which were not only money spinners but considered worthy of detailed study and analysis by literary critics and psychologists, so that there was already a considerable literature on the Stride phenomenon.

They chatted easily for a few minutes then Helen said, 'You live in a beautiful place, Mr Cleeve, and you seem to have a delightful garden.'

'Are you interested in gardening – either of you?'

Wycliffe said dryly, 'Helen is, and I'm learning.'

Cleeve chuckled. 'I sympathize; it's the same with us. Patricia – my wife – is the gardener but I have to sort of caddy for her and make the right noises.' He broke off abruptly. 'Why don't you come over while you are here and let Patricia take you round? She never misses a chance to show off her garden.'

They displayed a proper reluctance, but allowed themselves to be persuaded. They were shepherded across the field, through a wicket gate into the garden of the house, and along a mossy path through a rhododendron tunnel which brought them to a door at one end of the long, rambling building.

Cleeve pushed open the door and they were in a garden room with a blue-and-white-tiled floor, ornamental white tables and chairs with striped cushions. Almost the whole of one wall was open to a courtyard garden where there was an ornamental pool and a fountain with Berniniesque figures.

'I'll find Patricia – do make yourselves at home. What can I get you to drink?'

They refused drinks.

'Later perhaps,' Cleeve said.

Helen whispered, 'What a charming man! But not a bit like I expected; he's so *ordinary*.'

Cleeve came back with his wife, a slimly elegant blonde. She wore a cornflower-blue frock which fitted without a crease and made Helen feel uncomfortable in her M & S slacks and blouse. But Patricia Cleeve was cordial in her welcome.

'David is quite right; I love showing off my garden but I get little opportunity. Most of our visitors are only interested in publication schedules, copyrights and royalties. But really a garden is not much fun unless friends come to look at it – don't you agree, Mrs Wycliffe?'

It seemed obvious that the two women would hit it off.

'Shall we start here in the courtyard?'

Cleeve said, 'I'm going to be selfish and cut the garden routine, if I may. I want to show Charles my workshop.'

A fairly smooth operation, but Wycliffe was in no doubt that it was one, and had been from the first moment of their meeting.

Cleeve took him along a corridor, elegant but severe, with disquieting pictures and institutional undertones, up a flight of stairs to a landing with doors opening off. Wycliffe could see into one room, a business-like office where a girl was sorting pages of typescript. Cleeve's own room was next door; large and L-shaped, a combination of office and library with creature comforts catered for, but it was in total contrast with what he had seen of the rest of the house: Edwardian; thick red Wilton on the floor, heavy mahogany bookcases, straight-backed leather armchairs and a huge desk with an inset leather top.

'Sit you down. You'll find my chairs comfortable. If a soldier marches on his stomach a writer writes on his backside, so I've made a study of chairs. You can lounge in one of these or you can sit at a desk – both in comfort; and you can push it around on its castors. I abominate those articulated swivel things which remind me of the dentist's. Darwin wrote his *Origin* sitting in one like this so that gives me a chance.'

He opened a drinks cupboard. 'What will you have? Whisky is my tipple.'

'A small one then – no water.'

Cleeve brought over the drinks; half a tumbler for Wycliffe.

They prepared to engage. Wycliffe said, 'This is good whisky.'

'Whiskey with an "e" – it's Irish. My publisher has a house in Kerry. I've no idea where he got this but, knowing him, I wouldn't be surprised if it was moonshine out of a Kerry bog.' Cleeve was watching Wycliffe, trying to gauge his responses, but Wycliffe was at his most bland, wearing what Helen called his 'well-meaning-vicar look'.

'Have you read any of my books?' The question came with a disarming grin.

'All of them, I think.'

'And?'

A thoughtful pause. 'I think they are extremely well written and compelling. Does that sound patronizing?'

'If it does, I asked for it. So you don't like my books, but do you take them seriously?'

Wycliffe drank some more whiskey with an "e": it

really was very good – smoother than the scotch to which he was accustomed. 'I take them very seriously.'

'But in official jargon you probably feel they tend to corrupt and deprave; is that it?'

'No, it isn't!' Wycliffe was short. 'Your books depress me because you write about a world without hope. God is dead; heaven is empty. I'm simple enough to hope and believe that there must be some chink of light in the darkness somewhere.'

Cleeve laughed. 'I've said already, this is my lucky day. Drink up! The prophet of doom and gloom! One critic called me Bunyan without a pilgrim.' He became serious again and looked at Wycliffe quizzically. 'A non-conformist background? Liberal-cum-Fabian Socialist? Don't be offended; it's no good if we waste time being polite. Have I got it right?'

'Just about.'

A satisfied smile. 'I'm out of the same stable. Totally backslid, I tell myself, but it sticks like shit to the proverbial blanket. It left Arnold Bennett too inhibited to indulge the one vice he really fancied – screwing nubile girls under pink lampshades. I must say it's never got me that way – stopped me, I mean.'

Wycliffe pursued his theme in self-defence. 'Even your "good" characters seem doomed through circumstance to add to the evil in the world—'

Cleeve cut in sharply. 'And that worries you? Don't you think it worries me? But I write about the world as it is – at least as I see it; a world with no sense of guilt because it has lost its sense of sin. After thirty years in the police you must surely go some of the way with that.'

Wycliffe smiled. 'I will admit I sometimes wonder if our generation was the last to be burdened with a sense of guilt. I don't think it follows that people no longer distinguish right from wrong or that the future is wholly black.' He emptied his glass. 'Anyway, now that the courtesies have been exchanged and the ice broken, perhaps you will tell me why I am here.'

Cleeve's face was like water which takes on the changing moods of the sky; the blue eyes and the fresh, open countenance could darken in an instant. They did so now.

'I do want something from you; something I'd be very unlikely to get from the nearest cop-shop – advice without strings. Your profession is one of those where it's very difficult to bypass the GP and get to the consultant direct.'

'Except by kidnapping the consultant.'

A brief smile. 'The fact is, my life is threatened. I know that sounds dramatic but I'm satisfied that it is the case.'

Wycliffe waited.

'The threats have come through the post – four so far, extending over a period of about nine months.' Cleeve's nervousness showed; he fingered his rather ragged moustache and looked at Wycliffe with obvious anxiety.

'Have you any idea who is threatening you?'

A momentary hesitation. 'None.'

'Is it David Cleeve or Peter Stride who is threatened?'

A quick, appreciative glance. 'Oh, Cleeve. Because of the kind of books I write all sorts of cranks send abusive and threatening letters addressed to Stride. I take no notice of them.'

The casement window was open and voices came from the garden below. Patricia Cleeve's, rather high-pitched but musical; Helen's softer, her words inaudible. Wycliffe felt irritated; they were on holiday and they had come, casually, to look at an archaeological dig, now they seemed trapped in other people's lives. He made an effort.

'So the threats are personal and you take them seriously. In that case I think you must have some idea why you are threatened.'

Cleeve picked up the whisky bottle. 'Let me top you

29

up!' Wycliffe refused and Cleeve replenished his own glass. 'I've told you I don't know who is threatening me.'

'May I see these threats – I suppose they take the form of letters or cards?'

'I destroyed them.'

Wycliffe was patient. 'You say you received the first one about nine months ago; when did you get the last?'

A frown. 'About a month ago. It indicated that time was running out.' He grinned self-consciously. 'Sounds like something out of Agatha Christie, doesn't it? "The end is near." '

'Is that what it said?'

'Of course not, but that is what it amounted to.'

It was obvious he was lying; at least suppressing most of the truth.

'Did these communications have postmarks?'

'Oh yes – all over the place – one was from London, another from Durham and the last was posted in Exeter. I think the third one came from Bristol – something like that anyway.'

Wycliffe took refuge in the official manner and sounded pompous. 'Mr Cleeve, if you want help from the police you will have to be more open with me. Originally you said that you wanted my advice – it's this: whatever the circumstances, if you think you are in danger, you must be completely frank. Without more to go on it isn't possible for me to tie up for your protection men needed elsewhere.'

Cleeve said quietly, 'I am not asking for protection; I don't want it.'

'What, then?'

He leaned forward across the desk and spoke with great seriousness. 'I want to be sure that if anything happens to me – if these threats are carried out – my family will not be plagued by the police. You understand?'

'I'm not sure that I do.'

Cleeve sighed. 'It's not easy to explain; that is why I'm talking to you instead of some cloth-eared detective sergeant in the nearest nick. If a man in my position is murdered the police will dig into his private life and find God knows what reasons for suspecting his relatives and close associates – money, jealousy, sex . . . I don't have to tell you what the family of a murdered man has to go through if there is any mystery about the crime.' A twisted little smile. 'I don't have to tell you either what may come out when the lid is lifted off that Pandora's box which we call family life.'

'You are saying that if you are murdered the police should look for suspects outside the circle of your family and friends.'

'Exactly! I would rather they didn't look at all, it wouldn't do me any good, but that would be too much to hope for. I've thought of putting this in writing and attaching it to my will or something of the sort, but when you turned up out of the blue it seemed too good a chance to miss.'

He was smiling, a nervous, tentative smile. 'I'm trouble enough to my family alive; I don't want to haunt them when I'm dead.'

Wycliffe was brusque. 'There is very little I can say to you, Mr Cleeve. Your obvious course is to allow the police to investigate the threats to your life and prevent them being carried out. If you decide to do this or if you have any more to tell me, you can get in touch at any time. I advise you to think it over.'

Cleeve nodded. 'The official line; I couldn't expect anything else but I've said my say and you will remember it if anything happens.' He got up from his chair. 'Now, let's see how the women are getting on.'

Wycliffe felt uneasy; even guilty, but what more could he do? His irritation increased. Why couldn't he and Helen have a holiday like anybody else?

They ate coq au vin with a green salad and drank a bottle of over-age Beaujolais in a restaurant close to the harbour. The other diners were mostly unisex boating buffs in blue jerseys and carefully bleached jeans with expensive labels on their bottoms. They wore canvas shoes and talked a cryptic jargon incomprehensible to the uninitiated. The meal was second-rate, but for the buffs it was the chance to talk that mattered. Wycliffe seemed preoccupied.

Over coffee Helen said, 'What exactly did David Cleeve say to you? You've been broody ever since we left them.'

Wycliffe looked around at the other diners, babbling away for dear life and none of them listening. It depressed him. A character in one of Cleeve's books had been made to say: 'Once people were individuals; they struggled; at least with the illusion that they might change things; now, unresisting, resigned, they're swept along by a great wave which must soon break.'

For Wycliffe, that was the real trouble with Cleeve's books, they focused the mind with the unrelenting intensity of a burning glass.

He muttered, 'I'll tell you later.'

When they left the restaurant the sunset was glowing red over the castle, and overhead the sky was pale blue-green. The air was silky and people were sitting out at tables in front of the pubs, feeling just a little awed by the vast stillness of it all. The trippers had gone home, there was no traffic, and the waters of the harbour mirrored the moored craft. Herring gulls, nicely spaced on the sea wall, meditated on eternity.

'Well?'

'He thinks his life is in danger.'

'You mean someone wants to kill him?'

'That's what he says. Someone is threatening him; he doesn't know who or why. Of course he's lying.'

'You mean he isn't being threatened?'

'I mean that if he is, he knows where the threats are coming from and why.'

'What are you going to do?'

He snapped, 'What can I do?' Then quietly, 'Sorry!

But unless he is prepared to give me the facts I can't spend police time on him; he doesn't even want it. Did you get any impression of the family from his wife?'

Helen considered; always careful about making judgements of other people, she made a dull gossip. 'She seems a very pleasant woman, fond of her children and interested in what they do.'

'And her husband?'

Longer consideration. 'I had the impression that she looks upon him not so much as a man and a husband, rather as a kind of monument or institution to be preserved.'

'Not much affection between them?'

'I don't know. People can become very attached to monuments and institutions even when they are something of a liability.'

Back at the cottage he lit his pipe and stood in the doorway, watching the dusk take possession of the creek, the hill opposite, the pine trees and the bay. Finally he turned away. 'I'll sleep on it.'

CHAPTER TWO

Sunday July 17th
They agreed to split up for the morning. Helen would walk along the coast path to St Just then on to Philleigh in time for a snack lunch at the pub and Wycliffe would join her there with the car.

'I want to find out what the local sergeant knows about the Cleeves.'

Sunday, a day like any other; there would be the same tourists, and even more trippers, the same parade along the waterfront, the same sailing and wind-surfing (given some wind) but it would all take a little longer to get started. Sunday is a sluggish day, as though God, unable to preserve His day of rest, has nevertheless applied the brakes.

As Wycliffe climbed Zion Steps to the house which was home and office for the police sergeant, the single bell of the village church called to worshippers with a blatant and monotonous insistence. In the chapel they were already singing. 'There is a land of pure delight . . .' Let's hope so.

Sergeant Pearce answered the door in his shirt sleeves, a grey-headed old warrior with his years of service recorded on his countenance like notches on the stock of a gun.

'Just a courtesy call,' Wycliffe said.

'I heard on the grape-vine that you were with us, sir.'

Wycliffe took him out for a drink and Pearce introduced him to a bar at the back of The Buckingham Arms.

'Non-emmet,' Pearce said. (The word emmet derives from the Old English for ant and is the Cornish vernacular for a summer visitor.)

The Buckingham presents a brash face to the waterfront but keeps a little bar at the back for locals.

Pearce explained: 'The emmet who strays in here soon begins to feel like a pork butcher in a synagogue – unless, of course, he's somebody's guest.'

They drank lukewarm beer, sitting on hard seats, but without space invaders, fruit machines or juke boxes, and with plenty of privacy. The bar had just opened and they were the only customers.

'They'll get busy later.'

Wycliffe mentioned the Cleeves.

'We hardly ever see Cleeve himself but his wife and daughter do a bit of sailing and they're members of the club. Mrs Cleeve seems a nice woman. Then there's a son – the children are twins – he's about quite a lot in the vacations. He's got a rebuilt MG which is the envy of all the young blood in the village.'

Pearce got out his tobacco pouch. 'I hear you're a pipe smoker – try some of this, sir. I grow it and cure it myself but it's not at all bad.'

They filled their pipes and smoked peaceably. Wycliffe found the tobacco pleasant; mild and sweetish to the tongue. Rum and molasses.

'Going back to Mrs Cleeve, she's got a brother in the village, a chap called Tull – Geoffrey Tull – he runs a herbalist's shop further down the Steps; you may have noticed it. He calls himself a naturopath, whatever that is. He seems to have a good business but I fancy he spends faster than he gets and I've heard that his sister has had to bail him out of trouble more than once.'

Wycliffe diverted the flow. 'I gather Cleeve isn't too popular with some people over these excavations.'

Pearce chuckled. 'The Roseland Celtic Society. Chairperson, Mrs Laura Wynn – she's got a shop on the

Steps too – jewellery, near the top. She's a strange one. If she was ever married I don't know what happened to her husband but it wouldn't surprise me if she'd eaten him.'

'Is the feeling over the dig very strong?'

Pearce scratched his cheek with the stem of his pipe. 'I doubt if the real Roselanders care a cuss either way, but some of the newcomers want a bit of colour in their lives and they've decided to revive what they call the Celtic tradition.'

'What do they do?'

Pearce was intrigued by Wycliffe's interest but he asked no questions. He took a swallow of beer and wiped his lips. 'Until this excavation lark started, not much that I could see. They have a bonfire on the Stone Field twice a year – Mayday eve and Hallowe'en, and I believe they go up there sometimes at sunrise to dance round in their nightshirts in a yoghurt-induced frenzy, pretending to be druids or something.' Pearce spoke with a vast tolerance of human vagaries bred of a lifetime in the force. 'I got to admit I was never up there to see.'

'And since the excavations started?'

'Ah! Officially I don't know anything about that as nobody made any complaint, but I understand they went up there two or three times in the early stages and pulled up all their markers – that sort of thing. It seems they've stopped that caper now and decided to play it legal; they're getting up a petition and talking about an injunction, though I can't think who'd put up the money for any court case.'

'I don't suppose it bothers Cleeve too much.'

'You wouldn't think so, but about the same time as they began talking about the dig in Henry's Field, Cleeve employed a firm of private inquiry agents to investigate Laura Wynn.'

'How do you know that?'

'A complaint from the lady herself about a strange

man asking her questions and talking about her to her neighbours. I made a few enquiries, asked around a bit, and it turned out to be Charlie Cox who used to be a DC at sub-division and now works for Sowest Security Services. Over a jar Charlie told me his agency had been briefed by Cleeve.'

'To do what?'

'To find out who the woman was and where she came from – that was all.'

Wycliffe looked at the empty glasses. 'Shall we have another?'

'No, sir; thank you. Not for me; I've had my ration for a morning session.'

'Me too; I'd like to get back to your office and use the telephone.'

In a neat little office, looking out over Zion Steps, where even the rubber stamp knew its place, Wycliffe telephoned his headquarters.

'Who's on duty in CID?'

'DS Watson, sir, but Chief Inspector Scales is in his office as it happens.'

'Good! Put me through, please.'

He talked to his deputy, John Scales. The usual smokescreen of words which takes the place of the sniffing ritual in lower animals, then: 'I want you to set going a few enquiries, John. Have you heard of Peter Stride?'

'Who hasn't? But he's not a favourite of mine at the moment. Jane has an American girl over here doing a PhD thesis on *The Man and his Work*. (Jane Scales was a lecturer at the university.) She can't get near him. Just a note from his secretary: "Mr Stride thanks you for your interest but he does not give interviews, neither does he furnish details of his private life. He prefers to be judged on his published work alone." '

'He may have a good reason for that! Anyway, I want you to find out what you can about him through the usual channels. You probably know already that his real name is Cleeve – David Cleeve; he's a little older than me, married to Patricia née Tull – an Oxfordshire family. She's several years younger. They have twin children, boy and girl, aged about nineteen . . . They've lived here for several years . . . No, I don't mind if he gets wind of our interest . . . As far as I know he hasn't done anything except tell me a half-baked yarn about his life being threatened . . . No, I'm quite prepared to believe he's being threatened but he won't give us enough detail to help him . . . Yes, it's pretty obvious he's afraid of incriminating himself in some way . . .'

That and a word to sub-division arranging for the Panda patrols to keep an eye on Roscrowgy, made him feel better. Not that it would do Cleeve any good if someone had decided to stem the flow of contentious masterpieces with a bullet or a loaded sock, but it was all he could do.

He joined Helen at the Philleigh pub for lunch and afterwards they crossed by the chain-ferry to Trelissick and spent the afternoon walking in the gardens and woods. Wycliffe grew nostalgic about life in the great days of houses like Trelissick, until he remembered that he would have been among the forelock-touching minions on the wrong side of the green-baize door.

A pleasant tea in a former barn with the chaffinches more than ready to go shares.

Monday July 18th
Cleeve was following his morning ritual, counting the pine trees. The sun was shining directly into his room and it was already hot. He opened the window and let in the fresh air along with the sounds from outside, the gulls screeching, the shouts of children playing in a garden further down the hill, a helicopter pulsing distantly, somewhere over the bay. For most people it was another summer's day; for him it was Monday July 18th and he was waiting for Milli to bring in the mail.

She came at last, wearing a sleeveless frock with shoulder straps and a plunging neckline, more provocative than if she had been nude. But today he hardly noticed.

The routine 'Good morning!'

Milli said, 'There are a couple of queries from Lester about a TV serialization of *Medicus* you'll have to look at. Apart from that. . .'

'Leave it on the desk with the others.'

On the way out she stopped. 'Are you all right?'

'Why shouldn't I be?'

A shrug of the bare shoulders.

After an all but sleepless night he had been up since first light and from eight o'clock he had felt like a man living on borrowed time, as though the minutes, the seconds, were being doled out to him with miserly reluctance. Once more he seemed to bestride two worlds.

He crossed to his desk; the Cleeve mail was there, five or six envelopes . . . the third was white, addressed in block capitals, postmark Truro. He opened it, the card was there but it was in two pieces; a Jack of Diamonds roughly torn across. In the margin of each half, the date: Monday July 18th and the number 5.

After a while he returned the torn card to its envelope, unlocked the bottom left-hand drawer of his desk and added the envelope to the four others contained in the cigarette box. Automatically he checked the other contents of the drawer: his pistol, three clips of ammunition, the current volume of his journal, and a slim file of documents.

He closed the drawer and locked it. For a while he stared out of the window, watching a squadron of herring-gulls perform breathtaking aerobatics as they mobbed one of their number who carried a coveted morsel of food in its beak. He reached a decision and went out into the corridor, calling to Milli.

'I'm going out.'

'Out? What if Lester phones?'

'Tell him.'

'Tell him what?'

'You'll think of something.'

He collected his stick and let himself out of the house by a little-used side-door, crossed the garden, and passed through the rhododendron tunnel and the wicket gate to Henry's Field. There he followed a path diagonally across the field to the wooden shed. He raised his stick in salute to the students at work on the dig, and came to the shed and the narrow, rutted lane which led in from the road. He continued down the lane and reached an area of woodland, part of what was once a much larger area preserved for shooting. As he entered the trees he felt calmer; there was an atmosphere of claustrophobic seclusion and remoteness which brought to mind the sombre fairy-tale forests of childhood and, paradoxically, made him feel safe.

He came to a house in a clearing, pushed open the slatted gate and walked up the garden path. The garden had run wild, a paradise for butterflies and bees. An old wicker chair with sun-bleached cushions stood by the front door; the door was open and Cleeve could see into the dimly lit interior of the cottage. A table covered with a green chenille cloth, shared between an ancient Remington portable, a pile of books, and a sleeping tabby cat. Peace descended upon him like the holy dove.

'Anybody home?' He tapped on the door with his stick.

A moment, and Kitson's lean figure emerged from the kitchen at the back, stooping to clear the low lintel. In an old cotton shirt and trousers which were too short he looked like a broomstick man.

'Ah! The squire on a tour of inspection of his property.' The voice was soft and the words were accompanied by a smile which, because of his disfigurement, involved only half his face.

Years of mortifying self-consciousness had established a conditioned reflex so that he usually contrived to present his uninjured profile.

'Aren't you going to ask me in?'

Kitson turned back into the house and Cleeve followed him into the front room which was a combination of living- and work-room. Sparsely furnished, with just the table and three or four chairs, the room overflowed with books; there were shelves everywhere. Two small, square windows looked out on the garden wilderness and in each was a jam-jar of wild flowers – foxgloves with flowering shoots of meadowsweet.

Cleeve was tentative. 'I know you don't like day-time visits . . .'

Kitson said, 'You're here now. What about a drink? Elderberry, dandelion or blackberry . . .'

'Christ! I should have brought a bottle.'

'Yes. The squire should never visit empty-handed.' The gentle and whimsical manner seemed to belie his words.

Kitson went into the kitchen and came back with a bottle and glasses. They sat on the hard wood chairs – Windsor strutbacks, and Kitson poured two glasses of slightly viscous purplish wine.

'Elderberry; said to ease the bowels.'

Cleeve said, 'My bowels won't need easing today.'

Kitson sipped from his glass. 'My calendar says Monday July 18th. I can guess why you're here.'

Cleeve nodded. 'You guessed right.'

But he felt relaxed here as nowhere else. There was an atmosphere of timeless serenity and for a little while it was possible to believe in Shangri-La and Santa Claus.

Kitson earned a meagre living, translating Russian texts for publishers and others.

Cleeve, self-absorbed, said, 'It's an uncomfortable feeling, Roger – unnerving. I would never have believed it could have affected me so.'

41

Kitson smiled. 'You're a fraud, Davy! You write as though it needed more courage to live than to die but, come the crunch, and you tremble before the Old Reaper like the rest of us. "Be absolute for death", Davy, then "either death or life shall thereby be the sweeter".'

Cleeve laughed despite himself. 'You always were a Job's comforter, you old devil!'

On that same Monday the Wycliffes crossed to St Anthony and visited Place House, site of an ancient Celtic religious foundation, made holy in the first place, according to local tradition, by earlier visitors of greater distinction, none other than the boy Jesus and his uncle, Joseph of Arimathaea. Later visitors are supposed to have included Henry VIII and his new bride, Ann Boleyn, completing a honeymoon begun at Hampton Court. Now it can look with condescension on other houses whose only boast is "Queen Elizabeth slept here."

Tuesday July 19th
A hot, sticky night; the Wycliffes had tossed and turned in bed, disturbing each other, then at first light they had fallen into a dead sleep and awakened unrefreshed.

They planned to drive to Pendower, to walk the coast-path to Portloe, and return to the car by way of Veryan.

'Have we got the map?'

'It's in the car.'

'The binoculars?'

'They're on the window-seat.'

'We're ready then. . .'

The telephone rang and Wycliffe answered it. Sergeant Pearce.

'Divisional Inspector Knowles's compliments, sir. He'll be over as soon as possible. He's notified headquarters, but as you're here he thought you should be told. . .'

'Told what?'

'There's been a death by violence, sir – here in the village; suspected murder.'

Wycliffe thought of Cleeve and his heart missed a beat. 'Who?'

'A young woman found dead on her bed.'

'How did she die?'

Pearce was cagey. 'There's some doubt about that, sir – not straightforward at all. Dr Hodge spoke of poison which, he said, was not self-administered.'

Wycliffe looked out of the little latticed window. The sun was still shining on the water and on the fields beyond; there were still dinghies whistling for a wind, and people continued to pass to and fro along the waterfront, but he was no longer part of it.

'Where is she?'

'Mount Zion Steps; two doors down from my place. The house is in two flats and hers is the lower one.'

'Who found her?'

'The milkman, and he came to my place to telephone for a doctor. It wasn't until Dr Hodge had seen her that there was any thought of foul play.'

'All right; I'll meet you at the house shortly.'

He looked across at Helen; she was standing by the window with her back to him but when she turned round she was already resigned. 'A murder case?'

'It looks like it; too early to say for certain. What will you do?'

'Don't worry. I may drive into Truro if you don't want the car, or I could take the ferry to Falmouth.'

He telephoned John Scales.

'Ah! I'm glad they got hold of you, sir. . .'

It was all arranged. Initially, Scales was sending Detective Sergeants Smith and Lane with three constables. 'I'll get two more DCs off to you later in the day, sir.'

Detective Sergeant Lane – Lucy Lane, a recent recruit to his squad. Wycliffe professed freedom from sex prejudice but he recalled Dr Johnson on the subject of women preachers – 'like a dog walking on his hinder legs. It is not done well; but you are surprised to find it done at all' – and reserved judgement.

Time would tell.

'What about Franks?' Franks was the pathologist.

'I caught him at the hospital; he's hoping to be with you about midday.'

Wycliffe turned once more to Helen: 'I'll be off then.'

Helen said, 'A floral shirt and light-fawn slacks might raise a few eyebrows, don't you think?'

He had to change.

The little house was half-way up Zion Steps, almost opposite the jewellery shop where Helen had bought her brooch. It was like being suddenly transported backstage from a seat in the stalls.

The sombre granite frontage had been tarted up with bright-blue paint on the woodwork of windows and door. Pearce was waiting for him outside.

'Better go round the back, sir.'

A little way down, there was a passage giving access to a narrow lane running along the backs of all the houses in the block, and the house of the dead girl had a yard from which blue-painted steps gave separate access to the upper flat.

Pearce pointed to a ground-floor sash window, open several inches at the bottom; the curtains were drawn but didn't quite meet. 'She's in there, sir; that's her bedroom.'

'Who is she?'

'Celia Dawe – a girl in her early twenties; a real eye-catcher, the sort men turn to look at in the street – women too, for a different reason.'

'Local?'

'Yes. She was an orphan, brought up by her uncle and two maiden aunts – the Borlases, who keep the photographer's shop further up the steps. She's been away for a few years but she turned up again last

44

season. Jack Polmear, the landlord of The Buckingham Arms, gave her a job and let her have this flat which used to be his mother's until she died a year or two back. There's an old lady in the top flat still – Maggie Treloar – she worked for the Polmears for donkey's years.'

'The girl didn't go back to her relatives?'

Pearce scratched his long nose. 'I don't think it would have worked; she probably left in the first place because she couldn't get on with her uncle and aunts – they're an odd family, great chapel people and probably very strict.'

'Have they been told?'

'Dr Hodge went over there. I thought I'd better not leave here more than I had to.'

'This chap Polmear seems to have put himself out for the girl.'

A sly grin. 'Jack's wife divorced him a year or two back but as long as I've known him he's had a succession of girl friends; this one is just the latest in line.'

'Was she a tart?'

Pouted lips. 'I wouldn't say that; I think she looked on a man as security. Incidentally, she's been seen about a lot with young Cleeve since he came home on vacation a few weeks ago.'

'I gather the milkman found her?'

'Yes, it seems they had an arrangement; if she wasn't up and about when he came he was to bang on her bedroom window. He did this morning but got no reply, then he saw her through the gap in the curtains. He realized something was wrong when she didn't wake and tried the back door; it wasn't locked and he went in. . .'

'Have you got his statement?'

'No, when the doctor came he went on with his round but we can pick him up.'

'Is there access to this yard other than through the alley from the Steps?'

45

'Yes, the back lane continues up into Chapel Street.'

Wycliffe found it hard to realize that he was starting on a murder inquiry. So far these people were not real to him; he still felt detached, as though he were reading about them in a newspaper; he was still on holiday.

'Let's go inside.'

Through a small kitchen which was modern, though none too clean; the remnants of a fish-and-chip take-away on the table; dirty dishes in the sink.

Pearce said, 'Apart from this and the bathroom she only had the two rooms – a little parlour facing out on the Steps and her bedroom overlooking the yard.'

In the passage Pearce pushed open a door and they stood just inside the girl's bedroom. There was a carpet on the floor; a double bed and a dressing table took up most of the space. A television set on a stand was placed at the foot of the bed; the clothes she had been wearing were in a little heap on a tub chair, and there was a floor-to-ceiling cupboard, presumably her wardrobe. White curtains were drawn across the sash-window but they did not meet and the window itself was open a little at the bottom so that the curtains were stirred by a draught. Despite the fresh air, there was a stale smell blended of cosmetics and woman.

Celia Dawe, completely naked, lay on her right side; a grubby sheet and a duvet trailed over the foot of the bed; her shoulder-length blonde hair spread over the pillow. There were no obvious signs of injury or violence but her features were contorted as though in a spasm of pain.

'She was lying on her back,' Pearce said, 'but Dr Hodge shifted her. You see he's marked a small punc-ture wound in her left buttock.'

A reddish ring, apparently drawn with the girl's own lipstick, surrounded a tiny puncture high up on the left buttock where the hips began to narrow to the waist.

The puncture itself was at the centre of a brown spot like a mole.

They were standing by the dressing table which was littered with cosmetic bottles and jars. Pearce pointed to a glass specimen tube lying in the lid of a jar of face cream. In the tube was a little dart-like object which seemed to consist of a fine needle in a brass holder. The needle was stained brown as though by rust.

'Dr Hodge found the dart on the floor by the bed; he reckoned it must've dropped out of the wound and rolled there.'

Wycliffe examined the tube, removed the stopper and sniffed. 'Nicotine!'

'That's what the doctor said, sir.'

There was nothing they could do until the technical people had done their work so they went out into the yard.

'You haven't had a word with the old lady upstairs?'

'No, sir, I haven't had a chance but I'll do it now.'

Wycliffe said, 'Leave it. There's something else I want you to do. We shall need an incident room; I'd prefer a large room or a small hall – somewhere with a bit of space. I hate those caravan things where you're afraid to breath for fear of upsetting somebody else's cocoa. Any ideas?'

Pearce nodded. 'I'll see what I can do, sir.'

The divisional inspector had left again with his DC, relieved to be let off so lightly. Wycliffe had said, 'It's too early; I'll let you know if I need more local assistance, it depends on the amount of leg-work. At the moment I want Pearce freed of normal duty and assigned to me. In addition, you can leave me your uniformed man to defend us from snoopers.'

The truth was that he preferred to work with a small team of his own men.

Now he was going up Zion Steps to the photographer's shop. Tourists were plodding up and ambling down in a thin stream, women with sun-reddened skins, paunchy men and bored children. Nobody showed the slightest interest in what might be happening in the little house with the blue paintwork, but that could change once word got round.

A tall, bald-headed figure threaded his way among the tourists; an animated scarecrow, his head and face were terribly scarred on one side; Kitson, carrying a plastic bag, doing his shopping. Mutual recognition and acknowledgement.

It was hot, Wycliffe could feel the damp patches under his arms and he promised himself a cold beer at lunchtime.

W. Borlase and Son, Photographers: faded gilt lettering on a brown fascia; a double-fronted shop with one window devoted to wedding photographs and child studies while the other was filled with historical photographs recording the life of Roseland through more than a century.

Joseph Borlase stood in his shop, a little back from the door, watching the approach of his visitor. He was a soft, fleshy man of about fifty with the unformed features of a plump baby; he wore a fawn linen jacket, a white shirt with a bow tie, and dark trousers. He saw Wycliffe pause for a moment outside, sizing the place up, then the door opened and a bell sounded discreetly. Everything in the shop was both dusty and discreet, the potted palms, the framed photographs on the walls and displayed on easels, the ornately carved screen with velvet curtains which separated the shop from the studio; the place could scarcely have changed in 50 years.

Wycliffe introduced himself. 'I think Dr Hodge broke the news of your niece's death . . . I'm very sorry . . . I understand that you and your sisters are her next-of-kin – is that correct?'

Borlase was sweating though it was cool in the shop; there were beads of sweat under his eyes and he wiped them away with a silk handkerchief from his breast pocket as though they were tears.

'Celia's parents were killed in an accident when she was three . . .' His voice was soft as melting butter. 'My sisters and I brought her up . . . My sisters are a good deal older than I . . . it wasn't easy.'

Wycliffe said, 'I don't know what Dr Hodge told you but we suspect that your niece was murdered.'

'Murdered!' A murmured exclamation of horror.

'Did you think she had died a natural death?'

'What?' The blue eyes were troubled. 'Dr Hodge mentioned poison . . . I thought it must have been an accident. Perhaps that she had taken her own life – not murder . . .' His words seemed to hang in the air, breathy and moist.

'Your niece left home several years ago, I believe. Where did she go?'

Joseph rolled his handkerchief into a ball and was kneading it with both hands. 'I don't know, super-intendent . . . After breakfast one morning she went out and never came back . . . We found that her clothes were missing . . . She was eighteen. Three days later we had a card with a London postmark. It said that she was well and that she wouldn't be coming home . . . We heard nothing more until at the beginning of last summer she arrived back in the village.'

'Didn't she offer any explanation of where she had been or why she had come back?'

'She never came near us – we heard she was back from neighbours and then she came to live just a few doors away. She never came to see us.'

'Did you or your sisters go to see her?'

He looked mildly shocked. 'It wasn't our place . . . After all we'd done for her, to be treated like that!' He wiped his face once more; his pores seemed to ooze moisture.

'So you have had no contact with her since she came back?'

'None.'

'For practical purposes, Mr Borlase, I have to ask whether you are willing to act as next-of-kin – there will be formalities, the body will have to be identified, there will be an inquest and arrangements to be made for the funeral.'

A sigh. 'I quite understand. I hope I know my duty.'

Wycliffe looked round the shop with its air of dusty, fossilized gentility. Celia Dawe had lived in the place with this man for fifteen years of her life. 'Is there anything you would like to ask me, Mr Borlase?'

'Ask you? No . . . I don't think so . . . There is, perhaps, one thing . . . I mean her belongings.'

'What about her belongings, Mr Borlase?'

'I wondered . . .' He hesitated. 'Shall I be able to claim them? I'm sure that my sisters will feel . . . I mean things of family interest . . .'

'If she has left no will I imagine all her property, whatever it is, will come to you and your sisters eventually.'

It was evidently not what he had hoped to hear. The handkerchief was kneaded more vigorously. 'Perhaps I could come over and go through her things . . . I mean, we ought to know exactly what her circumstances were . . .'

Wycliffe was puzzled. He said firmly. 'I'm afraid there can be no question of that until our investigation has gone a good deal further than at present. Of course, there is nothing to stop you getting in touch with your solicitor regarding your rights.'

He shook his head with unaccustomed vigour. 'No! No, we wouldn't want to do that . . . I merely thought . . . The whole business is so very painful.'

Wycliffe decided to leave it there. Borlase came and stood on the step, watching him as he crossed over.

Cleeve was at his desk; he had the typescript of *Setebos* in front of him but it was no more than an excuse, he had scarcely turned a page for the morning. He was not drinking either, he was waiting. Since half-past nine when Milli brought the mail he had seen no one and no one had telephoned. Unless he gave specific instructions it was rare for him to be undisturbed for so long.

The windows were open and from time to time he went over to stand, looking out. Not a cloud in the sky, the sun blazing down, the air shimmering in the heat, and everywhere, silence. A strange silence it seemed to him, even a conspiracy of silence. He dismissed the fanciful notion but without conviction. He looked at the long-case clock which he wound religiously every Saturday morning – ten minutes to eleven. In ten minutes Milli would bring him his coffee. Perhaps then . . . Milli had her own way of gathering news; he suspected her of operating her own KGB in the village.

The night of Monday July 18th . . . last night. An incredible coincidence and an incredible stupidity on his part; he could almost believe that the events of the night had been a dream.

The old clock cleared its throat, as it always did a couple of minutes before striking, and just then there was a tap on the door. Milli came in with the coffee on a little tray.

'Do you really want this? Or is it too hot for coffee?'

'Don't I always have coffee?'

She shrugged. 'As you like. Do you mind if I have a shower? It's sticky in that room.' She squirmed inside her frock and her hard little nipples protruded through the thin material like beansprouts.

She was signalling; he could have her if he wanted, as he had done before, still wet from the shower. He was tempted, but this was not the time.

He said with contrived casualness, 'By all means have a shower if you want one. No calls?'

'No, it's quiet this morning.' She paused, looking at

51

him. 'All right, I won't be long. I'll switch the phone through.'

He could imagine what she would do in the shower. 'Little whore!'

He laced his coffee with whisky. Two or three minutes went by and there was another tap at the door; he thought it was Milli, back on some pretext, but to his astonishment it was Patricia. He couldn't remember the time when she had come to him in this part of the house.

As always, Patricia looked relaxed and cool. 'I hope I'm not disturbing you?' Her calm gaze took in the whole room and he was sure she had not missed the lingering fragrance of whisky.

'Of course you're not disturbing me! Sit down. Will you have something? Coffee? A drink?'

It was absurd, he was treating her like a visitor.

She remained standing, aloof. 'I was in the village this morning and I met Nancy Hodge – the doctor's wife.' Patricia was never sure how much he knew of the village. 'Hodge was called out this morning to that little house on Zion Steps which Polmear turned into flats . . .' Her eyes were on him, unwavering. He sat at his desk, gently stroking the ragged ends of his moustache.

'Celia Dawe – Borlase's niece – has been living in the bottom flat and working at The Buckingham . . . The milkman found her this morning, dead on her bed.'

'Dead? What did she die of?' His voice sounded unreal.

'That's the point. Hodge called in the police and now your friend Wycliffe is down there. Nancy hinted that they think the girl was murdered.'

'Murdered? That is ridiculous!'

'Why is it ridiculous?'

He realized that he had been too emphatic. 'Well, who would want to murder the girl?' Feeble.

Patricia did not relax her gaze. 'I'm worried, David.'

'Worried?'

A flicker of annoyance. 'Please don't fence with me! You think if you close your eyes you can't be seen.'

Cleeve spread his large freckled hands on the desk and seemed to study them.

Patricia went on: 'There is Andrew to consider.'

'Andrew?'

'You must know that he has been seeing a lot of that girl since he came home this time. That at least will be common talk in the village.'

Cleeve said nothing. Patricia remained standing; she had gone as far as she was prepared to go.

'You remember that we shall have guests this evening?'

'I hadn't forgotten.'

The headquarters party arrived; they trooped into the back yard of Celia Dawe's flat led by Detective Sergeant Smith – the squad's photographer, fingerprint man and resident Jeremiah. He was trailed by Detective Constable Shaw – the administrative assistant, and two DCs carrying gear – like porters in darkest Africa. Smith would take charge at the scene-of-crime; Shaw would look after communications and records.

'We had to park a quarter of a mile away.' Smith, the eternal victim.

Wycliffe said, 'Is DS Lane not with you?'

'She's coming in her own car.' This, too, seemed a matter of grievance.

Franks, the pathologist, was not long after the police party. By contrast, Wycliffe had never known the plump little doctor anything but cheerful. He was ruled by two passions, women and fast cars, and age had not withered nor the years contemned.

'Seventy minutes from the hospital, Charles! Not bad over these roads.'

Wycliffe, whose speedometer rarely touched 60, was unimpressed. 'One of these days a bright lad in traffic

53

will stay awake long enough to book you. I only hope it happens before you kill somebody.'

Franks grinned. 'Still the same old Charles! Where is she? It is a she, isn't it?'

Wycliffe led the way into the house. Smith had already taken a number of shots of the room and the body; now he would record each change of position during the pathologist's examination.

Franks looked down at the dead girl. 'She was beautiful, Charles! "The nakedness of woman is the work of God . . . The lust of the goat is the bounty of God." You wouldn't approve, you old Puritan! But Blake said that – it's poetry . . . What's the hieroglyph on her bottom in aid of?'

Wycliffe pointed to the specimen tube containing the dart. Franks picked it up and examined it through the glass, then took out the cork and sniffed.

'Nicotine, my God! Fancy stuff, Charles. It's a long time since we've had a decent poisoning – gone out of fashion. Too much bother; needs a bit of nous – planning. Easier to clump somebody over the head.' He held up the little tube. 'Who has a go at this? Me or Forensic?'

As always, Wycliffe reacted to Franks with gloomy disapproval. 'You know better than that. You do your Stas-Otto on the tissues and leave the clever stuff to the whiz-kids at Forensic.' After a moment, he added, 'I suppose there's no harm in you taking a look before passing it on.'

Franks said, 'You'll want to know whether she had a man.'

Wycliffe waited in the yard. The professional callousness of pathologists made him uncomfortable. But things were beginning to move. After a while, Pearce came back wagging his tail like an old spaniel with his master's slippers. He had found a little building once used by the village school, now in planning limbo.

'Where is it?'

'In Chapel Street at the top of the Steps. It belongs to the chapel and they're always glad to make a few pounds by letting it.'

'Good! Put DC Shaw in the picture and let him get on with it. I want you here.'

Shaw would arrange for a pantechnicon to bring furniture, office equipment and a communications unit from central stores.

Detective Sergeant Lucy Lane put in her appearance; this would be the first time she had worked directly under Wycliffe. She had applied for a vacancy in Serious Crime Squad from a divisional CID and, with an ear for his conscience and an eye on the discrimination acts, Wycliffe had agreed to the appointment. Her qualifications were impeccable, beginning with an honours degree in English Literature. She had the vital statistics of a Miss World and at first had been a major distraction in the duty room, with cases of the wandering hand as well as the wandering eye. In the end she had put a stop to it in a single memorable sentence; she said simply, to all within earshot: 'If you want sex in your work you can play with each other or with yourselves, not with me.'

Wycliffe gave her her instructions: 'I want you to brief yourself with the local man, Sergeant Pearce; let him put you in the picture about the place and the case. Then you can start on house-to-house with DC Curnow to assist. There's an old lady who lives alone in the flat above this; she might have something to tell us. Obviously we want to know whether anybody saw or heard anything last night – they probably didn't; but we also want gossip. Don't turn your nose up at gossip. More than half the leads in a case like this stem from it.'

The dark eyes were innocent.

'Yes, sir. I remember you making that point in a lecture you gave when I was in training school, way back in '78.'

First blood to the lady.

Franks's preliminary examination did not take long and he rejoined Wycliffe in the yard.

'You can have her shifted, Charles. In my opinion she's been dead between fifteen and twenty hours, which puts it between nine and two last night. The only sign of injury is the puncture wound and what I've seen is consistent with her having died of a quick-action poison injected into her system. Nicotine would fill the bill very well and that dart stinks of the stuff. Of course I'll be able to tell you more when I've done the PM and the tests.'

He wiped his bald head with a silk handkerchief. 'God, it's hot! Nicotine – where would he get it? It used to be used by horticulturalists as a pesticide but I don't know if it still is – you and Helen are the gardeners. Vets use it as a vermifuge . . .'

'Surely penetration of the skin by a needle simply dipped in nicotine wouldn't be fatal?'

'No; there must be more to that dart. You're after a man of ideas, Charles, and God knows, there aren't many of them left. Murders these days are merely brutal. The Borgias invited their victims to dine; this chap coaxed his into bed – I like that.'

'She definitely had a man with her?'

'Definitely! I might be able to tell you his blood group from the semen, though much good that will do you at this stage.'

The mortuary van came to the top of the Steps and the girl's body had to be carried up on a stretcher, providing a brief diversion for the sightseers. End of Celia Dawe who left home at eighteen for the big city but came back to her village five years later to work as a barmaid and sleep with her boss. Wycliffe muttered irritably, 'Stupid youngsters! Chasing rainbows!'

But now they could get on.

Wycliffe went back to the flat. Smith and his assistant

were creating havoc in the bedroom, looking for unconsidered trifles. Smith was good at his particular job because he could be single-minded about little things; no detail would escape him, his problem was to see the broader picture.

Wycliffe poked about in the kitchen. Celia had not been a housekeeping girl. The cupboards were empty except for a few basics – tea, coffee, sugar, a packet or two of breakfast cereal and a few tins. She had probably eaten most of her meals out. In the bathroom, the bath and basin had a soapy rim and the loo cried out for that wonder liquid which kills 'all known germs DEAD!'. Knickers and bras were draped on a string stretched over the bath.

He went into the front room – the parlour; a dreary little room with a window looking out over the Steps. No sun and little enough light. It was furnished with a dusty three-piece suite, a sideboard, a table ... There was a carpet on the floor and framed prints of soulful maidens looked down from the walls. Even on this hot July day it smelled of damp and disuse; it was almost certainly as Polmear's mother had left it. The girl had used the flat only as a place to sleep.

Wycliffe let himself out by the front door and stood for a moment looking up and down the narrow street, taking it all in afresh. Subconsciously he was beginning to see the place through the eyes of a local. Opposite was the shop where Helen had bought her brooch, and he was aware of being watched by the lady with the long blonde hair. She must be wondering what he had to do with the happenings across the road. Next door to the jeweller's was the photographer's and it was in those rooms with the bay windows over the shop that Celia Dawe had spent most of her childhood.

Feeling more at home he strolled down the Steps to the waterfront and the lounge bar of The Buckingham. The pub did a good trade in light lunches; most of the tables in the bar and in the walled courtyard were occupied by people eating crab or prawn salad, cold meats, or grilled fish. He chose the prawns and found a table in a corner by the bar. He wondered where Helen was lunching and felt hard done by at missing his holiday in such ideal weather.

Waitresses in blue nylon overalls flitted between the tables with trays held high. He felt conspicuous in a suit. Behind the bar a middle-aged man, running to fat, kept an eye on it all. He wore a white shirt, a bow tie and black trousers: Polmear, the landlord. His fair hair was thinning but carefully combed to disguise the fact. His eyes rested momentarily on Wycliffe, registered his presence and moved on.

Wycliffe took his time over the meal; drank two glasses of chilled lager and followed this with coffee. By that time customers were dwindling, a bell sounded. 'Last orders for drinks, please.'

The waitresses were beginning to clear the tables; Wycliffe went over to the bar where Polmear was lighting a cigarette.

'Mr Polmear?'

Recognition, not of the man but of his mission. 'You are . . .?'

Wycliffe told him: 'I think you know why I'm here.'

'Yes, it was a shock.'

'I would like to talk to you in private for a few minutes.'

Polmear called through a hatch to another bar. 'Chris! Take over here for a bit. . . This way.'

Wycliffe followed him into a little office where there was just room for a desk and two chairs; no natural light. 'Will you have something?'

'Not now, thanks.'

Polmear tapped ash from his cigarette into an ashtray advertising lager.

'You've known her a long time?'

'Since she was a kid – three or four years old. Her

parents were killed in an accident somewhere up north and she came to live with her aunts and uncle – the Borlases – they're a brother and two sisters.'

'You've taken an interest in her since she came back?'

A shrewd look. 'I gave her a job and found her somewhere to live.'

'Altruism?'

Polmear trickled smoke through his thick lips and watched it rise. 'Not altogether; I did feel sorry for her – she was down on her luck but I also thought she'd make a good barmaid, and she did; she had looks, a pleasant manner, an eye for the till and, when necessary, she knew how to cool it.'

'Couldn't she have gone back to the Borlases?'

A broad grin. 'You must be joking! I mean, she stuck it as long as she could the first time round. The Borlases have to be seen to be believed and he's as kinky as they come, in spite of his chapel-going.'

'So Celia Dawe was simply an employee of yours whom you helped in various ways?' Wycliffe at his most bland.

Polmear grinned. 'You know damn well she was more than that; the whole village knows I spent most nights up there. It suited us both, I'm divorced and Celia had got into the habit of having a man in her bed.'

'Were you there last night?'

He looked shocked. 'My God, I wasn't! I haven't been up there for more than two months.'

'Why not?'

'Because she found somebody else. That was fair enough. She was looking for security and she knew she couldn't expect it from me. She told me she'd taken on somebody else and that was the end of it as far as I was concerned. No hard feelings; I've never gone short.'

'Who was this other man?'

'I don't know – none of my business.'

'But I expect you could make an informed guess.'

He shook his head. 'Straight up, I couldn't. They must have kept it pretty quiet because I never heard a whisper. Now, I suppose, he's done for her. She was an unlucky kid – never got it right.' His manner was relaxed and natural, concerned but not nervous. He was playing with a ball-point, flicking it in and out. 'She liked to play it rough: some women do; I suppose he went too far and strangled her.'

'She wasn't strangled.'

'No?'

'She was poisoned.'

'*Poisoned!*' Polmear was incredulous. 'Then I'm a long way out . . . If that's the case it sounds like a woman. . . . Are you sure it wasn't an accident?'

'Could her new bedfellow have been young Cleeve?'

Polmear shrugged. 'It started before he came home on vacation. It's true she's been running round with the boy but I guess that was fun, not business.'

'When did you last see her?'

'Last night when we closed.'

'Was she her usual self?'

'She seemed so to me; she was in the other bar and I didn't see a lot of her.'

'One last question. Have you any idea where and how she spent the years she was away?'

Polmear lit another cigarette. 'I know she was in London and that she had several jobs; she had a spell in a strip club then, through her boy friend, she got bit parts in the theatre. By the time she decided to chuck it and come home she was sharing a flat in Bayswater with a girl friend and working in a café in Queensway . . . Come to think of it, she used to hear from that girl so you may find letters.'

Wycliffe left the pub and joined the crowds on the waterfront. The holiday circus was in full swing, the car park was full, boats peeled off from the quay, laden with their quota of emmets, to 'cruise round the creek and view the lighthouse' or 'tour the harbour and docks at Falmouth'. Laughs, cries, shouts and occasional shrieks came from the shingle beach, now at its greatest low-tide extent. Village, creek, castle and pine trees shimmered in the afternoon heat.

He was beginning to get some sort of picture of the dead girl – of whom he had never heard until that morning. Like thousands of others she had set out with little more than an undiscriminating greed for life. Such a girl might, conceivably, end up being strangled by a lover; it was a credible climax. But this girl had been poisoned – poisoned by someone who had carefully and deliberately planned to murder; someone with a knowledge of poisons and access to one of the most lethal; someone with the ingenuity and skill to prepare a dart which must have functioned as a miniature hypodermic.

Not a crime of passion but of cold, festering hatred.

The man who had slept with her on the night of her death was the most obvious suspect but, in Wycliffe's view, not the only possibility.

He saw the bedroom in the eye of his mind; the bed across the window, with only a couple of feet of space between; the window open at the bottom to the yard, the flimsy curtains scarcely stirring; the night sultry and still. The girl on the bed quite naked.

He sensed that this would be a plodder's case, nothing to be gained by running round in ever diminishing circles to meet the fate of a certain legendary bird, but step by step; stone on stone.

Back to the present. He had been leaning on the sea wall staring at nothing. In his sombre suit he must have looked like an undertaker at a party. A few feet away a woman painter in water colours had set up her easel; her colours were spread out on a little tray and a water-pot dangled from a hook. It needed courage, so nakedly to expose one's talents.

Wycliffe made for Zion Steps. As he passed the herbalist's he was recalling his encounter with Cleeve. Within three days of his arrival in the village on holiday he had been consulted about threats to a man's life and confronted with the murder of a girl. Coincidence? Reason said 'Yes', but instinct, cautiously, 'Perhaps not'. Was young Cleeve's association with the dead girl a significant link? Cleeve had made a deep impression on Wycliffe and though his first reaction was antagonistic he sensed the man's profound disquiet, his self-disgust, and wondered what the cause might be.

At the girl's flat Smith was still in the bedroom, his assistant, DC Edwards, had been assigned to the other rooms. The bedroom looked as though the removal men were expected at any moment. The dressing table had been cleared of cosmetics and toiletries and in their place was an array of labelled polythene envelopes, large and small. Smith, wearing his rimless half-glasses, sat on the stripped bed writing in his notebook – always an exercise in copy-book script which magistrates and even judges had commended.

'Anything to tell me?' One had to be careful with Smith, a too-precise question might elicit a long exposition of some side-issue while more vital information waited in the queue.

Smith got up from the bed, removed his glasses, and pointed to his envelopes. 'There's a lot of stuff to go through when I get back.'

'Anything of immediate interest?'

Smith smoothed his lantern jaw. 'She was saving money.' He picked up one of the envelopes. 'Building Society pass-book. In the past year she's paid in four thousand pounds, a hundred or two at a time, and she didn't do that on a barmaid's wages, even allowing for tips.'

'Anything else?'

Smith looked over his collection in the manner of a connoisseur selecting his best pieces. 'A few letters –

not many – but one recent, from a girl she seems to
have been with in London. That might mean something.' He searched through another envelope and came
up with a two-page letter written in large, round hand
and almost devoid of punctuation. 'I've marked the bits
which might be interesting.'

Wycliffe skimmed the lines. 'It looks as though you
was right to go back you seem to have struck it lucky
for once. I never heard of him but I wouldn't would
I. The boy seems nice even if he is a bit wet but I think
you could make trouble that way . . . What about your
uncle. Have you seen him again . . . Yes I would like
to come down for a week in September if I can get time
off then . . .'

The letter was signed 'Liz' and there was no address.

*I never heard of him but I wouldn't would I. The boy
seems nice even if he is a bit wet but I think you could
make trouble that way* . . . The boy was obviously young
Cleeve. Could the other, of whom Liz had never heard,
be his father? *You could make trouble that way.* By
running father and son in tandem?

Wycliffe shrugged. Perhaps he had Cleeve on the
brain.

Polmear had said that Celia had worked at a café in
Queensway; if necessary the Met would find the café
and from there it should be possible to find Liz.

Smith was scratching his grey cheek with an earpiece
of his glasses – one of many idiosyncracies which
would have endeared him to a cartoonist. He said, 'I
had a visitor this afternoon, sir – the girl's uncle who
keeps the photographer's shop. He wanted to help in
sorting through her stuff. I told him we could manage.
He seemed upset.'

Wycliffe went through to the back yard; he wanted
to satisfy himself that it would have been practicable
for the killer to enter the yard and approach the open
window of the girl's bedroom without any great risk
of being seen.

The yard was too small to swing the proverbial cat but it was private, only overlooked by windows belonging to the two flats and, standing close to the bedroom window, one was shielded from view in the upper flat by the projecting landing at the top of the stairs. Wycliffe stood there without being noticed by Smith who was sitting on the bed with his back to the window.

A blue-painted door in a stone wall opened into the back lane. Wycliffe let himself out and walked up the narrow, grass-grown track which had a step or two at intervals, until he joined Chapel Street. He was satisfied that at any time after dark the killer would have been very unlucky to be spotted if he approached the house that way.

CHAPTER THREE

In the chapel schoolroom Shaw had worked a transformation; it had already acquired the atmosphere of a duty room in a rather sleazy nick with the traditional amenities: battered furniture, ancient typewriters, buckled filing cabinets, and tin-lids for ashtrays. On the whole it was a convenient arrangement, certainly preferable to those mobile rabbit hutches where it is scarcely safe to sit down without warning. There was even a little cubby hole with a window which would serve as an interview-room. There had been three or four calls from press and radio, routed through subdivision. Shaw had handed out Wycliffe's prepared statement to the effect that a young woman had been found dead in bed in suspicious circumstances, and that the police were investigating the possibility of foul play.

Wycliffe was facing the prospect of coming to terms with the Lane girl and regretting the loss of his old sergeant – now inspector – Kersey. ('You lose your best men in the promotion stakes.')

There she was, sitting at one of the typewriters, looking cool and competent in a butcher-blue frock which seemed right for her colouring. He had to admit that she dressed sensibly; that she had a professional look, crisp and clean as a new banknote, which was more than could be said for some of her male colleagues.

Shaw was duty officer and Sergeant Pearce was helping DC Edwards with his share of the scene-of-crime report. Two old-timers got together! Add Pearce's service to Edwards's and you had a lifetime.

Shaw said, 'Cuppa, sir? Tea or Instant?'

The chipped mugs were lined up, plastic spoons at the ready; home from home.

Shaw went on: 'Dr Franks would like you to ring him at this number, sir, and Mr Scales rang to say that Potter and Dixon will be here sometime this evening.'

Wycliffe was put through to Franks.

'How's this for service, Charles?' Franks full of himself as usual. 'Your girl died of nicotine poisoning – no doubt about that. No doubt either that it was injected by that dart which was really a miniature hypodermic, crude but ingenious: a bit of brass tube, sealed at one end and fitted with a hardwood plunger, well greased and pierced with a sawn-off length of hypodermic needle. The nicotine was contained in the tube behind the plunger and as the needle entered the skin it was forced through into the tissues. Not exactly a precision job, but effective. I estimate that it delivered the equivalent of sixty milligrams plus of the pure alkaloid. I expect the boffins at Forensic will set up all sorts of elaborate gadgets to demonstrate how it worked, but you can take it from me the girl died because that thing was jabbed into her backside.

'What puzzles me is why he didn't use an ordinary hypodermic; they're easy enough to come by. I suppose it would be a bit awkward, going to bed with one and biding your time . . . but the more you think of it the more extraordinary it seems that a man should choose that way of murdering his mistress.'

Wycliffe said, 'We are assuming that she was killed by the man who slept with her.'

'Surely that's the most likely?'

'I don't know. What is the external diameter of the brass tube?'

'External? I can't say offhand, but I made a detailed

sketch of the thing before passing it on. I'll check.' He was soon back: 'Almost exactly five millimetres – why do you want to know?'

'Just curiosity.'

Franks sighed. 'Well, if it wasn't the guy who was screwing her then your case really is wide open. I wish you joy, Charles.'

As Wycliffe put the phone back on its cradle he muttered to himself, 'Not that wide.' The killer must have had access to nicotine and the knowledge and manual dexterity to contrive a suitable dart for its injection. Added to that, he had, presumably, sufficient acquaintance with Celia Dawe to generate a motive for murder. Really a fairly neat set of crossbearings.

He! Always he! But might not the killer have been a woman? It is a cliché to say that poison is a woman's weapon, but statistically true. And there was something about the sustained rancour suggested by the careful and lengthy preparation which pointed, perhaps, to a feminine cast of mind.

He had been standing in the middle of the room, hands in pockets, brooding; now he turned to Lucy Lane and tried out his thoughts after bringing her up to date.

She met him half-way.

'I agree, it's hardly the way a man would murder his mistress.' She had a way of wrinkling her forehead as she spoke which gave her words an added seriousness. 'All the same, the man who was with her must have been there up to a short time before, if not actually when she died, and you would expect him to come forward.' She hesitated, then went on, 'As to the feminine cast of mind when it comes to nursing a grievance, my brother teaches in a school where three male members of staff haven't addressed a single word to each other in fifteen years.' She grinned. 'But I suppose you would call them "old women" anyway.'

Wycliffe laughed. 'Speaking of old women, have you seen Borlase yet?'

'Borlase and his two sisters. I saw them in the house-to-house routine and I'm just writing up my report. They're a weird trio and I feel sorry for any girl brought up by that lot. Incidentally, the old lady who lives above Celia Dawe's flat says Borlase has been to see his niece several times since she came to live there and that more than once she's heard voices raised as though they were quarrelling.'

No surprise there. He had suspected as much. 'She may have been trying to blackmail her uncle – perhaps succeeding. He was desperately anxious to take possession of what he called "her things" and when I turned him down he had a go at Smith, offering to help with the sorting out. He's obviously scared of what we might find, but in point of fact Smith has almost finished there and we've found nothing that need worry him.'

Wycliffe had perched himself on the edge of her table, now he got out his pipe and started to fill it; a sure sign that he was relaxing his guard. 'Did you get anything from the old lady in the top flat about the girl's night visitor?'

'Nothing. She either couldn't or wouldn't help. She said she went to bed to go to sleep and that was that.'

'Anything else?'

She shuffled through her papers. 'Nothing much. I talked to Laura Wynn, the woman who runs the jewellery shop.'

'Boadicea.'

A polite smile. 'She's certainly a dragon; I didn't get beyond the shop and I had very little to show for a ten minute fencing match. Her attitude was: "Surely, with girls like that, murder is an occupational hazard." She says she saw nothing and knows nothing.'

'What do the neighbours say about Mrs Wynn?'

'What don't they say! They call her "the duchess".

It seems she has a habit of casually referring to "my family" as though she belonged to the landed aristocracy. Among her other accomplishments she tells fortunes – not for money, of course! "Just leave a little something for charity." But according to her neighbours, her charity begins at home and stays there.'

Wycliffe said, 'You know she was investigated by a private detective working for Cleeve?'

'Sergeant Pearce told me. I think there might be more to be got out of Mrs Wynn.'

'Then perhaps you should try again.'

A small smile. 'With respect, sir, I think you would inspire greater confidence in the lady.'

A working relationship? Something like it, anyway. A start. He had to admit that he wouldn't have got a more concise or shrewder summing up from any of his men. And she had tolerance, a quality he looked for in all of his staff.

He gave her her instructions: 'I want you to tackle the nicotine angle – people who would have access to nicotine through their work – horticultural, veterinary or agricultural . . . The county advisory services would probably help in identifying trades in which the stuff is used. Then there are others likely to have the knowledge and resources necessary to extract nicotine from tobacco leaves as grown, or as sold for smoking. I don't think it's all that difficult. . .

'Anyway, you've got enough to be going on with. I think we'll let Borlase simmer for a while and I'll talk to Madam Laura later.'

He left the Incident Room and walked down Zion Steps. It had occurred to him that few people could be in a better position to extract vegetable poisons from their source than a practising herbalist. Of course, it was too obvious; no man in his senses would risk drawing attention to himself so blatantly . . . and yet, enterprising criminals, especially the clever ones, often have a blind spot. In any case,

Wycliffe was too old a copper to ignore the obvious.

For the first time he looked at Geoffrey Tull's shop with more than casual attention. A colourful sign showed a bouquet of herbs, apparently well painted, but he was too ignorant to identify them. The bow-fronted window exhibited only a printed card with an ornamental border of which the text read: 'Infusions, decoctions, extracts, tinctures and tablets, prepared on the premises from finest ingredients. Consultations by appointment. Geoffrey Tull MB, BCh.'

Beyond a low screen at the back of the window he could see into the shop. A large number of little varnished wooden drawers with white-enamelled labels and, above them, shelves with rows of glass bottles carrying gilt labels. It was reminiscent of a shop in a city museum: 'Pharmacy – circa 1910.' The era of Seidlitz powders, castor oil and ipecacuanha wine.

Although it was half-past six the notice on the door read 'Open'. He entered and a bell buzzed somewhere as he stood on the mat, but there was no response. The shop was elegantly neat, the glass jars gleamed in the dim light and there was an attractive smell of aromatic herbs. The labels on the drawers and bottles read like an index to one of the herbals; a cornucopia of healing.

'Can I help you?'

A voice almost at his elbow. Geoffrey Tull was tall, somewhat overweight, with a carefully trimmed moustache. He had his sister's colouring though his features were plump and soft, the face of a spoilt child.

'My name is Wycliffe – Detective Chief Superintendent Wycliffe.'

'Oh, yes?'

'I am investigating the murder of Celia Dawe.'

'Your sergeant has already spoken to me. I knew the girl, of course, but I can tell you nothing which isn't common knowledge.'

'You have heard how she died?'

'I have heard rumours – no more.'

There was something familiar about Tull; not that Wycliffe had ever seen him before, but he belonged to a type, a type once familiar in seaside hotels in the company of widowed or divorced ladies. Not a crude con-man, rather a professional companion for well-to-do lonely women.

'She died of nicotine poisoning; the nicotine was injected into her body by means of a hypodermic device.'

'I see.'

Getting nowhere, Wycliffe tried another approach. 'You are a registered medical practitioner?'

'I am medically qualified but I practise only as a naturopath. I am not in medical practice.'

An evasion; he had probably been struck off.

'You prepare your own medicines?'

'I prepare most of my herbal prescriptions.'

'So you have a laboratory or dispensary – something of the sort?'

'Something of the sort.'

'Have you any objection to showing me where you work?'

Tull did not reply but he moved aside to allow Wycliffe to pass between two counters to a door at the back of the shop.

'Through here.'

The room, looking out on the back yard, was more like a kitchen than a laboratory.

Tull said, 'Most of my preparation work is in the nature of cookery. As you see, I use slicers, shredders and mincers to deal with leaves, roots and stems. The heating is done on an electric hotplate . . . I suppose one of the main differences is that I use glass utensils exclusively, though most of these are bought at kitchen shops.'

'What about distillation?'

71

A faint smile. 'Few of my preparations involve distillation but I am equipped.' He opened a cupboard door. 'See for yourself. For distillation I use ordinary chemical glassware – flasks and condensers. I also have apparatus for boiling under reflux in certain extraction processes.'

His manner was casual, teasing. He closed the cupboard door. 'You see, Mr Wycliffe, I have quite enough equipment to extract nicotine from tobacco but I have never had occasion to use it for that purpose.'

Patronizing bastard! Wycliffe was becoming irritated but Tull was no fool, he hadn't put a foot wrong.

'You live alone?'

He received a long cool look before an answer. 'I do.' A brief pause, then: 'I think I've answered all your questions frankly, Mr Wycliffe, so if you will excuse me, I am expecting a patient.'

'Do you have an assistant?'

'I do. She looks after the shop while I am dealing with patients who come for consultatiòns, but she finishes work at five-thirty.'

'Does she have anything to do with the preparation of medicines?'

'Nothing whatever.'

'You receive your patients here?'

'Certainly not! I have a consulting room upstairs.'

'Perhaps you will give me the name and address of your assistant.'

He would have liked to refuse but realized there was no point. 'Sonia Penrose, 4 Veryan Close. I hope . . .'

'Yes?'

Tull shook his head. 'Nothing.'

The shop doorbell sounded and a moment later a woman stood in the doorway of the dispensary.

Tull said, 'Oh there you are, Mrs Wynn! Do come in, Mr Wycliffe is just leaving.'

The statuesque proprietor of the jewellery shop.

Outside, Wycliffe wondered how much his suspicion of Tull was due to dislike.

The Cleeves and their guests were taking coffee in the paved courtyard by the ornamental pool: Cleeve and Patricia, her brother Geoffrey, the archaeologist Gervaise Prout, and Roger Kitson. Andrew had not put in an appearance at dinner and Christie had excused herself immediately afterwards.

Patricia explained: 'She is very upset about the dead girl.'

Otherwise there had been no mention of Celia Dawe.

Carrie Byrne was in the house supervising two daily women from the village who stayed on to help whenever the Cleeves were entertaining.

The air was warm and sensuously soft; heavy with the scent of dracaena palms in flower. Colours were muted by the dusk, and water trickled musically from an incontinent Cupid into the pool.

Cleeve had been drinking before, during and since the meal; now he was flushed and his eyes were heavy. He had himself in hand but he was edgy and from time to time his temper showed in barbed sallies. Patricia, by adroitly changing the subject or deliberately misunderstanding her husband's words, had so far avoided unpleasantness.

Prout sat erect in his cane chair, his suit almost white – like tropical 'drill', a pukka sahib. Through dinner they had talked largely of the dig and he had bemoaned his lot as a 'prehistoric' archaeologist with no written records to help in interpreting his finds. 'Think of some of those classical chaps with a library of contemporary literature at their backs!'

Later, by some quirk or, perhaps, by intent, the conversation had turned to herbal medicine and Cleeve had made a couple of snide jokes about his brother-in-law, referring to him as 'our resident shaman'. Now Kitson, in a threadbare suit, his long body half

73

coiled in his chair, his injured profile turned from his audience, was holding forth on remedies to be found in the great herbals of the Chinese Sung. Kitson was an encyclopaedia of unlikely information and he had that rare gift which can make a railway timetable interesting.

Cleeve said, 'When I was getting together background for *Medicus* I remember being impressed by the number of really virulent poisons which could be extracted from quite common plants.'

Prout, apparently anxious to make himself agreeable, said, 'Yes, it really is remarkable. I've often wondered why we bother so much with legislation about the sales of poisons when anybody with a bit of nous can prepare extremely toxic alkaloids from plants which grow freely in hedgerows and gardens. Isn't that so, Mr Tull?'

Tull had seemed to be absorbed in contemplation of the carp in the pool and he looked up, startled, at being addressed directly. There was an awkward silence while he studied Prout as though trying to decide whether some innuendo had been intended, then he said, 'I am not interested in toxicology.'

Kitson gave a shrill little laugh. 'I think you two are at cross-purposes. Gervaise is amazingly well informed about the migration of Celtic tribes over the face of Europe two thousand years ago but not so well briefed on today's or yesterday's news. I doubt if he has heard that the Dawe girl was poisoned by one of his toxic alkaloids.'

Prout flushed with annoyance but it was Cleeve who demanded in a harsh voice, 'Where in hell did you get that tale, Roger?'

Patricia's voice warned: 'David!'

But Kitson was unperturbed. 'I never reveal my sources.'

Tull said, 'I told him.'

Cleeve turned on Tull. 'You? Is it true?'

74

Tull, clearly annoyed by Cleeve's manner, contrived to keep his dignity. 'Of course it's true! The superintendent told me that the girl died of nicotine poisoning.'

'And did the superintendent say that she had been murdered?'

'He did.'

Cleeve was frowning and intent. 'Did he say how the stuff was administered?'

'By some hypodermic device.'

'Why should he tell you all this?'

Cleeve's manner was offensive but Tull's calm replies were an effective rebuke. 'I assume it was because he thought I would have the knowledge and resources to extract nicotine from tobacco and might therefore rank as a suspect.'

Cleeve looked like a man who had received a considerable shock but he laughed self-consciously, beginning to feel foolish. 'A suspect. I see! Well, well!' His eyes travelled round the little group. 'Who's going to help me out with this brandy?'

When Wycliffe got back to the cottage, Helen was in the kitchen, wearing an apron, ready to get to work.

'Ah, you've come! I was afraid you would be late. How do you feel about having a meal here instead of going out?'

'I doubt if I could keep awake in a restaurant.'

'A rough day?'

He yawned. 'It didn't feel much like a holiday. What have you been doing?'

'I went across to Falmouth on the ferry and I've been extravagant. We're having fresh salmon steaks, cooked in white wine. There are a couple bottles of Muscadet in the fridge. If you feel like sampling it you can pour me some; I shall only need a little for the salmon.'

Just like home; drinking in the kitchen while the food was being prepared.

They had their meal in the front room with its latticed windows open to the waterfront so that voices of passers-by sounded as though they were in the room. They ate their salmon with small boiled potatoes garnished with parsley and they finished the Muscadet.

Wycliffe began to feel human. 'And for dessert?'

'Peaches. There's clotted cream if you've given up worrying about your cholesterol.'

Coffee, and then a walk. A circuit of the village, returning down the hill by the castle in time to see the estuary and the whole western sky glowing red.

Red sky at night; shepherds' delight. Emmets' too.

Early to bed.

Wednesday July 20th

Wycliffe was a small boy again, back on his parents' farm; the little square window overlooked the farmyard and he could hear the cows' hooves pattering on the cobbles. His mother's voice came from downstairs: 'Charles! Charles! You'll be late for school again!' His mother had been the only member of the family who, like Helen, refused to call him Charlie.

It was Helen calling up the stairs. 'It's half-seven, Charles!'

A fine day as promised but, according to the radio, a temporary change on the way, with drizzle and coastal fog in the outlook period.

'I'll make the most of today,' Helen said. 'There's a trip across the bay to Helford.'

It was almost nine before he arrived at the Incident Room in Chapel Street. Two more DCs, assigned from headquarters, had arrived – Dixon and Potter, known to intimates as Pole and Pot in reference to Dixon's height and Potter's paunch. Potter was duty officer, and alone. He did not hear Wycliffe come in; only a close encounter detached his feet from the table and his attention from the sports pages of *The Sun*.

'Sorry, sir!' He reached for the log. '08.33 hours: message from Mr David Cleeve of Roscrowgy. He would like to see you as soon as possible; he will call here at your convenience or be available at Roscrowgy at any time to suit you.'

'Very accommodating of him. Where is DS Lane?'

'Due on at 10.00 hours, sir, with Edwards, Curnow and Shaw. DC Dixon has gone round the back to the loo.'

'A veritable hive of activity.'

'Yes, sir.' After a moment, Potter added brightly, 'Coffee, sir?'

'No.' He sat at his table, sucking the end of his ball-point and brooding over Celia Dawe. The girl had been mercenary; she had slept with men as an investment in security and hoarded her gains. Her upbringing probably accounted for that. Otherwise there was nothing special about her but her looks. Only by being murdered did she stand out from the crowd in false perspective. Who would have cause to hate or fear such a girl enough to plan and contrive her death with such patience and care?

Lucy Lane arrived, wearing green, and cheerful with it. 'Good morning, sir! Another lovely day.'

He preferred the morose taciturnity he was accustomed to from his male colleagues. He answered glumly.

She went to her table, opened her shoulder bag and took out a bulky envelope. 'I think this is what has been worrying the Borlases.'

She emptied the contents of her envelope on to her table. Wycliffe went over. About 20 full-plate photographs; all of girls of different ages either nude or scantily clad; a voyeur's collection. Then he realized that they were photographs of one girl – of Celia Dawe, a record of her growing up from the age of three or four to early maturity. The quality was high and though the studies were intimate they were neither vulgar nor obscene. All the same, they made Wycliffe feel uncomfortable, as though he had stumbled into the very private world of a young girl. He had to admit that in all his years in the police he had never seen anything quite like them.

'How did you get them?'

'Luck, sir. I thought it might be useful to talk to the other girls who worked at The Buckingham, so I looked in there yesterday evening. Well, they couldn't or wouldn't tell me much about her. It was obvious they didn't like her, probably because she slept with the boss. Anyway, as I was leaving, one of the girls asked me what was to happen to Celia's belongings because they needed her locker. In the season they have a staff of five women and three men and each of them has a locker for personal things. Of course I didn't have her keys but Polmear found a duplicate. Her locker contained an overall, a raincoat, an umbrella, a pair of shoes, and these.'

'Good for you! What do you make of them?'

She turned the prints over, puckered brow. 'At least they explain what Borlase was so agitated about. He couldn't afford to have these passed round among his chapel friends.'

'Do you think his sisters know about them?'

It was a silly question and she looked surprised. 'They must have done; this was going on for thirteen or fourteen years. I imagine they were glad to keep his rather mild sexual vagaries in the family. I don't suppose they did anybody any harm.'

'Not the girl?'

'I shouldn't think so. I doubt if he touched her; he's a brooder, not a doer. It would be enough to have her to gloat over; and for her it would be routine. On Thursday night you wash your hair; Friday is bath night; and on Saturday afternoon or whenever, you strip and pose for uncle. She might have thought it a bit odd as she got older but she would be used to it.

I doubt if these were among her reasons for leaving home.'

Wycliffe told himself that women in general and this one in particular were full of surprises. He said, 'All the same, it seems likely that she was getting money out of him on the strength of the pictures. In other words, he had a motive.'

The brown eyes looked incredulous. 'For murder? I can't honestly see Borlase as a killer unless one imagines a homicidal rabbit.'

Wycliffe laughed; their relationship was beginning to gel. 'Do you want to follow this through?'

He thought of Borlase's torturing embarrassment at being questioned about his photographs by a girl, and decided he deserved it.

But Sergeant Lane had other ideas. 'In the long run I think there's more to be got out of his sisters and they're more likely to talk to you than me, sir.'

'I'll think about it. Meanwhile Cleeve wants to see me.'

'About the case?'

'What else? I suppose you know he's Peter Stride, the author?'

'I had heard.' Drily.

'You know his work?'

'I'm an addict; I took him for my special paper in finals.'

'Good! You may have a chance to get to know him better.'

Wycliffe was regretting that he would have to talk to Cleeve before he had news from John Scales of the man's background but, on cue, the telephone rang.

'Mr Scales for you, sir.'

'Well, John?'

'I've got something on Cleeve at last; it doesn't amount to much – nothing you'd think he'd want to conceal unless he really is a very shy bird. No biographical titbits in any of the tomes which list the works and whims of the literary. I got on to him finally by chance, through a chap who works on the *News*. A couple of years back he thought of doing a piece on the man but he came up against the same brick wall as Jane's student. It made him inquisitive and he did some poking around but the game wasn't worth the candle and he packed it in. Anyway, he gave us a start and we were able to carry on where he left off. David Paul Cleeve was born in Bristol, September 5th 1931, son of David Gordon Cleeve, solicitor's clerk and Elizabeth née Cotterell. Nothing so far on his childhood or education but in either '47 or '48 he joined the staff of the local paper as a trainee journalist. National Service was still in force then but he was exempted on medical grounds – he was an epileptic. He's still remembered on the paper as the reporter who had fits – he had one in a council meeting.

'In 1953 he moved out into our territory at Exeter, and set up as a freelance, contributing to newspapers and writing articles for magazines. But by the time he published his first book – *Xanadu* in October 1955 – he was living in London. *Medicus* followed in '57, *Magistra* in '59 et cetera.

'In April 1962 he married Patricia Elizabeth Tull at a register office in Oxford, a successful author, already very well-heeled. They lived in Surrey, then in Dorset, and moved to Cornwall in '74 or '75. Of course by then they'd had their twin children who were at boarding school.'

'Is that the lot?'

'I'm afraid so up to now.'

'A blameless career in fact.'

'It looks that way. Do you want the enquiry kept open, sir?'

Wycliffe hesitated. 'I'm seeing Cleeve later this morning so carry on unless you hear differently.'

They talked for a while about other cases then Scales, with good-humoured cynicism, wished him a happy holiday.

Wycliffe said to Potter: 'Ring Roscrowgy and tell them I'm on my way.'

He decided to walk to give himself time to think.

He left the Incident Room and turned up the hill by the chapel, leaving the tourists' village behind. Larger houses modestly concealed their virtue behind high dry-stone walls topped with escallonia in crimson flower. Only the bees disturbed the stillness and in the dry, fragrant heat it would have been easy to believe that he had the Mediterranean at his back instead of the English Channel. But his mind was on other things.

David Cleeve, Peter Stride . . . Why was he bothering his head about this man? Did he believe that Cleeve had killed the girl? He had no reason to think so, and yet . . . '*I never heard of him but I wouldn't would I. The boy sounds nice even if he is a bit wet but I think you could make trouble that way . . .*' The gospel according to Celia Dawe's friend, Liz. He had asked the Met to contact the girl. But even if Cleeve was sleeping with Celia Dawe was there any reason to link her death with Cleeve's past and the nebulous threats he had been so coy about?

He left the villas behind and came out on the *ros*, or heath, which gives Roseland its name. He walked on past the gates of Roscrowgy until he could see what was happening in Henry's Field. They were there, working like beavers preparing for a flood. Nothing had changed except that there were posters on boards set up in the hedge: 'Stop this desecration of land sacred to the Celtic People!' Followed by small print explaining how to set about doing it; all nice and legal.

Wycliffe retraced his steps and went through the white gates and up the long drive to the house. It brought him to a different entrance from the one Cleeve had taken him to – how long ago? Just four days! He was about to ring the bell when the door was opened by Cleeve himself.

'I happened to see you from the window . . . good of you to come.' Bland good manners which failed to conceal an underlying anxiety.

Wycliffe followed him along a short passage which joined the main corridor, then up the stairs to the study. The little dark girl looked up and saw them as they passed the open door of her office.

'Sit you down . . . whisky?'

'Not just now, thanks.'

A wry smile. 'I suppose not. You won't mind if I do? I shall probably need it.'

Nothing had changed; the sunlit creek, the estuary, the white-sailed yachts weaving their slow patterns on a smooth sea. In the study the smell of polished wood, of leather, of books and whisky . . .

'You wanted to see me?'

'I had to. Of course, it's about this girl – Celia Dawe. All this talk of her being murdered – poisoned.'

'You knew her?'

Cleeve made an impatient movement. 'Let's not beat about the bush! If you haven't heard already you soon will; I've been sleeping with her.'

'You visited her at her flat?'

'A couple of times a week over the past two months.'

'At more or less regular intervals?'

'Usually Monday and Thursday of each week.'

'You are being very frank.'

'I need to be. I was beginning to wonder when I was going to be haled off to the nearest cop-shop – "a man is helping the police with their enquiries". All this nonsense about murder . . .'

'Were you with her on the night of Monday/Tuesday – the night she died?'

Cleeve fingered his moustache, belatedly hesitant at the final fence. 'Yes, I was.'

'Then I should warn you –'

'To hell with that! I want to tell you what happened, then you can tell me what it's all about.' He paused, fiddling with his whisky glass, twisting the crystal tumbler between finger and thumb. 'I was with her when she died and I can see no way in which she could have been murdered.' He broke off and looked at Wycliffe. 'They're talking about nicotine poisoning – injected. Surely that would be quick acting?'

'Very.'

'Then there is no way she could have been murdered! I can't understand how all this started . . . I'm putting myself in your hands, I've got to rely on you to believe what I tell you.'

Wycliffe said nothing and Cleeve paused to collect his thoughts. When he spoke again it was in a different vein, he even summoned up a grin.

'I wonder how much you know about women. I suppose most men imagine themselves to be experts but I don't mind admitting they defeat me . . . You know those boxes of assorted chocolates with a little chart to tell you what's inside the different shapes? I need something like that in dealing with women; it's too late when you've bitten through the chocolate coating . . . Looking at that girl you'd have thought all that was needed was a match to the blue touch paper but, in fact, she was frigid. She put on a damned good act, but an act it was, and in a dozen subtle ways she let you know it . . . I always thought she was laughing at me; she was clever, I think she got a kick out of it, but it was tantalizing – humiliating, I suppose . . . A man likes to think . . .'

He looked at his glass which was empty. 'Are you quite sure you won't?' Wycliffe shook his head and Cleeve pushed his glass aside. 'I suppose I'd better not either. I've had enough already.'

He shifted heavily in his chair. 'I was going to say that on Monday night it seemed different.' He looked boyishly embarrassed. 'I thought I'd made it – you understand? I mean, all the signs, the sort of thing they can't fake – that shuddering spasm . . . Then she went limp and I must admit, my only thought was, "Got you this time, my girl!" '

Wycliffe found it hard to remember that he was listening to the creator of *Medicus*, and not to any man only haltingly articulate on the subject of his sexual experience. An author without his typewriter is a soldier without his gun.

'She was dead.'

The words hung uncomfortably in the air.

It was hot and getting hotter. Cleeve was red-faced and sweating; he got up and opened a window, letting in the sounds from outside with a breath of air and the smell of freshly cut grass. Someone was mowing the lawns.

He returned to his chair. 'It took me minutes to realize what had happened, and when I did I thought she must have died of heart failure or a blood clot or something of the sort. . . I did all I could—'

'Except call a doctor.'

He nodded. 'I was a fool, but I couldn't face it, and once I was certain nothing could be done . . .' He hesitated. 'I was right, wasn't I? Nothing could have been done?'

'As it happens, you were right.'

'Then I don't understand all of this talk of murder – of poison. She died in my arms – literally, and I was with her for about two hours before that. You see, it's not possible.'

'The girl was killed by a dart made from part of an ordinary hypodermic needle set in a brass tube which held the nicotine. It functioned like a miniature hypodermic syringe. The needle entered the girl's left buttock and the poison was injected into her system. Subsequently – perhaps when you moved away from her, the dart fell out and rolled onto the floor where Dr Hodge found it.'

Cleeve was looking at him in ludicrous astonishment. 'I suppose you know what you are talking about, but I was there—'

Wycliffe cut him short. 'The sash window of the bedroom was open a little at the bottom?'

'Yes, it was; I remember the curtains moving slightly but I don't see —'

'She could have been killed by someone in the yard; someone standing by the window.'

'You mean that someone reached in and plunged that thing into her when we were . . .'

'I think it's more likely that the dart was fired from some sort of air weapon or spring gun.'

Cleeve had lost his high colour and for a moment Wycliffe wondered if he would faint. It was some time before he could speak then he said in a low voice: 'So she really was murdered! Murdered while . . .' It was obvious that he was deeply affected, unable to come to terms with what he had been told. All his 'man-to-man-let's-settle-this-together' attitude had deserted him. He got up from his chair and made a slow circuit of the room, pausing now and then to stare at books on the shelves then, abruptly, he turned to Wycliffe. 'Have you any idea who did it?'

'None.'

'Or why?'

Wycliffe shook his head. 'I can think of no reason why anyone would want to murder Celia Dawe, can you?'

He looked startled. 'Me? Of course not! I've told you, I couldn't understand this talk of murder.'

Wycliffe was impressed by the change in the man. Celia Dawe had died in his arms yet he had been sufficiently detached to gossip, even make little jokes, but now that he understood how she had died he was overcome. Wycliffe thought that he knew the reason for that.

'What time did it happen?'

A moment to consider. 'Between half-past one and two; I can't put it closer than that.' He came back to stand by his chair, looking down at Wycliffe. 'So

85

you believe me – my version of what happened?'

Wycliffe made a small movement with his hands. 'It's too early to say; I can say that, in the light of what I already know, what you have told me is believable.'

Cleeve nodded. 'That's all I can expect. Thanks. What happens now?'

'You will be invited to make a statement. I suggest you come to the Incident Room in Chapel Street this afternoon. One of my officers will be expecting you and you will be asked about the events of Monday night and invited to make a statement in writing. Shall we say at four o'clock?'

'I'll be there.' He seemed to answer mechanically, preoccupied with his thoughts.

Wycliffe went on: 'At the same time I want you to allow your finger-prints to be taken.'

Cleeve looked surprised. 'Finger-prints? I've admitted being in the room with the girl; my prints are probably all over the place.'

'All the same we shall need your prints for comparison purposes.'

A shrug. 'As you wish.'

Wycliffe allowed a silence to drift on. Cleeve resumed his seat and the two men were once more facing each other across his desk. When Wycliffe spoke again his manner was less formal.

'Have you thought any more about our conversation on Saturday?'

'What? Oh, yes, I'm getting a security man to patrol the grounds at night.'

'Have there been any more threats?'

'No – none.'

'Do you feel at greater risk because of what happened to Celia Dawe?'

Cleeve reacted sharply. 'Why do you ask me that? Why should I?'

Wycliffe was matter-of-fact. 'Because since I told you that Celia Dawe had been murdered and explained how it was done, you have been wondering whether the dart that killed her found its intended target. That is reasonable. After all, it would be a very odd coincidence if, while your life was being threatened, the girl who shared your bed was murdered in an unrelated incident.'

Cleeve's powerful hands were lightly clasped, resting on the desk. A craftsman's hands, stout fingers, square ends. He seemed to be studying his hands and did not raise his eyes. 'Of course the idea occurred to me.'

'And?'

He shook his head. 'I don't know.'

Wycliffe got to his feet. 'You must think about it; but whatever you decide, now that I know you were with the girl, I have to look at the case from a new angle. Unless there is fresh evidence soon, which makes sense of the girl's murder, we shall assume that you were the intended victim; then your reticence about these threats will have greater importance.'

'Is that a warning?'

'Not a warning. I'm pointing out the direction our enquiries will take, and giving you the chance to make your voluntary statement as complete as possible.'

'I see.'

'Once we know the nature of the threats you received and once you have told us something of the reasons behind them, we can provide you with whatever protection is needed.'

Cleeve, too, got to his feet. 'I shall be at the Incident Room at four o'clock. I'll see you out.'

They walked down the long, inhospitable corridor and Cleeve saw him off at the front door. Wycliffe felt depressed. Sometimes it seemed to him that his was a degrading occupation, exposing the nakedness of men, the deceits and evasions of the weak and the pathetic deviance of the wicked; pinning out their sins, like insects in a box, and saying, 'This is what you are!' Not that he would condone crime, but sometimes he yearned for a more inspiring concept of justice, perhaps like the classical Chinese – the restoration of the pattern.

Back to earth: he was convinced now that his hunch had been correct, that the little dart had been carefully and cunningly contrived to be fired from an airgun or something of the kind. Franks had said that the external diameter of the brass tube was close to five millimetres and that meant it could be fired from a variety of air and spring weapons. Further than that, he was convinced that it had been aimed at Cleeve, not at the girl.

It was twelve-thirty – time for lunch and, on the spur of the moment, he decided to try The Vegetarian.

It was comfortably full and he was asked to share a table with a man of about his own age, a lean man of saturnine countenance. He looked at the menu; the waitress said: 'The sweet-corn-and-cheese-bake is our special today.'

'All right. Are you licensed?'

'No, but you can have fruit-juice, tea or coffee, or various herbal drinks.'

Depressing. 'I'll have coffee later.'

The saturnine man said, 'I've never understood why vegetarianism and total abstinence seem to go together.'

'I'll start with the soup.'

'Are you ready for your main course, Dr Hodge?'

Dr Hodge. The eyes of the two men met and Dr Hodge smiled. 'I think it's Chief Superintendent Wycliffe . . .'

They talked about the village.

Hodge said, 'I've been here for twenty years. It's not a village, it's a suburb without any urb to be sub to; a cosmopolitan collection of people with nothing in common but the conviction that they've escaped from something – from what, they're not quite sure. Interesting though. You'll need a side-salad with that bake thing when it comes. There aren't many of the original inhabitants left and those that are don't count any more; no more than mice in the woodwork.'

Wycliffe lowered his voice though there was no need; people were chattering nineteen to the dozen. 'You found the dart.'

The waitress came with the doctor's main course – a three-egg omelette with a brown-bread roll and butter. High cholesterol. 'My wife won't let me have eggs at home; says they're bad for me. Yes, cunning little thing, wasn't it? Somebody spent the whole winter concocting that, brooding on it. They're great brooders hereabouts – nothing else to do in the winter. But why the girl? That's what puzzles me. She was a good-looker but apart from that she was ordinary enough. The trouble was she had old-fashioned ideas – she thought somebody would be fool enough to set her up and keep her for what they could get in bed. It's funny; some of these girls don't seem to realize that sex is off ration now so there's no longer a black market. Leathery!' The doctor was prodding his omelette. 'Cooked too slowly; they're usually better at it here.'

'Do you mind if I ask you a professional question?'

'Why not? Everybody else does.'

'Would you say that epilepsy – *grand mal* epilepsy, where the patient is subject to recurring seizures – is curable?'

Hodge shrugged. 'It depends; every case is different, but for a young person who submits to treatment and behaves sensibly, the prognosis is good.'

'Is there a chance that he might be able to come off drugs and lead a normal life?'

'In many cases – yes.'

'Alcohol?'

A quizzical look. 'Oh, no, I'd strongly advise anybody with a history of epilepsy to lay off the booze.'

'For good?'

'Certainly, he'd be tempting providence otherwise.'

'Thanks.'

They finished their meal.

'If you and your wife are still here on Saturday afternoon, you might care to come sailing . . .'

Back in the Incident Room he briefed DC Edwards to take Cleeve's statement. Edwards was slow but nothing got past him and he had the integrity of an elephant. 'Also, get hold of Sergeant Smith and ask him to be here to take Cleeve's prints – I want them checked with CRO immediately.'

At a quarter to four Wycliffe pushed open the door of the photographer's shop, the bell buzzed, but no one came. He went through to the studio at the back, pushing aside the velvet curtains: a camera on a stand, various lamps and screens and an assortment of studio props dating from the 'twenties. Carpeted stairs to the floor above.

He could hear the photographer's voice, softly insistent. He stood at the bottom of the stairs and called: 'Is anyone at home?'

An interval, and Borlase came to the top of the stairs, wiping his mouth with a table napkin. Afternoon tea: the photographer's too-solid flesh needed frequent nourishment. He was anxious, startled.

'Mr Wycliffe!'

'Don't bother to come down; I'll come up.'

Before Borlase could stop him he was at the top of the stairs, on a landing with several doors. Two of the doors at the back were open, one to a gloomy kitchen and the other to a dining-room, furnished in oak which would have been thought handsome 60 years before. Smells of cooking, stale clothes, dust, and dog blended uneasily.

Borlase's sisters had come on to the landing to see what was happening.

'This is my sister, Helena, Mr Wycliffe.' Tall, gaunt and grey, supporting herself. 'And this is Posy.' Younger and stouter than Helena, having split a packet of genes with her brother.

'This is Mr Wycliffe, the gentleman from the police.'

Helena rounded on her brother. 'I know who he is; the question is, what does he want?' Her voice was harsh and masculine.

The photographer, embarrassed, said, 'Perhaps you will come into the dining-room, Mr Wycliffe . . .? Will you join us in a cup of tea . . .? Are you sure?'

On the table was a plate of sandwiches, another of sausage rolls and a third of dough buns.

A yellowish dog of dubious provenance, an obscene-looking creature, patchily bald, roused itself from sleep on the hearth-rug and lumbered across to Wycliffe, wagging a truncated tail. Wycliffe took a large envelope from his bag with a police inventory tag stuck to the outside. The photographer brushed crumbs from his shirt front, his gaze riveted on the envelope.

'I think these are what you are looking for, Mr Borlase.' Wycliffe slid the photographs on to the table top.

Borlase was speechless; he squeezed his napkin into a ball and began to knead furiously.

Helena glared at the photographs, then at Wycliffe, finally at her brother.

'How did he get hold of these?' The voice was menacing.

Wycliffe said, 'You told us lies, Mr Borlase. You said you hadn't been in touch with your niece since her return; in fact, you've been to visit her several times and, on more than one occasion, you quarrelled.'

Borlase shook his head helplessly and little beads of sweat appeared on his forehead and lips. 'It was the photographs, Mr Wycliffe . . . I had to get them back. She took them when she went away and she was threatening me. When a painter paints a nude, it's art, but when a man like me, a photographer . . .' He picked up one of the prints. 'This is work of very high quality, Mr Wycliffe – any authority would tell you . . . You have to believe me; there was nothing . . . it was entirely innocent, I assure you . . .' The weak, rather sensuous mouth was trembling.

'Then why did you allow your niece to blackmail you?'

He shuddered. 'Blackmail! Dear God, I assure you—'

Wycliffe's expression was blank. 'An unpleasant word, but still not so unpleasant as murder.'

'Murder!' A whisper; his voice all but let him down completely. 'You can't think that I . . .'

Helena hammered on the floor with her stick and shouted. 'Will you tell me how *he* got them? You said you'd made her give them back!'

It was Posy's turn. With a grim I-told-you-so smile, she said, 'You should never have gone to see her in the first place, Joe! You wouldn't have gone if it had been left to me, but other people knew better.'

Helena snapped: 'If people listened to you they would never do anything, not even keep themselves clean.'

They were laying the foundations for a future quarrel in which Joseph's role would be no more than that of a carcass squabbled over by jackals. But there was no time now. Helena concentrated on her brother; her wrinkled lips quivering with frustrated rage:

'Five hundred pounds you said you gave her! What happened to the five hundred pounds?'

'She took the money but she wouldn't give me . . .' Words failed him.

Helena shouted and banged her stick on the floor. 'Fool! Fool! Liar!'

And Posy said, 'They really will come to lock you up one of these days if you go on like that, Lena.'

Lena and Posy. A long time ago they must have been young girls, a few years' difference in their ages; Lena, slim and dark; Posy, fair, plump and rosy-cheeked. In fact, there was a hand-coloured enlargement of two such girls over the mantelpiece.

But it was not his sisters who were worrying Borlase

at that moment, but the seemingly impassive policeman. He turned to Wycliffe.

'Celia said they were photographs of her, so they were hers, and if I wanted them back I would have to pay for them. Then, when I gave her the money she asked for . . .'

'But why did you want them so badly? Surely you had negatives?'

The photographer raised his hands in helplessness. 'You don't understand, Mr Wycliffe! She threatened to show them round the village! In a place like this I would never live it down; they would say that I . . . that I . . .' His voice broke in a sob and he covered his face with the wretchedly crumpled napkin.

His sisters watched him and Helena said, 'Murder? You can see for yourself. He couldn't step on a cock-roach!'

Wycliffe was feeling grim. He gathered up the photographs and replaced them in the envelope. 'These will be retained until the case is over; then you will have them returned to you. It would have saved a lot of trouble, Mr Borlase, if you had told us the truth in the first place.'

Early in his career he had discovered that if one has greater sensitivity than a punch-bag, humiliation recoils. Ashamed of this scene he turned to the window and stood looking out, giving them a chance to recover some semblance of dignity.

From the window he could see down into the yard next door. Laura Wynn was in her workshop, bending over a sink, her golden hair like a crown. The houses on this side of the street had long narrow gardens. The Borlases' was a wilderness but Laura Wynn had put hers in grass and not far from the house there was a little gazebo.

'Keeping an eye on her?' Lena's harsh voice at his elbow. Incredibly, after all that had gone before, her manner was relaxed and conversational. 'You should!

She and her cats! She's been there two years and still nobody knows who she is or where she came from. You should ask her what she was doing the night Celia was murdered – prowling round till all hours.'

'You said nothing about that to Sergeant Lane.'

She sniffed. 'Perhaps I forgot.'

'Well, you've remembered now; what did you see, and when?'

'I've told you. It was Monday night. I'm an old woman and I can't sleep. My bedroom is in the front and sometimes I get out of bed and sit in a chair by the window for a bit. I saw her in the street, wearing some dark-coloured dressing-gown sort of thing.'

'What was she doing?'

'She was crossing the street when I saw her.'

The photographer had recovered sufficiently to intervene. 'I think Lena should tell you that Mrs Wynn is often out at night, looking for her cats. She's got four Siamese and they wander away.'

To Wycliffe's surprise Helena did not seem to resent the interruption. She said, 'That's as maybe, but it's funny why she had to go down the alley that leads round to the backs of the houses.'

'You saw her go down the alley?'

'It looked that way to me.'

'You either saw her or you didn't.'

She shrugged. 'It was dark on that side of the street.'

Wycliffe said, 'I shall have to ask you to make a statement about this. It's obviously important to get it right. Are you sure—'

She interrupted. 'I don't trust her. She calls herself Mrs but there's never been any sign of a husband nor talk of one and she came here in the first place because of that man, Cleeve.'

'Because of Cleeve? What makes you say that?'

She looked smug. 'It was obvious. She hadn't been in the place five minutes before he way paying her visits and staying half the night. I thought he'd set her up here.'

'And you no longer think so?'

'If he did, it didn't last long – not more than four or five months; then he stopped going there. It wasn't long after that they started on about digging up Henry's Field and she was all against it – spite!'

She was a thoroughly unpleasant old woman but what she said made some sort of sense.

'I'll send someone to take your statement, Miss Borlase.'

'Suit yourself!'

Borlase came with him to the shop door. 'I hope . . .'

'Yes, Mr Borlase?'

'Nothing, I'm sorry.'

Wycliffe found himself out on the Steps with a sense of relief, wondering why people, families in particular, contrive their own peculiar hells.

He arrived back at the Incident Room as Cleeve was signing his statement. Cleeve in checked shirt and khaki slacks, looking like the lord of the manor who has called on his steward to sign a few boring documents before proceeding to more interesting concerns. Edwards, sitting opposite him across the table, was respectful but firm.

'The declaration at the start, then each page separately, sir, then the declaration at the end.'

Cleeve signed with a flourish and a gold pen, disregarding the miserable little ball-point he had been offered. When the last signature had been given he looked up and saw Wycliffe.

'Oh, it's you, Mr Wycliffe.'

'Good afternoon, Mr Cleeve.'

Very formal, Wycliffe took the statement and turned over the pages, unhurried. When he had finished he said, 'I see you have included nothing fresh in your statement.'

'No, it covers the same ground we discussed this morning – everything relevant as far as I can recollect it.'

Wycliffe nodded. 'There will be two men on duty round the clock – in the grounds close to your house, if you will allow it, otherwise outside.'

'Am I under observation, house-arrest, or what?'

'You are being given police protection.'

'Am I free to come and go as I please?'

'Of course! But I shall be grateful if you will keep my men informed of your movements, for your own safety.'

'I see.'

When Cleeve had gone, Wycliffe talked at length to Lucy Lane.

'Cleeve must know as well as I do that Celia Dawe was killed in an attempt on his life. He must know too that the attempt could only have been made by someone with an intimate knowledge of his movements.'

Lucy Lane thought he seemed preoccupied, unsure of himself. He stood by one of the windows, watching the unexciting life of Chapel Street. Another meal time loomed and the emmets had drained away from the streets as though someone had pulled the plug on them. A grey-haired woman stood in her open doorway, staring at nothing; a dog sniffed along the pavement; a man in a blue jersey went by, carrying three or four mackerel strung together by their gills.

'The attempt on Cleeve's life must have been made by someone intimately acquainted with him and his routine.' Wycliffe repeated the words to himself as though to lend them emphasis. Yet Cleeve's whole point at that first, fortuitous meeting had been that he was being threatened by someone outside the circle of his family and friends . . .

In any case, there could hardly be many who could claim close acquaintance with the man. Who were the initiates? Patricia and the twins, the brother-in-law Geoffrey Tull, the housekeeper Carrie Byrne, and, according to Helena Borlase, Laura Wynn. Were there others? What were Cleeve's relations with Gervaise Prout? With the mutilated Kitson?

Whether or not the attempt on his life had arisen from something in his past, whoever made it must belong to the here and now.

Wycliffe sighed. He had committed men to Cleeve's protection; he had little choice once it became obvious that the man's life really was under immediate threat. With or without Cleeve's co-operation the obligation remained, but whether the protection could be effective was another matter.

CHAPTER FOUR

Thursday July 21st

Wycliffe was standing on the edge of a trench; it could have been part of the dig in Henry's Field or it could have been a grave. Lying in the trench was a man, fully dressed. It was Cleeve and he was looking up at Wycliffe with an enigmatic smile. Wycliffe felt giddy and was afraid of falling into the trench; at the same time there was a ringing in his ears. Helen's voice came, peremptory but irrelevant:

'It's the telephone, Charles!'

Consciousness returned. The telephone. It was ringing downstairs; no bedroom extension in the cottage.

'Damn!'

He went down the narrow, break-neck stairs, mumbling to himself. It wasn't completely dark, just light enough to see the time by the wall-clock with the brass pendulum: four forty-five.

It was Pearce. 'I'm ringing from Roscrowgy, sir.' He spoke in a low voice as though concerned not to be overheard. 'There's been a fire on the Henry's Field site, the wooden shed they use as an office and museum has been burned down. The brigade was on the spot before me, and Bert Chinn, the fire officer, says it was burning so fiercely when he arrived that he suspects arson.'

Wycliffe was not pleased to be woken at dawn to be told that the Celtic Society might have had an unscheduled bonfire. He muttered something under his breath.

'Sir?'

'Never mind. What do you want me to do? Arrest the Wynn woman?' Heavily humorous.

But Pearce had saved his real news. 'I knew you wouldn't want to be got out of bed just because Laura Wynn might have got the bit between her teeth, but there may be more to it than that, sir. It looks as though Cleeve is missing.'

'Missing?'

'It seems that way.'

'Either he is or he isn't. What about our chaps who are supposed to be patrolling the place?'

'It was one of them who spotted the fire and phoned the brigade, but it looks as though Cleeve must have given them the slip. When the son went to tell his father about the fire, father was nowhere to be found. Mrs Cleeve is obviously worried but I can't get her to admit that she hasn't a clue where her husband is. I think she's afraid of starting something then having him turn up saying, "What the hell?" '

'All right. You were quite right to phone; I'll be along.'

He went back upstairs and groped for his pants.

'You've got to go out?'

'They think I'm the fire-brigade.'

The weather had changed – only temporarily, according to the forecast – the creek was obliterated by heavy mist, and moisture condensed out of the chill morning air. He seemed to be the only human being out of bed. His car was parked behind the cottage on a little rectangle of beaten earth advertised as 'space for car' – barely space enough to manoeuvre into the narrow lane, so testing his modest driving skills to near their limit. He cursed silently, and the engine was dubious about this early start on a damp morning. Further up the hill the mist became a fine drizzle.

Henry's Field was a dreary prospect; the large wooden shed had collapsed in on itself and was no more than a tangled heap of carbonized timbers, still smoking and steaming. The firemen had decided that the fire was out but they were in the cab of their tender, maintaining a watching brief. No sign of the archaeologists; the flaps of the bell-tents were down and the curtains of the caravan were drawn. Henry's Field was a depressing sight and Wycliffe decided it could hardly have been a health resort for its Iron-Age occupants.

Pearce was waiting. He nodded towards the tents. 'They've gone back to their sleeping bags.'

'What did Gervaise Prout make of it all?'

'Prout isn't here; he went off early yesterday and he isn't expected back until lunchtime today – some university meeting. It seems he took the site records with him to show his mates. Just as well, otherwise they would have gone up in smoke too.'

'So who's in charge?'

'Young fellow called Wrighton; Prout's assistant; all hair and glasses, looks at you like an owl.'

'What does he have to say?'

'That the fire must have been started deliberately; that there's no way the place could have caught fire otherwise. The lighting is electric, powered by a pocket-sized Jap generator in that dog-kennel over there and it's switched off at night.'

'Anything inflammable stored in the hut – petrol? Paraffin?'

'According to Wrighton there was a five-gallon drum containing about two gallons of paraffin. They use it for the generator.'

'And one of our chaps raised the alarm – at what time?'

'He logged it at 02.07.'

Wycliffe shivered; the chill dampness seemed to be seeping into him. Hard to believe that only the day before the site had been sweltering under the sun. He looked at his watch. 'Half-past five. Have the

100

Roscrowgy contingent gone back to bed too?'

'I very much doubt it, sir.'

'Then I'll try talking to them. I want you to find out from the fire officer when this debris can be handled without people getting choked or burned. If necessary, get them to damp it down some more. I would like somebody down from Forensic this afternoon – somebody with experience of arson.'

Pearce seemed surprised. 'You're taking this very seriously, sir.'

'Yes.'

He left Pearce and crossed the field to the wicket gate, he passed through the rhododendron tunnel where water dripped from the foliage and as he emerged from the tunnel one of the uniformed men on duty came towards him.

'PC Julian, sir.'

Wycliffe, becoming an expert on the brogues of the two counties, placed him as a Camborne man.

'I spotted the fire, sir. I was doing my rounds behind the house when I saw a glare in the sky somewhere over Henry's Field. It was clear then, the mist came in just before dawn. I reported in on my pocket-set and Control alerted the brigade. I heard them arrive ten or fifteen minutes later.'

'You didn't go over to the site?'

'No, sir. I talked to my mate and we decided our brief was here. I hope we did right?'

'In the circumstances – yes. Did you wake the people in the house?'

'We thought about it, sir, then decided not; but at about half-two or a bit later, young Cleeve turned up; he'd been to some party in Truro and he'd seen the fire on his way home. He was a bit shirty because we hadn't told his father and went off to do it.'

'And?'

Julian shifted uneasily. 'Well, his father wasn't there, sir.'

'When did you last see Mr Cleeve?'

'Neither of us have seen him since we came on at ten, sir. With respect, it's very nearly impossible to keep this place boxed up between the two of us. Altogether, there are five doors—'

Wycliffe said, 'I know; I'm not blaming anyone.'

He walked on towards the house. There were lights in several of the windows, competing with the grey morning. He rang the bell and the door was answered by a youth immediately identifiable as Andrew Cleeve because of his likeness to his sister.

'Mr Cleeve?'

The boy was pale, and hollow-eyed with tiredness. 'You are Mr Wycliffe – I think my mother will be relieved to see you.'

He took Wycliffe's raincoat and led him through a large drawing-room to a small boudoir which opened off it; an hexagonal room, plainly furnished: a dove-grey carpet, a business-like desk and a couple of spoon-back chairs; the whole redeemed and relieved by an Ivor Hitchens flower study over the fireplace and a bowl of pink roses on the window-sill; the office of an up-market headmistress. Patricia Cleeve was fully dressed, pale, but apparently composed.

'Mr Wycliffe, I'm so glad you've come; I scarcely know what to do.' She said this in the manner of a lady putting at ease a guest who feels that he has arrived at an awkward moment. 'May I offer you something?' She made sure that he was comfortably seated. 'Thank you, Andrew.'

Wycliffe refused refreshment though he would have given a great deal for a cup of black coffee. 'I expect you are very concerned for your husband.'

She arranged her dress to cover her knees. 'I must admit that I am, and very puzzled.'

'You would have expected him to tell you if he intended to stay out?'

'Of course! We don't share a bedroom because we

have different sleeping habits but he usually tells me if he intends to spend the night or any part of it away from home.'

Different sleeping habits . . . the night or any part of it – no beating about the bush; these are the facts; why pretend otherwise?

'You have no idea where he might have gone?'

'No.' She considered carefully before enlarging. 'In the circumstances, I was very surprised to hear that he had gone out.'

She did not say, 'with that girl lying dead', but her meaning was clear.

'Sometimes in the past he would take a stroll round the grounds before settling down for the night but not, I think, recently.'

'Can you tell me when you last saw your husband?'

'At our evening meal which we have at seven-thirty. Afterwards he went back to work as usual.'

'You have been to his room?'

'His bed has not been slept in.'

With caution, Wycliffe said, 'When you were speaking to Sergeant Pearce earlier he had the impression that you were reluctant to admit that you had no idea where your husband was.'

A little smile. 'Was it so obvious? I'm sure you will see that my husband would not have welcomed a hue and cry about nothing.'

'Since then, something has occurred to change your attitude?'

She played with her thin gold wedding-ring, twisting it round and round on her finger. 'Only that some hours have gone by and he still hasn't come home.'

She was superficially calm but underlying nervousness showed in her restless hands. She went on: 'When you were here on Saturday you had a private conversation with David and I'm sure he must have confided in you to some extent.' She added with a shrewd smile, 'Otherwise I hardly think you would be interested in

103

a man who has been missing from his home for only a few hours.'

Wycliffe nodded. 'And by the same token, if he hadn't taken you into his confidence, you would probably be less anxious now.'

She swept back her blonde hair with an impatient movement. 'I assure you, Mr Wycliffe, that David doesn't share his troubles with me; he seems to think that it is his duty to shield me from worry, which of course means that I worry all the more.' Her voice became brittle. 'You are probably in a better position to form an opinion about what danger he may be in than I am.'

'Is he on friendly terms with anyone in the neighbourhood whom he might conceivably have visited last night?'

She considered her reply. 'Leaving aside his affairs with women, about which there can hardly be any secret, there is only one person he is in the habit of visiting, that is Roger Kitson. I think you met Roger, he was with David when you were at the dig on Saturday. Roger has a little cottage in the plantation and David often goes there; they seem to have a lot in common. But he wasn't there last night; Christie and Andrew went over to enquire. We tried to telephone but Roger's phone is out of order. Since then they've been searching the whole area in case there's been an accident of some kind. I gather that Roger has been out too.'

Wycliffe was thinking that the mating game brings together strange partners. This woman, perceptive, forceful, but restrained; probably tantalized by sex though prudish by nature . . . she must have had a hard time with her brilliant, often sombre, always wayward and egocentric husband.

Wycliffe said, 'Forgive me, but I suppose there is no possibility that he was visiting another woman?'

A faint smile. 'I think not.' She added after a moment, 'He would allow a decent interval.'

'Could he have left the area for any reason? Simply cleared out?'

She looked surprised. 'Walking? The cars are in the garage, and as far as I can tell he had only the clothes he stood up in.'

Difficulties easily solved with money but he did not press the point.

He allowed a minute or two to pass before putting his next question and she waited, quite still now.

'Do you think there may be a connection between your husband's absence and the burned-out hut?'

'If there is I can't imagine what it could be.'

Wycliffe thought: That makes two of us. He said: 'Yesterday afternoon he came to the Incident Room and made a statement in connection with Celia Dawe's death. The statement did not incriminate him but it makes him a key witness so he is certain to be called to give evidence at the inquest and at any trial there may be.'

She looked at him, her blue eyes non-committal. 'So?'

'Do you think he would have been very upset at such a prospect?'

'I'm sure that he would. David has an intense dislike of publicity which amounts to a phobia; he even tries to prevent it being generally known that Peter Stride and David Cleeve are one and the same.' She smiled, as at the whims of a child. 'He never gives interviews, never fills up biographical questionnaires, and his photograph doesn't appear on the dust cover of his books.'

Wycliffe thought: Let it go at that for the moment. He dispensed balm with professional skill and it was received by one adept in the art of acknowledging courtesy with grace . . . 'I know that you will do all that is possible, Mr Wycliffe.'

Wycliffe got to his feet; then, as though the thought had just occurred to him, he said, 'Do you know if your husband, as a young man, was subject to epileptic seizures, Mrs Cleeve?'

She too was standing, and she looked at him in astonishment. 'David? What makes you ask that?'

'Was he?'

'If he was, he told me nothing of it and there has never been the slightest suggestion of anything of the kind since our marriage. I would like to know—'

Wycliffe cut her short, gently but firmly. 'We have to think of every possibility.'

Andrew Cleeve was waiting for him in the big drawing-room. 'I'll see Mr Wycliffe out, mother.' The boy clearly doted on his mother and wanted to save her from distress as far as he could.

In the hall he helped Wycliffe on with his raincoat. Wycliffe said, 'Walk back with me to the site.'

It was obvious that Andrew was waiting for a chance to talk.

'Take a coat or something, it's quite wet out.'

Andrew went to a hall cupboard and came back, struggling into an anorak that was already wet.

Outside, it was the boy who spoke first. 'Do you think that something has happened to father?'

'I don't know what to think; what is your opinion?'

The question took him by surprise. 'I don't know . . . he's been very odd lately. Since I've been home this vacation he's hardly been outside the grounds except . . . It's true he never went out much. Then he's been talking of employing a security johnny to patrol the grounds at night; he says it's because there have been one or two burglaries in the neighbourhood but I can't help feeling he's scared of something . . .'

'Do you get on well with your father?'

He thought about the question or, perhaps, about the answer he would give, then he said, 'No – not really.'

'Rows?'

'Not rows; we just keep out of each other's way.'

'Is this strain something new? Is it connected with Celia Dawe?'

In a dead-pan voice the boy said, 'So you know about that; I suppose you are bound to.'

'I know about your father and Celia and about you and Celia.'

'Yes, and that's what caused the trouble. I don't want to say much now but it's disgusting! He's more than old enough to be her father and, in any case, it's so humiliating for mother.'

'You weren't madly keen on the girl?'

They passed through the wicket gate and were able to walk side by side over the wet grass.

'I liked her; she was good fun but it wasn't serious for either of us. She was a really nice girl who'd had a very rough time and I felt sorry for her. But first Polmear, then my father, treated her like a tart.'

'How did you find out about her and your father?'

'She told me. She was very straight about it; she wouldn't let me take her out until I knew the situation. I thought that was very honest.'

Wycliffe thought that there might be other words to describe it but he said nothing.

'So your father sometimes went out at night if he didn't by day.'

'Yes! Sneaking out of his own house like a delinquent schoolboy!' He was silent for a while and they came to a halt in order not to reach the fire-tender before they had finished their conversation. 'Of course, the rules that apply to ordinary people are not for The Great Writer. I know that sounds harsh, but all that crap makes me sick!'

'There are many people, all over the world, who think your father is a great writer.'

'So what? My tutor at university is internationally known as a geologist but he's an ordinary, pleasant chap; he takes his wife and kids on holiday, he watches telly, and when he gets drunk he does it in company because he's enjoying himself – not alone in his room as an outlet for creative frustration.'

'But don't you think that the emotional demands on a first-rate writer or painter or musician are probably greater than those on your geologist?'

The boy shrugged. 'Possibly; I don't know, and I don't want to know. I prefer to be stupid and live like other people.'

Wycliffe changed his ground. 'Do I need to tell you that your father didn't kill Celia Dawe?'

The young man seemed to consider this for a while though he made no comment but after a little more time the question came, hesitant and a little fearful, 'Was he with her that night?'

'I'm not going to answer that; I've said more than I should already. Now, you must tell me something. Did Celia say anything to you which might have implied that she was frightened of someone or threatened by them?'

'Never!'

'Did she talk about her uncle?'

'Only about the way she was treated by him and her aunts.'

'Ill-treated?'

'Not exactly that; they were incredibly old-fashioned and she was made to dress and behave as if she was living when they were young. Even after she was sixteen, there was a row if she didn't go to chapel every Sunday, and she had to tell them exactly where she was going before she was allowed to go out of an evening. It was Victorian!'

'I understand you spotted the fire on your way back from Truro at about half-past two this morning.'

'Yes. I'd been to a sort of farewell party to a chap I was at school with; he's off to work in Tunisia . . . I know it sounds a bit heartless with Celia and all that . . .'

'It's natural enough; I shouldn't let that worry you.

You didn't see anything unusual along the road – apart from the fire, that is?'

'No, nothing. In fact I don't think I saw a soul – not a thing on the road – from Tregony home.'

Wycliffe thanked the boy and they parted. Andrew turned back towards the house and Wycliffe continued across the field. There was more activity on the site: unisex students in all manner of dress, looking damp and dismal, drifted to and fro between the tents and the screened-off wash-ups and loos. Near the burned-out hut Sergeant Pearce was in conversation with a sturdy, bearded young man with a mass of curly black hair and king-sized spectacles; presumably Prout's assistant.

Pearce turned to Wycliffe. 'Mr Wrighton tells me he knew nothing of the fire until a student came banging on the door of the caravan where he was sleeping. By that time the fire-tender was already entering the field.'

Wrighton looked at Wycliffe, solemn and anxious. 'I must admit to being a very sound sleeper.' He confessed it as a fault.

Wycliffe said, 'I suppose this is a major set-back for your work?'

The young man removed his glasses to wipe them and blinked myopically. 'I shouldn't think so. Ours won't have been the first hut to be burned down on this site; it must have been a fairly common occurrence when the original inhabitants were in possession.'

'But they weren't archaeologists working to a budget.'

A quick smile. 'They weren't insured either. No, most of our artefacts are pretty durable; they wouldn't be here otherwise after so many centuries. I expect most of our finds will turn up again in the debris. Luckily all our instruments are kept in the caravan.'

'And your records?'

The glasses were replaced. 'Ah, there we really had some luck. Dr Prout had the bulk of our records with him and I was working on the current stuff in the caravan last night.'

'I understand that you and Dr Prout live in the caravan, but that he is away.'

'Dr Prout is away and he'll be returning some time this afternoon, but I only sleep in the van when he's away. At other times I'm in the tents with the others.'

'Is he here most nights?'

'Oh, yes, he's never away more than one or two nights a week. Although he only lives at St Germans and could, I suppose, go home every night, he prefers to stay on the site.'

'Tell me how you spent yesterday evening.'

'I was in the caravan writing up our log. I worked until about ten-thirty, then I made myself a hot drink and went to bed and to sleep.'

'Did you see Mr Cleeve at all?'

'No, I didn't; he hardly ever comes here in the evenings.'

'When you went to bed, had the students settled down for the night?'

A tolerant smile. 'No, they certainly had not. On Wednesday evenings there is a disco in the village and they went off in a body. I understand they came back at about half-past eleven but I'm afraid I didn't hear them.'

'How many students do you have on the site?'

He considered. 'Let me think . . . yes, twelve – ten of them, six girls and four boys, are living in the tents; the other two are local and one of them is Christie Cleeve.'

Wycliffe thanked him.

'If there is anything more I can do . . . I'm sure that Dr Prout would want me . . .'

'We may ask you for a written statement later.'

Pearce's owl seemed to Wycliffe more like an earnest, myopic teddy-bear.

Back in his car, Wycliffe put through an RT call to

division, asking for additional men. No point in ringing Forensic until the witching hour of nine a.m.

It was still a little short of eight o'clock when he let himself into the cottage. The mist showed no sign of clearing and a very fine rain had spread down from the hill. No sailing today; no trippers; no cruises round the docks or to the lighthouse.

Helen was in the kitchen, in her dressing-gown.

'Coffee?'

Her auburn hair was set off by the blue of her dressing-gown and he thought how young she looked to be the mother of grown-up children. He kissed her on the nape of her neck.

'What was that for?'

They sat on stools in the kitchen, eating toast and drinking coffee.

'What happened? You said something about a fire.'

'The archaeologists' hut has been burned down – almost certainly with malice aforethought. More important, it looks as though Cleeve is missing.'

Helen paused with a piece of toast half-way to her mouth. 'Missing?'

'It seems he went out late last night and he hasn't come back.'

'You've talked to his wife?'

'Yes. She didn't miss him until they were all woken up about the fire. They don't sleep in the same room.'

Helen nodded. 'I thought there was something. Poor woman! With all her breeding she couldn't hide the fact that she had her troubles. It can't be easy living with a man like Cleeve. Since we were there I've thought about them a lot; it's one thing to read the work of a man who is obsessed by the evil in the world but it's quite another to have to live with him.' She grinned. 'I suppose there are worse things than being married to a policeman.'

After a pause she said, 'Do you think there's a

111

connection between the fire and Cleeve's disappearance?'

Wycliffe sighed. 'I wish I knew.'

'Surely in a village of this size, a murder, arson, and a missing man, all in the space of three days, are more likely to be linked than not?'

He nodded. 'You'd certainly think so, but piecing them together is another matter. It reminds me of homework we used to get at school: "Put the following incidents into a story of three hundred words—".'

'Taxis and hire-cars in Roseland itself and the district up to and including Truro and St Austell; you'll need a description of Cleeve and of the clothes he was wearing when he went out. If we haven't found him by late afternoon I shall issue a press release then we can ask for public co-operation – anyone driving along the A3078 after 20.30 hours last night blah blah . . .'

Lucy Lane was making notes. 'You really think he's cleared out of his own accord?'

'Or he's under the debris of the burnt-out hut, or he's lying injured or dead somewhere in the neighbourhood, or he's been kidnapped by the little green man with an Irish accent.'

'Sorry, sir.'

'No, it's me.' Wycliffe sighed. 'After talking to him yesterday I feel I should have kept closer tabs on him. Then there are the watermen.'

'Watermen?'

'Down at the harbour. It's not impossible that he took a boat, his own or somebody else's. We also want to know where everybody was yesterday evening and night. I've asked Division for more men.'

'Anything else?'

'Yes. Laura Wynn's Celtic circus. It seems that somebody set fire to the hut and arson is arson whether or not it is connected with Cleeve's disappearance. So: anybody seen loitering in the neighbourhood with a dangerous box of matches . . .'

'But seriously—'

'Seriously, you get from Pearce a list of Laura's dyed-in-the-wool activists and make 'em account for themselves. It will be a waste of time but "no stone unturned" and it might teach 'em a lesson.'

Six constables, including three dog-handlers with their dogs, arrived from Division and were allocated to Sergeant Pearce to work over the fields and lanes, the cliffs and shore lines to the north of Roscrowgy – the area within which Cleeve might conceivably have walked and met with some mishap without being found. Before turning them loose, Wycliffe telephoned Patricia to make sure there had been no news. In telling him there had not she effectively hid whatever feelings she may have had under the veneer of her impeccable manners.

Dr Bell, an old friend at Forensic, telephoned to say that Horton, the fire expert, would be on the scene by three o'clock. He also confirmed that the dart had probably been projected from some sort of air or spring gun: they had found traces of oil on the brass tube probably from the barrel of the weapon and, more significantly, tiny fragments of hard wax adhered to the blank end of the tube, almost certainly a substitute for the flaring of the pellets normally fired from airguns, which stops them sliding down the barrel.

The killer had thought of everything.

Tests were being carried out to determine the effectiveness of the dart when fired from different types of air weapon.

Wycliffe said, 'The killer couldn't have counted on an open window and a naked target. He might have had to wait for his victim to leave, fully dressed. What about the effectiveness of the dart then?'

Bell was definite. 'I think it would have penetrated all but the thickest clothing and remained effective when fired with a modern airgun or pistol.'

For an hour Wycliffe created an atmosphere of unease in the Incident Room, standing about, brooding, drinking cups of Potter's coffee and smoking. He spoke with two reporters who were quite content to be briefed with the details of Celia Dawe's murder; they showed no interest in the fire, and had not yet heard that the country's most controversial and best-selling author was missing from home.

Cleeve missing. Since yesterday's encounter Wycliffe had been convinced that Celia Dawe was the accidental victim of a dart intended for Cleeve. The middle of the night, the lighting poor, the killer nervous, and the two bodies on the bed anything but still; a sudden convulsive movement on their part had probably reprieved the man and condemned the girl. Polmear, landlord of The Buckingham, had said it: 'She was an unlucky kid – never got it right.' Wycliffe hadn't been a policeman for nearly 30 years without knowing that there were such people – Fate's preferred targets.

But it was Cleeve, missing or not, on whom the investigation must concentrate now.

He said to Potter: 'I'm going to talk to Laura Wynn.'

The mist had thickened; on the Steps visibility was less than 20 yards; a sea mist with the tang of salt. Invisible, a jet-fighter ripped through the air above the mist – in yesterday's weather. In this steep narrow lane between granite cottages it was easy to imagine that the figures looming out of the fog were fishermen returning from sea; in fact they were disgruntled emmets in plastic macs, wondering what there was to do but eat. Now and then the fog-horn on the lighthouse boomed out like some monstrous animal in its last sad hours.

Wycliffe pushed open the door of the jewellery shop and stepped down into the well-like area in front of the counter. A moment or two went by before Laura Wynn appeared; Laura in working rig – blue nylon overall, her hair caught back in a youthful ponytail, no torque, no bangles. Probably she did not expect customers in such weather and she looked at him without enthusiasm.

'Mr Wycliffe, isn't it?'

'I would like to talk to you, Mrs Wynn, in connection with the murder of Celia Dawe.'

She indicated by the slightest movement that there was nothing stopping him.

'It would be more convenient if we could sit down.'

She seemed on the point of refusing but changed her mind. She went to the door, lowered the catch and changed the sign to closed. 'This way, then.'

Through the door at the back of the shop, along a narrow passage to a room which looked out on the back garden. A pleasant room, white walls, chintz upholstery, shelves on either side of the chimney-breast filled with zany books. The pictures were framed reproductions of mediaeval illustrations of the Arthurian legend. She indicated a chair on one side of the empty fireplace and sat herself opposite him.

'I've already told your detective that I know nothing of the dead girl or of the people she associated with.'

A woman striving to achieve a serenity which did not come naturally to her; one could imagine her attending yoga classes, and dutifully consuming her fruit and fibre with live yogurt. At least she had achieved a clear eye and an intimidating gaze. Not a woman who had spent much of her life with men.

'You are acquainted with David Cleeve?'

It was obvious that the question came as a surprise. 'Why should—'

Wycliffe was firm. 'Perhaps you will allow me to ask the questions. Of course you don't have to answer them but I hope you will. This is a murder inquiry and I assume you wish to help.'

'All right. As we live in the same village it would be surprising if we were not acquainted.'

'Do you know that he was on intimate terms with the dead girl?'

A hardening of the facial muscles. 'It doesn't surprise me.'

'But did you know?'

A momentary hesitation. 'No, I did not know.'

'You were out on the Steps very late on the night of Monday/Tuesday.'

'So?'

'What were you doing?'

'I was looking for Tripitaka. Although he has been neutered he is very wayward at night.'

'Did you go down the alley which leads to the backs of the houses opposite?'

'A short distance – yes. I called Tripitaka and suddenly he was there at my feet. I picked him up and came back here.' Her manner was detached, objective.

'What time was this?'

'About half-past twelve.'

'Did you meet or see anyone while you were out?'

'No one.'

She was a good-looking woman – splendid was the word; too statuesque for Wycliffe's taste, but she might well have been a challenge to Cleeve. A modern Hera. Wasn't it Hera who annually renewed her virginity at the Argos spring? Women like Laura never really lost theirs and he suspected that this was true of Patricia too. Psychological virgins.

'David Cleeve is missing.'

'Missing?'

'He went out last night and he hasn't come back.'

She looked incredulous. 'You think something has happened to him?'

'That's what I'm trying to find out.'

'But why come to me?'

'The big wooden hut on Henry's Field was burned down during the night. Arson, by the look of it.'

A worried frown. 'You don't think that any of our people would do such a thing?'

'No? It seems they've been pretty active on the site before now.'

'But nothing wilfully destructive!' Anxious, shocked.

He moved in. 'I suspect that you knew Cleeve before you came to live here.'

Hesitation. She was saved from immediate reply by the arrival of one of her tribe of cats, a wicked-looking seal-point. The creature leapt on to her lap, flexed its claws in a way which must have been painful, and settled down, sleek and graceful as a snake.

Laura made up her mind to be co-operative, though her manner was more aggressive. 'I suppose I shall be badgered until I tell you, and I've nothing to hide. When I was at school I lived with my mother in a flat in Exeter. We had been deserted by my father who went off with another woman. David Cleeve and a friend moved into a flat on the same landing.'

'What year was this?'

She reflected. 'It must have been early in the summer of 1953, I remember the city was decorated for the coronation. They were still there when we left in September '54.'

John Scales had established that Cleeve moved from Bristol to Exeter in 1953 and set up as a freelance journalist. Now, here he was pin-pointed in an Exeter flat with a friend. Nice when the wires crossed on target.

'Where was this flat?'

'In Mellor Road – number fourteen. The houses in Mellor Road were four-storey Victorian town houses and most of them had been converted into flats. They're all gone now – replaced by modern flats, half the size and ten times the price.'

'Cleeve would have been about twenty-two at that time?'

'I suppose so, about that.'

'This friend he lived with . . .'

'A young man of about the same age. He was called John – John Larkin. They were journalists of some sort and they were both writing books.' She seemed slightly embarrassed. 'At that time I had visions of becoming a writer and I was impressed.'

'Did you know them well?'

She shook her head. 'No, we just met occasionally on the stairs. I was never in their flat or they in ours. I was only a schoolgirl and my mother didn't like me talking to them; she thought they were a bit odd.'

'I suppose they chatted you up?'

She frowned. 'No, it wasn't like that. We talked about books and they used to tease me about being serious. Anyway, when I was seventeen we moved to London and a bit later I went to the School of Art and Design.' She smiled, a rueful little smile. 'No more writing.'

'Did you see either of them again?'

'No, it wasn't until just after I came to live here – David came into the shop to buy a present for his wife and I recognized him.'

'After nearly thirty years?'

'Why not? People don't change all that much.' She smiled, softened by recollections of youth. 'I got mixed up, though, and called him John.'

'These two, when you knew them in Exeter, how were they living? Lots of friends – parties – girls?'

'No, nothing like that; they lived very quietly. Of course they were out a lot because of their work. They seemed quite well off; one of them had a car and not so many people did then.'

'I suppose your mother remembers them?'

'Mother died before I came to live here.'

'Perhaps you will tell me your maiden name?'

She hesitated, then made up her mind. 'I've never been married. I adopted the "Mrs" to avoid unwelcome attentions.'

'That's understandable. Did Cleeve seem pleased to see you again?'

'He didn't remember me at first.'

'And afterwards?'

She actually coloured. 'I saw him from time to time.'

'Do you know what happened to his friend – John Larkin?'

'No; I asked him, but it seems they lost touch. Not long after we left Exeter David moved to London himself and published his first book – *Xanadu*, the one that made his name. It was strange, I suppose, I actually read all the Peter Stride books without having the least idea that they had been written by him.'

'Can you give me the names of other people who were living in the Mellor Road flats who might remember the two young men?'

He got three names. Progress of a sort; at least a Knight's move.

As he was leaving he asked to see her workshop. She looked doubtful, but led him to a room which had been built onto the kitchen. Not very big but meticulously arranged to make use of every inch. Two benches, one for the metalwork, the other for enamelling. Tiny tools – snips, pliers, various little hammers, some of metal others of hard wood, tweezers and tongs; doll-size anvils and vices; a kiln and another little furnace; bottles labelled with cabalistic signs containing the enamelling colours . . . No doubt at all that Laura would have found the making of the dart well within her capability.

'Very interesting – thank you.'

Lunch, he thought, at The Buckingham.

The Buckingham was full of people and talk; waitresses dodged between the tables while people queued at the bar for drinks. Wycliffe hovered at the entrance to the lounge bar and was instantly spotted by the all-seeing Polmear. A signal to one of the waitresses and he was piloted to an alcove where there was a table laid for one – presumably for Polmear, when he found time to eat.

'The plaice is very good, sir. Fresh-caught this morning . . . With a side-salad . . . dressing? . . . And a lager?'

Near the end of the meal Polmear came and sat opposite him, nursing a bottle of brandy. 'To sweeten the coffee.'

Wycliffe said, 'Weather not so good today.'

'I'm not complaining, a couple of days a week like this and the money just rolls in – they've nothing to do but eat and drink; but if the weather stays bad longer than that they think about going home.'

The ethology of the emmet.

'Progress?'

Wycliffe shrugged.

Polmear said, 'I hear they had a fire up at the dig last night.'

'I heard that too.'

Polmear poured brandy into balloon glasses. 'Since you told me about Celia, I've been thinking: it could have been a jealous wife. There are women who can't take that sort of thing . . .'

Whatever Polmear had or hadn't known before, he knew something now.

'Thanks for the brandy.'

Wycliffe strolled along the waterfront; he found the tangy mist invigorating. One of the ferry boats was berthing with hardly anyone aboard. He turned up Zion Steps, loath to get back to the grind. The herbalist had a 'Closed' notice in his glass door; the vegetarians were champing away; the jewellery shop and the photographer's had a sealed look. In the Incident Room Dixon had taken over from Potter.

'Coffee, sir?'

'I'm awash already.'

He stood by one of the tall, narrow Gothic windows

of the little building, looking out into the grey gloom with a morose unseeing gaze.

In a murder case the rules are clear; you look to the oracles, the Three Wise Monkeys of criminal investigation: Motive, Means and Opportunity, and the greatest of these is Motive. He had asked: Who had a motive for murdering Celia Dawe? And the oracle had remained dumb. Now it seemed the question should have been: Who had a motive for killing Cleeve? But the oracle was no more communicative.

Cleeve had been threatened and there had been an attempt on his life; now he was missing.

Wycliffe brooded on Cleeve. The reporter on the local paper who had 'fits'; the freelance in Exeter, sharing a flat with another journalist, John Larkin; the schoolgirl Laura Wynn, living in the same building. Then, London, *Xanadu, Medicus, Magistra* . . . fame, marriage, the twins, Roseland . . . no more fits.

Patricia had said, 'If he was (an epileptic) he told me nothing about it and there has never been the slightest suggestion of it since our marriage.'

There was another remark playing hide-and-seek on the fringes of his consciousness, a remark someone had made recently. He made an effort of memory – almost always fatal to the trapping of such will-o'-the-wisps – and failed. He thought it might have been something from Laura Wynn but could get no further.

Perhaps it would come back if he stopped trying.

He turned to Potter. 'See if you can get Mr Scales on the telephone.'

Scales would be in his – Wycliffe's – office, sitting in his – Wycliffe's – chair. It was an odd feeling; somehow the job seemed more important when someone else was doing it. When he sat in that chair he felt at everybody's beck and call; when someone else sat there they seemed to acquire a certain eminence. Absurd!

'I've got the address of the Exeter flat, John, but it's been pulled down.'

Scales already had men working on the Exeter angle, so far without success, but with the address and the names of occupants contemporary with the two young men they might do better.

'Has Horton arrived yet, sir?'

'I'm expecting him at any moment.'

'No news of Cleeve?'

'No, the search party is out and as soon as Horton arrives we shall start turning over the debris of the fire. Keep watching this space, John!'

A man had come into the room and was talking to Potter. Wycliffe reconized Horton, a dark, undistinguished little man with whom he had worked before and admired for his self-effacing manner as well as for his professional skill. He did not look like a veteran of the courtroom but he had a reputation among criminal lawyers for never getting ruffled and for never being jockeyed into saying more or less than he intended.

They shook hands. 'Are you coming with me to wherever it is?'

'I'll run you up to the site.'

Henry's Field was a bleak prospect. The drizzle had stopped but the landscape was obliterated by mist, and the fog-horn on the lighthouse punctuated the silence with its eerie blast. They were working on the dig and figures were dimly visible through the mist. It was arranged that the earnest Wrighton would work through the debris of the hut with the police to rescue the second-hand artefacts.

Horton cast a professional eye over the tangled mass of carbonized and charred timbers and seemed mildly surprised.

'This is important?'

'If there is a man underneath.'

'A funeral pyre?'

'Could be.'

Horton turned to the two men who would do the heavy work. 'All right, you can get started. As you work, try to cause a minimum of disturbance and lay the timbers out in order as you remove them.'

Wycliffe walked over to the dig. Christie Cleeve was the first to see him. 'Is there any news?'

'I'm afraid not.'

She looked grey-faced and heavy-eyed. 'Mother says it's better for me to carry on here.'

'I think she's right and I'll make sure you know the moment we hear anything.'

Gervaise Prout's slim figure emerged from the mist, his white hair glistening with moisture. 'Mr Wycliffe! I'm so glad to see you.' He turned to Christie: 'Jane has found something at number five and she's not sure what it is, see if you can help her.'

The girl went off.

Prout said, 'I feel so annoyed with myself for not having been here, but I really had no option. There was a symposium in Exeter at which I had to read a paper.'

'I don't see what you could have done if you were here.'

Prout made a gesture of impatience. 'It's such a blow to our work when it was going so well.'

'Are you thinking of the loss of your hut or the disappearance of your patron?'

He received a quick appraising glance as though Prout suspected him of sarcasm but Wycliffe's bland features gave nothing away.

'I was referring to the loss of the hut.'

'I understood from your assistant that it would be no great set-back because you had the bulk of your records with you and the rest were in the caravan.'

A frown. 'Wrighton is an enthusiastic youngster, a good field-worker in the making, but he has no idea of administration and its problems.' Prout rubbed his bony chin until it shone like a little red apple. 'I was deeply shocked to hear about Cleeve. What does it mean?'

'That he went out last night and didn't come back.'

'You know no more than that?'

'At present, no. We are searching the neighbourhood, so far without result.'

'Do you suspect foul play?'

Wycliffe shrugged. 'Do you? You probably know the man and his circumstances better than I.'

Prout seemed to resent having his question turned back on him. 'I'm naturally very concerned. David is not only our patron here but I may say that he has become a friend. Have you spoken to Kitson?'

'Not yet. You think he might be able to help?' Naïve.

'I don't know . . .' After a pause he went on, 'I certainly have the impression that David and Kitson are very close.'

Wycliffe was casual. 'I suppose that is natural; two very intelligent men, living as neighbours . . .'

Prout would have liked to let it go at that but he was urged on by the desire to seem well informed. 'You may be right but I feel there is more to it than that . . . Whenever David visits the dig, Kitson is rarely far away and one frequently comes upon the two of them in seemingly intimate conversation. What really strikes me as odd is that David seems to defer to him in a way that he would do to nobody else.'

Wycliffe recalled the curious moment of strain when, on his first dig, returning to the hut with Prout, they came upon Cleeve and Kitson in earnest discussion.

Prout had talked himself into yielding confidences. 'You may think it petty, but raising funds even for a small project like this is difficult – one has to nurse one's patron, to catch and hold his interest . . . It is true that we have sufficient money for the present dig but I had interested Cleeve in a more ambitious scheme . . .'

'And Kitson talked him out of it?'

'I'm sure that he did.' Prout had his eyes on the wall of mist which all but hemmed them in. 'Altogether, I felt that Kitson must be a . . . must have very considerable influence on David.'

'Are you suggesting that there might be something sinister in their relationship?'

Prout shied away from that like a frightened colt. 'Not sinister! Of course not! I'm merely saying that for Kitson to have so much influence over David he must know him better than anyone else. I suspect that they have known each other a long time – certainly before Kitson came here to live.'

Wycliffe said, 'Do you know anything of Kitson's background?'

Prout prodded a clump of heather with the toe of his bespoke fell-walkers. 'I met him for the first time when I came here to talk to David about the dig eighteen months ago.'

'But you've been making a few enquiries among your academic friends – quite natural in the circumstances.'

Prout let this pass though he looked uncomfortable. 'I really know very little about him. He doesn't seem to have a formal academic background. I gather that he translates Russian and other Slav languages for anybody who will pay him and he's made something of a reputation as a linguist. I've heard that he undertakes hack-work for scholars in the field of Slavonic studies – manuscript reading, indexing, proof checking – that sort of thing.'

Wycliffe guessed that he had got all that he was likely to get from Prout and he was anxious to move on. 'Thank you for being so helpful. I shall treat what you have told me in confidence.'

The Land Rover which had brought the searchers from Division, parked on the skyline at the highest point in the field, looked grotesquely enlarged by the mist. Sergeant Pearce was in the cab, a map spread in front of him, a flask of coffee on the seat beside him; he was monitoring the search through the personal radios of his men.

'This has worked well, sir. Very few radio blind spots and no blisters on my feet. Unfortunately, no luck either. They've covered the ground we mapped out for them and, in any case, I shall have to call them off for refreshment shortly.'

'Don't send them back until you hear from me.'

'You don't think he can be out there, sir?'

Wycliffe growled something unintelligible. Why did they all ask questions as though he had a crystal ball?

He plodded through the heather and joined Horton by the burned-out ruin. Already a large quantity of charred timber had been laid out on the ground and the site was looking less like a Guy Fawkes bonfire which had been caught in a deluge.

Horton said, 'I think we've found what you are looking for.'

CHAPTER FIVE

Thursday July 21st

It was a moment before Wycliffe, peering down through the still considerable tangle of carbonized wood, saw a human foot; a foot burned through to the bones of the toes but, for the rest, still enclosed in the ghostly remnants of a shoe. The leg, dealt with in the same freakish manner by the fire, was visible to the knee, but what-ever remained of the body was hidden under more charred timbers.

'Is that what you expected?'

Wycliffe was subdued. 'I think this is the man we are looking for.' He glanced across at the industrious Wrighton, squatting on his haunches, sorting through ashes and rubble with no eyes for anything else. 'Does he know?'

'No.'

'Then find some pretext to send him away. I don't want the news to get around until we are sure. Another thing: it's possible that he died in the same way as the girl – injected with nicotine by a hypodermic dart. Obviously it's vital to find the dart if there is one.'

He went over to the Land Rover and made a number of calls on the RT; to the coroner; to Franks, the pathologist; to the local GP; to his headquarters and to the Incident Room.

Another half-hour and the body was completely uncovered. It was Cleeve; no doubt about that. In the whimsical way of fires, objects near the ground had suffered less actual burning than others higher up, probably due to the reduced oxygen supply. Horton said, 'A body takes a lot of burning.'

All the same, Cleeve was no sight for the public gaze and Wycliffe posted Pearce and his men to keep people away until the screens were delivered.

Dr Hodge, the local GP, came in his battered Metro, bouncing over the rough ground. He got out, slammed the door, and came to stand, looking down at the remains of the dead man. He muttered: 'Is it Cleeve?' Then he turned to Wycliffe, 'If at first you don't succeed, try, try again – is that it?'

'We don't know how he died yet.' Wycliffe was terse.

'No, but we can make a good guess.' Hodge rubbed his dark chin, always a little in need of a shave. 'Well, it makes more sense; I couldn't believe that anybody would take that trouble over a silly girl. Poor little so-and-so! Ah, well!' The doctor sighed. 'I suppose you've notified the coroner?'

Wycliffe made his way across to the dig. He spotted the auburn head in one of the trenches and was immediately seen himself. Christie was like a young doe, alert to the slightest signal. She came to him, frowning, anxious, 'You've heard something?'

'I'm afraid it's bad news.'

'Tell me.'

He told her. The news of her father's death did not come as a great shock, rather a confirmation of something feared; it was the circumstances of his death which distressed her.

She murmured: 'He died in the fire . . . in the fire . . .'

Wycliffe said: 'I'm sure we shall find out that your father was already dead when the fire started.' He added after a moment: 'I mean that. Now you must go to your mother.'

She seemed to hesitate and he said: 'Would you like me to break the news first?'

She shook her head. 'No, but I must find Andrew.'

Wycliffe was reminded of his own twin son and

daughter, several years older, but still in moments of crisis reaching out to each other. He watched her set out across the field to the wicket gate, deeply puzzled and distressed. In his turn he was being watched curiously by the students working on the dig; they must have realized that there had been some development.

Cleeve was dead and Wycliffe was in no doubt that he had been murdered, though he would have to wait for Franks to provide official confirmation.

Why had he gone out late at night knowing that his life was threatened? Wrighton, who had spent the evening working in the caravan, had not seen him, though his body had been found in the shed.

Lucy Lane arrived and he put her in the picture. 'I want you to be with me when I talk to Mrs Cleeve.'

Just short of the wicket gate they were waylaid by Dr Prout, very subdued. 'I've just this moment heard . . .' And then, 'I suppose it's too early to call on Patricia?'

Wycliffe agreed that it was.

Through the wicket gate and the rhododendron tunnel. The mist was lifting at last and, as is often the case on this coast, there was a prospect of a fine evening after a dismal day. He led the way round to the front door and rang the bell.

The door was opened by a woman Wycliffe had never seen before, a little brown mouse of a woman, probably still on the right side of forty but she would look very different at sixty. Her features looked pinched and he had the impression that a single harsh word would send her scurrying for cover, or that she might burst into tears.

Wycliffe introduced himself and Lucy Lane. She said, 'I am Mrs Cleeve's cousin; my name is Byrne – Miss Byrne.'

'I suppose you have heard?'

She nodded without speaking, eyes cast down like a nun.

'This is a distressing time for you all . . . I am anxious to find out exactly what happened last night and I hope you will answer a few questions . . .'

Another nod.

'Did you see Mr Cleeve at all?'

'We all had dinner together, as usual.'

'At what time?'

'At seven-thirty.'

She seemed so distressed that he felt heartless in questioning her. 'Can you tell me what happened after dinner?'

She made an obvious effort. 'The same as usual. David had a strict routine which he followed unless we had guests. He worked in the morning, then he was free until dinner. After dinner he would go back to work until midnight or even one in the morning.'

He saw with surprise that her eyes were glistening with tears.

'You were fond of him.'

She flushed. 'He was his own worst enemy. He was a hard-working man and except at odd times when he'd had too much to drink, a kind man – too kind, sometimes.' She turned her head away.

'Were you surprised to hear that he went out last night?'

She nodded. He was afraid that if he questioned her further she would break down. He said something soothing and asked her to find out if Mrs Cleeve would see them.

'She's expecting you.'

They were taken to the big drawing-room. 'I'll tell her you're here.'

A clock in the passage chimed and struck five. Several minutes went by before Patricia Cleeve came into the room. After being introduced to Lucy Lane she apologized for keeping them waiting, sat herself in one of the armchairs and smoothed her skirt.

'Christie and Andrew have each other; I've left them

together.' She was completely controlled but there was tension in every little line of her body.

Wycliffe repeated the usual phrases with obvious sincerity and she accepted his sympathy with dignity. Wycliffe thought: These are the forms, and she is the kind of woman to be strengthened and supported by their observance. No hiding away; no hole-in-corner grief, self-indulgent and destructive; there is a ritual for bereavement as for everything else.

'There are questions I shall have to ask you, some of them very personal, but if you would prefer to put it off until tomorrow . . .'

In a deliberate, emphatic tone she said, 'I would prefer, Mr Wycliffe, that you do whatever you think necessary to find out what is behind all this; how David came to die. It is certainly not pleasant to be interrogated but it is much worse to be kept in the dark . . . in the dark about almost everything.'

Wycliffe nodded. 'I understand.'

The windows of the drawing-room looked out on a terraced lawn, falling away to a fringe of trees and, beyond the trees, to the creek, the headland and the pines. The mist had vanished magically, like the lifting of a veil, and already a watery sunshine was restoring colour to the scene.

'As you know, your husband's body was found in the ruins of the archaeologists' hut – can you think of any reason why he would have gone there late at night?'

A slight shrug. 'No, I certainly cannot. It's true that he was more interested in the dig than he was willing to admit and I think Gervaise Prout sometimes worked very late but I understand he was away.'

Wycliffe cleared the decks. 'So far, of course, we have no evidence that his death was other than accidental but—'

She cut across his words. 'Please don't feel that you have to spare me, Mr Wycliffe. David was murdered.

131

You know that as well as I do. The horror of publicity he has had ever since I've known him arose from some sort of fear and in recent months that fear has been catching up with him. Although he would never discuss or even admit the existence of anything of the kind, I've no doubt in my mind that he believed his life to be threatened. When I saw how anxious he was to talk to you on Saturday, I hoped that he was going to tell you about it.'

Few women in his experience could have disciplined themselves to speak so objectively of a husband, recently dead.

'Up to a point your husband did confide in me; he told me that he was being threatened but he claimed to have no knowledge of the source of the threats or of any possible reason for them. He was extremely vague as to their nature though he did say that they had arrived through the post – four of them spread over the past nine months. When I asked to see these communications, whatever they were, he said that he had destroyed them.'

Lucy Lane had been sitting bolt upright in her chair, her bag on her lap, here eyes moving from one to the other, taking in every nuance of the exchanges; now she said, 'When someone makes that kind of complaint to the police, Mrs Cleeve, it usually means that he or she is well aware of who is threatening them and why, but without embarrassment or some incriminating admission they can't or won't speak out. With no facts it is impossible for the police to act.'

'Yes, I see that.'

Wycliffe said, 'And the situation hasn't changed so far as those threats are concerned; we still need to know more about them, which means that we must know more about your husband's past.'

She made a gesture of helplessness. 'But I know so little – virtually nothing about his life before our marriage.'

'And you feel that whatever made him so . . . so wary of publicity of any kind, must have occurred before you met him?'

She was emphatic. 'I do! Very early in our marriage I questioned him about it.' A wry smile. 'Needless to say, I learned nothing except not to ask such questions in the future.'

'Did you ever meet any of his relatives?'

'No, his father and mother were already dead; he was an only child and, though he admitted to cousins, I don't think he was ever in touch with them.'

'When did you first meet?'

'It was one Christmas, in London – Christmas 1961 it must have been. We were married the following April.' She smiled. 'It was hero-worship on my part. I had read his books and I was an eager disciple. I saw him as a genius.' She glanced across at Lucy Lane as she said this.

'Where was he living at that time?'

'When we met? In a bachelor flat off Gower Street. As far as I could tell he had few, if any, friends – a loose acquaintance with a couple of fellows in a neighbouring flat – they, in fact, came to our wedding, the only ones from his side.'

'Not his publisher or his agent?'

She spoke with deliberation. 'You may find this incredible but at the time of our marriage, David had never met either his publisher or his agent. All the business was conducted by correspondence.'

Wycliffe kept the questioning in a low key, allowing intervals of silence when the three of them sat, each apparently absorbed in private thoughts.

'This man, Roger Kitson – is he a recent acquaintance?'

Another frown. 'I think David has known Roger for some years. Very occasionally David had to go to London to deal with the business side of his work and when he came back from one of those trips he said that

133

he had offered the cottage to someone. That was nearly two years ago, and a month or so later Roger turned up and took possession.'

For a while she sat, looking down at her hands, clasped in her lap, then she raised her eyes and looked straight at Wycliffe. 'You must think it very strange that after twenty years of marriage I know so little about my husband but ours was not a conventional marriage. I've already said that I regarded David as a genius; certainly he was no ordinary man and he did not behave like one. He lived much of his life in a sort of limbo between imagination and reality and, as you will know from his books, the world of his imagination could be strange and terrifying.'

Her gaze shifted from Wycliffe to Lucy Lane as though the girl fitted more easily into the pattern of her thoughts. 'Even as a young wife I realized that I could not expect to monopolize any part of such a man – that it would have been inviting disaster to try.

'When we had the children I asked only that he would not allow the assertion of his own personality to blight or smother theirs and, in the main, he kept that bargain.' She made a small gesture with her slim hands. 'Of course, he had many women; there were occasional bouts of drunkenness, he was sometimes thoughtlessly cruel, and obsessively secretive . . . But I knew that he couldn't be otherwise; he was the man I married.'

She was looking down at her hands once more. 'I flatter myself that I understood his needs and that I made life easier for him. I saw that as my role. But you will see that I am not in a position to tell you much about him.'

Wycliffe was beginning to feel stifled in this atmosphere of reasonableness and studied calm which seemed to create its own peculiar tension. He admired the woman's self-control but it was unnatural. Oddly, he felt sympathy for Cleeve; such repression would probably have provoked him to either violence or obscenity and either response would have been incomprehensible to Patricia.

'What an extraordinary woman! I never really thought of him as having a wife, but a woman like that . . .' Lucy Lane in admiration.

They walked along the broad corridor with its disturbing pictures and erratic changes of level and climbed the stairs; Lucy all eyes. As they reached the secretary's office the girl came to the door and Wycliffe introduced himself and Lucy Lane.

Milli looked them over in cool appraisal. 'I know who you are.'

It was the first time Wycliffe had seen the girl at close quarters. 'I suppose you know that Mr Cleeve's body has been found?'

'Mrs Cleeve told me.'

'Did he seem much as usual yesterday? Or was he nervous, edgy – you know the sort of thing?'

She shrugged her thin shoulders. One had the impression that her body was infinitely pliable rather than jointed and, though she was perfectly proportioned, she was very small. She said, 'You were here yesterday, you saw as much of him as I did.'

'But you knew him, you could compare his behaviour with some sort of norm.'

'There was no norm; he was never the same two days together, it depended on how the work was going, whether he had slept the night before – even on the weather.' She added grudgingly, 'But he was upset yesterday. I noticed it when I arrived in the morning, then you came, and he was out most of the afternoon so I didn't see much of him.'

'Do you live in the house?'

'I do not! I live in the village but I have my lunch here.'

'With the family?'

'Of course.'

'How long have you worked here?'

'Nearly five years.'

'We shall be in the library for a while but I would like to see you again afterwards.'

She glanced at her watch. 'I finish work at half-past five and it's already quarter to six.'

'I won't keep you longer than necessary.'

For the third time in six days Wycliffe found himself in Cleeve's library, so much in contrast to the rest of the house.

Lucy Lane exclaimed in astonishment: 'It's Edwardian! I'd always imagined him against a background of white walls, steel-framed abstracts, and Giacometti figures on the bookcases.'

'That sounds more like his wife.'

Looking round the big room he experienced a mild elation and immediately felt guilty. The truth was that he always had a pleasurable sense of anticipation when he was able to look behind the scenes of another man's life. Asexual voyeurism, he called it – the vice which sells autobiographies, published journals and diaries. Wycliffe was one of that army of unassuming people who feel the need to match themselves against the grain of other people's lives; perhaps that was why he had found his vocation in the police.

Cleeve's desk was orderly: a thick wad of typescript in a limp cover, labelled *Setebos*, presumably the next novel in final draft, waiting for the author's finishing touches and seal of approval. But even without them, good or bad, *Setebos* would be 'Peter Stride's last and greatest masterpiece, published posthumously'. And if publication could coincide with a well publicized trial of his killer then the sky would be the limit.

Wycliffe said, 'Why Setebos, I wonder?'

'Setebos was Caliban's creator-god, and in Browning's

136

poem Caliban thought Setebos had created the world for his own amusement.' Lucy Lane, BA Hons (Eng Lit). Very prim.

'Ah!'

On the desk there was a crystal pen-tray with coloured ball-points and pencils; a paper-knife with an ivory handle in the form of a lion couchant, a memo pad, and two telephones . . . On the memo pad were three lines of notes: 'Lester . . . RC WE 9/8 . . . Saunders for Medicus???' The notes had been written in green and below them there was an odd little doodle of a man upside down.

'Ask Miss Who-is-it to come in.'

Lucy was looking at the bookshelves; she fetched the girl from the office. Milli came in and looked disapproving when she saw Wycliffe sitting in Cleeve's chair.

'I wonder if you can explain these notes?'

She glanced at the pad. 'I think so. Colin Lester is Mr Cleeve's agent and this is a memo to ring him; RC is Russel Cowdray, his English publisher. Mr Cleeve was arranging for Cowdray to spend the weekend beginning Friday August 9th here. Saunders for *Medicus* – that refers to dramatizing *Medicus* – one of Mr Cleeve's books – for TV. The company want to use Neville Saunders but Mr Cleeve wasn't sure they'd chosen the right man for the job.'

'And these notes were made yesterday?'

'Oh, yes.'

'Thank you; that is very helpful. But what about the little upside-down man?'

A ghost of a smile. 'That's typical of Mr Cleeve – a doodle.' She looked more carefully at the little drawing. 'I think it's a version of the hanged man in the Tarot pack. He thinks – thought in symbols, he really did. Even people who read his books (the inference being that Wycliffe was unlikely to have done so) don't realize the amount of symbolism there is in his writing.' She waved a hand vaguely. 'You'll find a whole section of the library devoted to books on the subject.' She paused. 'Is that all?'

'For the moment, thank you, but don't go home yet.'

So Milli was something more than an animated doll.

The room would have to be meticulously searched and this was a job for Smith but he wanted to get the feel of it, to glimpse the private world of David Cleeve. It wasn't possible to step into the dead man's shoes but from the things he kept close to him one could, perhaps, guess at the vision he had of himself.

The room was L-shaped and he had never seen the other leg of the L. Here there was a second window, looking out from the back of the house to a wooded area of the estate. As in the rest of the room the walls were lined with mahogany bookcases which reached to within a couple of feet of the high ceiling. There were eighteenth-century library steps with hand rails, and a long, polished table with several of the favoured straight-backed armchairs so that wherever one happened to be there was a convenient place to sit and look up a reference or make a note; there was even another telephone. One whole section of the bookcases was devoted to Cleeve's own works in a babel of languages and a rainbow pattern of jackets. An impressive card index stood next to a sinister electronic device with a blank screen, no doubt scheming a take-over.

There was a door in the end wall of the L. Wycliffe opened it and found himself in a bedroom, very simply furnished; aseptic like a private room in a hospital, but with a double bed. A wall-cupboard turned out to be a well-stocked wardrobe. There was a bathroom and a loo, accessible from the corridor as well as from the bedroom.

Wycliffe, hands in pockets, returned to the library and mooned about, feeling none the wiser. He was thinking of the young man who had started it all, the

138

acquaintance Laura Wynn had made in a block of Exeter flats. He had moved to London and, through his talent as a writer, he had become rich and famous, but after 28 years it seemed that he had still felt menaced because of something which had occurred in those early days.

He rejoined Lucy Lane. 'We must let Smith loose in here, and make a note to get Inspector Royal down. Somebody will have to look into Cleeve's affairs and cope with his lawyers.' Royal was the department's legal and financial expert.

They moved to Milli's office which she shared with two kinds of copier, a word-processor, a duplicator which looked like a space machine and, surprise, surprise, a finger-powered typewriter – no doubt in reserve like an oil-stove against a power cut.

'Is there a safe where Mr Cleeve kept valuables?'

She was filing correspondence and she did not stop in her work. 'If there is I don't know of it; he kept important documents and all his manuscript material at the bank.'

'What other rooms are there on this level?'

'Apart from the library and this office there is a stationery store, a bathroom, loo and bedroom.'

'Do the rest of the family come up here?'

She slammed shut the drawer of the filing cabinet. 'I've never seen Mrs Cleeve on this floor – that's not to say she doesn't come here. The twins used to come up here when they were younger – not now.'

'Does Mr Cleeve sleep up here?'

'I suppose so. I'm not here at night to see.'

'What is your impression of the household; do the Cleeves get on well together?'

She shrugged. 'So-so, like most families, I suppose.'

'You know that Mr Cleeve had other women?'

'It doesn't come as a surprise.'

'You?'

'On occasion.'

'Did Mrs Cleeve resent these relationships?'

'I don't know; I've never asked her.' She glanced at her watch. 'Now, if there's nothing more . . .'

The burned-out hut was now screened from the public gaze and two uniformed policemen, bored to their boots, stood guard. Franks's automobile, looking as though it had escaped from a James Bond film, stood at a sprawling angle to a line of other parked vehicles which included the mortuary van. Wycliffe recognized Smith's Land Rover among them.

The constables, galvanized into efficiency, saluted. Wycliffe passed behind the screens into more or less ordered chaos. Franks saw him and came over.

'Ah, there you are, Charles! I must say you go in for variety; a pretty tart on Tuesday and on Thursday, Britain's up-market answer to the horror comic. He'll be missed, Charles, and not least by those sharks at the Inland Revenue.'

Wycliffe said, 'You haven't shifted him yet.'

'No, there's a little problem of keeping him more or less in one piece. They're getting a plastic sheet under the body now.'

'I hope they're keeping their eyes open.'

'Horton is, and he won't miss much.'

The debris had been almost cleared away and four men in green overalls were bending over what remained of David Cleeve, manipulating the edges of a plastic sheet while Horton crouched, watching every move. Sergeant Smith was packing photographic gear into two custom-made holdalls of his own design.

The plastic sheeting was patiently edged under the body and folded over to make a secure envelope which was finally lifted clear and carried to the mortuary van. Inspector Knowles had arrived from sub-division and he would accompany the body and attend the post-mortem to maintain continuity of evidence.

End of an author. The rag-bag of contending emotions

and creative energy that was Cleeve had been obliterated, and in its place were the charred remnants of a body in a plastic envelope. Wycliffe, despite his years of experience, was always deeply shocked and angered by murder; he found it difficult to conceive of the arrogance which allowed one man to take all from another, leaving no possibility of restitution. And in this case his emotions were more than ever involved because he had known the dead man; just five days earlier he had been drinking his whisky.

Horton was beginning the detailed examination of the ground where the body had lain and, later, the rest of the debris would be removed and the whole area subjected to a minute scrutiny, as thorough as anything undertaken by the archaeologists.

Back in the Incident Room Wycliffe dictated a press release: 'The body of Mr David Cleeve of Roscrowgy in Roseland has been found in the ruins of a burned-out shed used as an office and site-museum by a group of archaeologists excavating in a field near his home. Mr Cleeve went out on Wednesday evening and did not return. During the night, the fire brigade was called out to a fire which completely destroyed the wooden shed and Mr Cleeve's body was discovered late on Thursday afternoon when the debris was being removed under the supervision of a forensic expert. The police are investigating the possibility of foul play.'

Wycliffe sighed. 'Once the press realize that David Cleeve is Peter Stride we shall have a hornet's nest about our ears.'

The routine of the case seemed to acquire a life of its own; nourished by large quantities of paper and by an increasing number of people. Every table in the Incident Room was occupied; reports were being typed, duplicated and filed; index cards, recording every item of information collected during the investigation, were lodged in the carousel; lists were prepared and compared . . .

DC Curnow was checking a list of people who, for one reason or another, used or had access to nicotine. As far as he could see, none of them had the remotest connection with the dead girl or with Cleeve. Another list recorded those who might have sufficient skill and apparatus to extract nicotine from tobacco leaves or from tobacco on sale in the shops; these included two teachers of chemistry and a former professor of pharmacology, but here again, there seemed to be no link with the girl or with Cleeve; the single exception was the herbalist, Geoffrey Tull.

Quite a number of people appeared on a third sheet – those likely to have the skill and tools necessary to contrive the dart, but few of these cross-checked with either of the other schedules and, of them all, only Laura Wynn was known to have been aquainted with Cleeve and Celia Dawe.

Wycliffe digested it all and was depressed. Sufficient unto the day – and it had been a long one. 'I'm going home.'

Helen was concerned for him. 'I had no idea when you were coming so I couldn't get anything ready but it won't take long, then early to bed!'

'Can't we go out?'

'Of course, if you really want to.'

Helen had heard good reports of a restaurant at Veryan and, encouraged by the dramatic improvement in the weather, they decided to eat there.

Veryan is a neat little village which somehow manages to escape the worst symptoms of the emmet plague. They had their evening meal in a small restaurant which offered a simple menu, the food well-cooked and presented, the wine sensible, and value for money. A vegetable soup, chicken-in-cider, followed by a delicious apple crumble and the cheese board. Half a bottle of German hock.

Helen said, 'This is definitely holiday eating; we mustn't make a habit of it.'

Wycliffe had been unusually silent; now he said, 'Cleeve is dead. They found him in the ruins of the hut.'

Helen was shocked but she said little, there was no point.

They were silent for a while then Wycliffe said, 'In the mirror – that couple who have just come in . . .'

Laura Wynn with her golden hair. (How long would she contrive to keep it like that?) Another green frock – she must think that green was her colour and certainly she drew attention from all over the room. The hair and the frock were discreetly garnished with jewellery from stock. Her companion was the herbalist, Geoffrey Tull, in a suit of fine grey cord. They were obviously known to the proprietor.

Wycliffe muttered, 'Those two together . . .'

'What about them?'

He made an impatient movement which meant that he didn't want to commit himself to words. 'Shall we have our coffee?'

When they were leaving they had to pass close to the other couple's table. Tull looked sheepish but Laura greeted them with the aplomb of a real duchess.

It was half-past ten when they got back to the cottage and quite dark. He had been up since before five that morning but he was disinclined for bed.

He said: 'I'll be up later.'

He opened the front door, crossed the road, and smoked his pipe leaning on the sea wall. The sea was quiet, just the ripple and swish of wavelets advancing and retreating over the shingle. Navigation lights and street lamps cut paths across the dark water and at 20-second intervals the lighthouse flashed. He counted the seconds through three or four cycles and got it wrong every time. It was then, by one of those subterranean tricks of the mind, that he remembered what it was that Laura Wynn had said, the remark he had tried so hard to recall.

It came as an anticlimax. She had been telling of her first meeting with Cleeve after more than 28 years, when he came into her shop and she had recognized him.

Wycliffe had said, 'After nearly thirty years?'

'Why not? People don't change all that much . . . I got mixed up though, and called him John.'

A natural enough mistake; on her own admission she hadn't known the two young men at all well . . . All the same, taken with the epilepsy . . ,

He went back indoors to the telephone and dialled John Scales's home number.

'I hope you are not in bed, John.'

'I should be so lucky! Jane is entertaining some of her departmental colleagues. Did you know that academic shop is even more boring than police shop? That academics have more expensive taste in booze and that they get tipsy quicker?' John sounded a bit tipsy himself.

'It's a very long shot, John, but there could be something in it. I want you to get somebody to check registrations of death in the Exeter area between September '54 and, say, June '55. The chap could have died in hospital and that might be a different registration district from his home address.'

'Does this chap we are talking about have a name, sir?'

'Yes: David Paul Cleeve, born September 5th 1931 at Bristol – will that do?'

Scales was impressed. 'So that's the way the cookie crumbles! I'll get somebody on it as soon as the office opens. Anything else?'

'Yes. I don't want Jane to break any professional confidences but I suppose she must know Gervaise Prout. If she does, I'd appreciate her off-the-record summing up.'

Scales chuckled. 'We've been talking about him recently, since he cropped up in this case. Jane knows him, though he isn't employed by the university. He's a freelance with private means. He's a bachelor, with a house near St Germans. It seems he's well thought of academically and he's got a knack for raising funds for his digs. He does some extra-mural work for the university and he's a visiting lecturer at several places. The funny thing is he's a bit of a joke, but nobody knows quite why.'

'Thanks, John. Enjoy the party!'

Wycliffe climbed up the narrow, twisted stairs to bed. Helen was propped up, reading a dog-eared copy of *Magistra*.

CHAPTER SIX

Friday July 22nd

A fine sunny day but with a light breeze; enough for
the sailing fraternity and for the wind-surfers, not too
much for the beach loungers. The emmets, convalescing
after yesterday's gloom, agreed with each other: 'We
were right not to go to Spain this year after all.'

Helen had decided on a rather special trip – up the
coast to Portscatho then on to the Gull Rock and the
Nare.

'It will be choppy.'

'You know I enjoy it.'

Wycliffe didn't, he was prone to sea-sickness.

At half-past eight he was walking up the Steps to the
Incident Room. Hardly anyone about; cats sprawled
elegantly on the sunny side, performing their morning
toilet; the postman was on his round; Borlase, with
bucket and mop, was washing down his shop-front.

A nervous 'Good morning' from the photographer.

Already the press-release had brought reporters with
photographers in tow and there was a group outside
the Incident Room.

'Is it murder? . . . Any connection with the girl? . . .
Is it true that he was scared of something? . . . Is that
why he was press-shy?'

Wycliffe made his way through. 'I can't tell you
anything because I don't know anything. As soon as
I have the result of the post-mortem I'll talk to you.'

In the Incident Room there was a feeling of being
under siege and it must have been the same at Roscrowgy

for there had already been a report from the man on duty about fending them off.

His table was dotted with little piles of paper neatly arranged. Horton had left a memo, preliminary to his full report. Wycliffe glanced through the clipped sentences:

'. . . fire almost certainly started in the area where the body was found. The initial intensity of the blaze suggests paraffin or similar . . . A 20-litre drum, screw-top missing, was identified by Prout and his assistant as the drum in which they stored fuel for the generator . . . it was said to have contained less than half that amount . . . Possibly that paraffin was poured over the body, then set alight . . .'

Nothing really new, he was waiting for Franks to pronounce.

Potter said, 'The chief for you, sir.'

Mr Oldroyd, the big-chief in person. 'You've run into a hornet's nest there, Charles! Sorry about the holiday. . . . The case is bound to draw a lot of attention and there will be plenty of sniping . . . Have you got all the assistance you need? I know you like to work with a small team. I'll do my best to keep the press off your back. Pity about Cleeve. I can't say I enjoyed his books but they were compulsive reading. They seemed to catch the spirit of our time, like Terry Wogan and sliced bread.'

The chief, dispensing moral support.

Another memo on his table informed him that CRO had no record of Cleeve's prints so he had never been convicted of any crime. A criminal record might have explained his fear of publicity and, perhaps, his fate.

Detective Sergeants Smith and Lane were at Roscrowgy with a DC to assist. Smith and the DC would make a systematic search of Cleeve's suite of rooms while Lucy Lane smoothed their path with the family.

Franks came through at last, and after the usual preliminaries, salted with Franksian cynicism, he said,

147

'I have had a hell of a job with this chap, Charles, but there's no real doubt; he was killed in the same way as the girl.'

'Have you found the dart?'

'Yes, among the odds and ends that were gathered up with the remains, but God knows where it got him.'

'Have you been able to do any tissue analysis?'

Franks laughed. 'Don't rush me, Charles! I'm fragile this morning. I've done preliminary tests on liver tissue and on muscle preparations taken from the rump – both show unmistakably the presence of nicotine. I've got other samples and later I may be able to give you some idea of probable concentration but I think you can take it that they poisoned Cleeve before they cooked him.'

That was what he wanted to hear, if not in those words. It would give the press something and be of some consolation to the family. He translated the pathologist's words for the benefit of the waiting reporters:

'The preliminary indications are that Mr Cleeve was poisoned and that he died before the fire.'

'Poisoned in the same way as the girl?'

'It seems so.'

'Are you saying that he was murdered?'

'This is now a murder inquiry.'

'That makes two.'

'Yes, I had worked that out.'

'Is it true that Stride made a statement to the police in connection with the murder of Celia Dawe?'

(Of course it would be 'Stride'; the public for whom these boys were working had never heard of Cleeve.)

'Yes, he did.'

'Was he wanted by the police in connection with that case?'

'No; his statement, along with facts already known to us, made it possible to eliminate him as a suspect.'

'Stride has always avoided publicity like the plague;

148

is it possible that something in his past caught up with him?'

A leak, or a shrewd deduction? Wycliffe said, 'I don't know the answer to that. There must be many reasons why a man would want to avoid publicity; I can think of several at this moment.'

They let him go, more or less good-humouredly, but a crowd was gathering and that would take up the time of another uniformed man who could be better employed.

Wycliffe drank Potter coffee and moped about the Incident Room trying to clarify his ideas. The case seemed to split into two – the Exeter end, where Sergeant Mitchell was digging into Cleeve's past and trying to establish a motive; and the Roseland end, where the murders had been committed and the job of the police was to identify the killer. Laura Wynn linked the two locations but was she the only one?

He let himself out into the sunshine; the reporters had gone but they would be back; the emmets had resumed their wanderings in search of God knows what – the Golden Fleece or the Second Coming. He turned up the hill towards Roscrowgy.

What if, after all, it turned out to be a purely local crime – even a family affair? Then what of the threats Cleeve had talked about? Were they real or had he invented them to draw attention to a danger which he saw but dared not name? With Cleeve out of the way Patricia would surely be a wealthy woman in her own right . . . Was it possible that someone – Tull, for instance . . . ?

He was wool-gathering. Cleeve's whole point had been that, whatever happened, it would have nothing to do with the family. But Celia Dawe and David Cleeve were dead and they hadn't been killed by remote control.

At the top of the hill he turned in through the white gates where there was a policeman on duty;

he walked through the garden and into Henry's Field.

Henry's Field was like a painter's palette, with splashes of yellow gorse, a whole spectrum of greens, and some synthetic purples from the heathers. Nature advertising her wares, blatant and shameless. The bees were busy, the students too; plump girls in tight bras and shorts in uneasy alliance with awkward angular youths.

They watched him pass and answered his wave with suspicious reserve. He wondered how Prout was managing without his hut.

He was taking the short-cut to Kitson's cottage; the path led past the ruined hut and joined the lane just beyond it. He continued along the lane and entered the trees – trees that were wind-blasted at first but rose later to the dignity of a high canopy. It was utterly silent. Abruptly he came upon the clearing with the cottage set in a neglected garden surrounded by a decaying fence. Wycliffe thought it might be a good place to live for anyone not bitten by the improvement bug.

Kitson was sitting in an old wicker chair by the front door, reading.

He looked up as Wycliffe pushed open the creaking gate. 'Ah! I expected you yesterday.'

They went into the living-room where a pleasant smell of stew came from the kitchen and one could hear a lid trembling on a saucepan that was simmering too vigorously.

'Excuse me, I must see to my lunch.'

When Kitson returned he sat at the table, one elbow resting on it, the injured side of his face cupped in his hand.

'You know, of course, that Cleeve's body has been found?'

Kitson said, 'I was over there last evening. My telephone has been out of order and it was only repaired this morning.'

'Was it out of order on Wednesday night when Cleeve went missing?'

'I don't know; I only found it out when Christie and Andrew came over in the morning to ask me if I had seen their father.'

'So you didn't telephone him on Wednesday night?'

Kitson's manner became more reserved, cautious. 'No, I did not.'

'Someone or something induced him to go out late at night and to cross Henry's Field in the dark.'

Kitson said nothing and Wycliffe went on: 'What was wrong with your phone?'

'The engineer said the line had broken opposite the hut where the fire was; he seemed to think it might have been something to do with that. The telephone to the hut came off the same pole.'

'When did you last see Cleeve?'

'On Tuesday evening. Periodically Patricia takes pity on her bachelor acquaintances and then she lays on a decent meal for them. She did on Tuesday.'

'Who were the bachelors?'

'Her brother – Geoffrey Tull – Gervaise Prout and myself. Prout, of course, is a bird of passage.'

Kitson had very dark brown eyes of bovine serenity, in sharp contrast both with his pallid skin and his almost bird-like awareness. He avoided looking at a companion directly and spoke, as it were, in profile so that he seemed to be talking to someone else.

'Have you known the Cleeves long?'

A quick glance from the dark-brown eyes before answering. 'I met David in London in '61, I think it was. That was before he married Patricia. He had a flat off Gower Street and he was spending his days at the British Museum reading room, getting together material for *Caliban* – his best book, in my opinion, but the one we hear least about. As it happened I was working in the museum too, but we actually met in a pub. We found that we had interests in common, and we've kept loosely in touch ever since.'

He spoke slowly with pauses between each sentence in the manner of a man who is much alone.

The room was long and narrow with low ceiling beams – two of the cottage rooms knocked into one. A paraffin lamp hung from gimbals over the table. The walls were lined with improvised shelving, loaded down with books, and there were books on the table along with a sheaf of manuscript notes and an ancient portable typewriter. Most of the books were in Russian or in some other language which used the Cyrillic alphabet. Furniture was minimal and basic. A tabby cat slept on one of the two window-sills, next to a jam-jar of wild flowers.

'So you've known Cleeve for more than twenty years; when did you come down here to live?'

'I moved in here nearly two years ago. I was fed up with London and I asked David if he knew of some little property I could buy or rent. He offered me this, so I cast off the ball and chain and here I am.'

'Did you see a lot of Cleeve?'

Kitson produced a little machine for rolling cigarettes and charged it with tobacco. He worked mainly with his right hand for his left shared in the injuries to the left side of his body and the fingers seemed to be stiff and poorly co-ordinated.

'He would drop in here three or four times a week, usually in the early afternoon.'

'And the last time?'

'The last time he was here on Monday morning, but that was unusual.'

'He had a particular reason for coming?'

Kitson extracted a passable cigarette from his machine, tapped it down, and lit it. 'Yes, he had a particular reason; he wanted somebody to talk to.'

'Something was worrying him?'

Wycliffe received a sidelong glance. 'I think you

know – at least the kind of thing I'm talking about. He told me he had spoken to you.'

'He told me a story about warnings or threats he had received through the post but he refused to give me enough detail to take any action.'

An emphatic nod. 'Exactly! According to him he had been receiving these things for months but he never discussed their nature or the reason for them. All I can say is that he got very agitated when one was due.'

'You mean that he knew when to expect them?'

Another quick glance. 'Didn't he tell you that? Oh, yes, he knew when one would come. Sometimes I wondered if it wasn't all in his imagination or even whether he was sending them himself, but he seemed genuinely scared and now he's dead.'

'He had one of these things on Monday?'

'Yes.' A pause while Kitson re-lit his cigarette which did not seem to draw very well, then he went on: 'Like a lot of highly creative people David lived in a world largely of his own imagining and, to some extent, signals from outside had to be tailored to fit.'

Wycliffe was looking out of the window through tiny panes which gave a chequered view of the sunny wilderness. Everything was still and the silence was so profound that one felt subdued by it – muted. He shifted irritably on his chair. 'But he is dead so it seems the threats must have been real enough and if you or I had persuaded him to talk he might still be alive.'

Kitson shook his head. 'I don't deal in "ifs". As I see it, we are born and we die, we have little say in either event so what gives us the idea that we can influence the bit in between, I don't know.'

'Did Cleeve ever speak to you of his life before you met?'

'We never discussed the past; I assumed that like me he preferred to forget what had gone by.'

'When you first knew him was there any question of him being or having been an epileptic?'

Kitson's astonishment showed in his face. 'Epileptic? I've never heard anything of the sort. Whatever gave you that idea?'

'Apart from these threats which he discussed with you, did he ask your advice on other aspects of his affairs?'

Pursed lips and a longish pause. 'David needed someone to talk to about himself and about his nightmare view of the world which, I believe, was genuine – and damned uncomfortable to live with. Sometimes it seemed to me that he felt guilty for being human; he would quote papa Nietzsche – "this disease called man" and all that . . . Once he said – no doubt he thought it up in advance – "We are God's sick joke; automata with a sense of sin." ' Kitson stubbed out his ailing cigarette. 'He was a man possessed by a tormenting spirit and his books were intended to be an exorcism, but they didn't work.'

'Do you think he talked to his wife?'

Hesitation. 'That's what he should have done. Patricia would have been a source of strength, but she was a woman and that would have injured Davy's self-esteem. In any case, he was afraid of her.' A short laugh. 'I suppose he needed an ego-boost from an neutral corner and he sometimes came here to get it.'

'Did you influence him in his dealings with Prout?'

A slow smile. 'Poor old Prout is an academic wheeler-dealer like so many of his colleagues these days, scrambling for grants and subsidies; he might as well be selling motor cars or replacement windows but it happens to be archaeology. David had little sales resistance.'

'One more question Mr Kitson, were you here the whole of Wednesday evening and night?'

'I didn't leave the cottage.'

Kitson came with him to the gate; so did the tabby

154

cat, stretching its legs and arching its back after a long sleep.

Wycliffe returned to Henry's Field and by the burned-out hut he stopped to look at the dumpy telephone pole perched on the hedge. A new length of wire marked the repair, while the line which had served the wooden hut was coiled and secured to the pole. He continued on, through the wicket gate and into the grounds of Roscrowgy. He rang the door bell and once again he was admitted by the cousin-housekeeper, more mouse-like than ever. She looked at him as though fearful that he might be the bearer of still more bad news.

'I've come to see my people who are working in the library; I know my way.'

She let him pass without a word and closed the door behind him. He walked along the now familiar corridor and up the stairs.

Milli's door was open and she saw him pass, glancing up from her work. Strange girl! Wycliffe wondered what would happen to her now. Probably Cleeve's literary executors would be glad to use her, in which case her future would be secure for a long time.

The library looked much the same except that Smith and Curnow were standing by the big table examining a heterogeneous collection of objects: their haul so far.

Smith complained, 'There's not much here to tell us about his present, let alone his past. According to the little vixen next door, he kept all his papers, including his manuscripts, in a safe deposit.' Smith had met his match in Milli.

Wycliffe pointed to two chargers for an automatic pistol which were among the collection. 'No gun?'

'We haven't found one and he's not a registered holder.' Smith picked up one of the chargers. 'These are Mauser 7.63 mm – what we used to call .30 in the days before we went continental. There are quite a few pistols which might fire them.'

Of course, it was quite likely that Cleeve had provided himself with a gun and that he had taken it with him on his late-night excursion, but no gun had been found.

'You might take a look at these, sir.' Smith handed him a cardboard box which had once held cigarettes. 'That was in the same drawer as the ammo, the only locked drawer in the desk. Take a look inside . . .'

Wycliffe lifted the lid and found several ordinary white envelopes addressed to Cleeve in block capitals. He glanced at the postmarks – Durham, Bristol, Exeter, London and Truro.

Smith said: 'Look in the envelopes, sir. Don't bother about dabs, I've been over them.'

Wycliffe slid out the contents of the envelopes on to the table – five Jacks of Diamonds. Each card was numbered and dated in one of the margins. One of the cards had been torn in two and was numbered and dated on both halves. All were from mint decks and were identical with each other except that the backs of two were pink while the others were blue.

'What do you make of them, sir?' Smith's questions were usually in the nature of a challenge.

'Not much.'

Wycliffe spread the cards out and arranged them in numerical order – one to five; the dates then read; Saturday September 4th; Tuesday March 8th; Friday May 13th; Thursday June 16th and, finally, Monday July 18th – the card which had been torn in two.

Smith said: 'Celia Dawe was murdered on the night of July 18th.'

'So?'

'I don't know.'

'Neither do I but it's worth remembering.'

Wycliffe stared at the five cards: five Jacks of Diamonds which had seemingly arrived through the post at irregular intervals over the past ten months and been interpreted by Cleeve as threats. There was something

156

melodramatic, something juvenile about it all – the Black Spot updated, yet Cleeve was dead and Celia Dawe had died apparently in a first abortive attempt to kill him.

Smith said: 'What about the intervals between the dates?'

'Work them out and see if they mean anything to us.'

Smith set to work, his glasses on the end of his nose. 'The interval between the first and second dates is one hundred and eighty-five days – near enough for six months; between the second and third, it is sixty-six days – just over nine weeks; between the third and fourth, thirty-four days – five weeks; and between the fourth and fifth, thirty-two days, or just over a month. Means nothing to me, sir.'

'Nor to me.' Wycliffe grinned. 'In *Alice* the jurymen added up the dates given in evidence and reduced their answers to pounds, shillings and pence.'

Smith did not smile. 'That would be before we went metric, I take it, sir.'

Wycliffe wondered, as often before, what went on behind that grey and gloomy facade.

They brooded over the cards then Wycliffe said: 'As it happens, the day of the week and the day of the month in the card dates correspond with the present year, but it surely meant more to Cleeve than simply the day on which they were sent. The intervals must have meant something too.'

Smith was staring at the cards over the tops of his glasses. 'You think these dates refer to events in the past?'

'I think they must do; otherwise what significance could they have? We might make a guess at the year.'

DC Curnow, a studious young man with old-fashioned ideas of self-improvement, was browsing through the books on the shelves. Wycliffe called to him: 'There's a whole shelf of *Whitaker's* just on your left, bring over a recent one.'

Wycliffe leafed through the almanack to find the perpetual calendar. 'If his wife is right, Cleeve's fears date from before their marriage in 1962.' His finger moved over the tables. 'Here we are, 1955 is the first year before that in which the days fit the dates; the one before that again in 1949. But in 1949 Cleeve was only seventeen – a bit young to start a feud which lasted through the rest of his life. My bet is that the card dates refer to 1955.'

Smith took off his glasses and polished them with a lens tissue. 'You are saying that the dates on the cards refer to events between September 1954 and July 1955 – is that right, sir?'

'I think it's a strong possibility.'

With magnanimity Smith said: 'You may be right at that.' He went on: 'There's something else in the same line.' He handed over a lapel badge in the form of a playing card club. 'This was also in the locked drawer.'

A pretty thing; the trefoil shape was done in black enamel and set in plaited gold wire. In the centre of the badge a gilt 'J' was embedded. A Jack of Clubs?

Wycliffe turned the thing over in his fingers. The whole business was acquiring an Alice-in-Wonderland zaniness. 'I'll give you a receipt for this and the cards.'

He was driven back to the Incident Room. No news from John Scales but Inspector Royal had arrived and Wycliffe put him in touch with Cleeve's solicitors.

Afterwards he walked down the Steps; the parade had thinned because it was lunchtime. The photographer and his sisters would be tucking in to something substantial – something with suet in it; Boadicea would probably be toying with a little steamed fish washed down with fruit juice. And Geoffrey Tull? What was the diet of naturopaths in captivity? To judge from Geoffrey's smooth, slightly oily skin, something rich. Perhaps in terms of food he and Laura Wynn would not see eye to eye, but in the matter of preparing a hypodermic dart charged with nicotine they could be an unbeatable combination.

It occurred to him that Cleeve had moved to the Exeter flat in '53 and that he was still there when the Wynns left in September '54 – the most probable date for the event recorded by the first card.

Having made himself diet-conscious by his speculations about food he settled for The Vegetarian and ordered an omelette with salad. Afterwards he walked down to the waterfront and went into a pub he had not visited before. He drank a pint of lager, standing at the bar, while a step away from him a group of reporters were having a liquid lunch, but they were far too busy talking shop to notice him.

Jack of Diamonds . . . Jack of Clubs . . . the sort of aliases young crooks might have fancied; tearaways with romantic notions of crime. A gang? The 'fifties were, after all, the era of the Teddy-boy, boot-lace ties and winkle-picker shoes.

By two o'clock he was back in the Incident Room and at a quarter-past John Scales telephoned.

'You've found the man who died twice, sir.' John in buoyant mood. 'David Paul Cleeve, born September 5th 1931 at Bristol, son of David Gordon Cleeve, solicitor's clerk, died October 12th 1954 in Exeter General Hospital of multiple injuries sustained in a road traffic accident earlier in the day.'

Wycliffe sighed with relief. 'Any details?'

'Some, but this goes back to the days of the old city force. Records stirred themselves and blew the dust off a couple of files. It seems that Cleeve had an epileptic fit in Queen Street during the morning rush-hour. The RTA report says he was struck by a bus as he fell, sustaining injuries from which he subsequently died without recovering consciousness. The body was identified by his flat-mate, John Larkin, and the next-of-kin was given as Elizabeth Cleeve, mother.'

'No question of foul play?'

'No hint of it. I've seen the inquest report. Cleeve's doctor testified that he was subject to epileptic seizures and that he was unreliable in taking his medications so that the seizures were not kept in check as they might have been.'

So John Larkin had become David Cleeve and David Cleeve had become the celebrated Peter Stride, one of the western world's best-selling and most controversial novelists. But why had he taken another man's name?

Scales said, 'This will be a meal ticket for the media when they get hold of it.'

But Wycliffe was not thinking of the media. 'You realize, John, that the stuff we scraped together on Cleeve's background no longer applies. The man who was killed on Wednesday night, who married Patricia Tull, and was responsible for the Stride canon, was John Larkin, and we knew virtually nothing about him except that he didn't have a criminal record. We start from there. I imagine Larkin had other than aesthetic reasons for changing his identity and we've got to know what they were. We've only got the Exeter flat as a starting point; I know it's nearly thirty years ago, but there must be people in Exeter who still remember him. Get some men on it, John, and see what you can do.'

The widow took the news with no outward sign of shock or distress and she made no attempt to contest it. She was silent for a while then in a resigned voice, she said, 'If what you say is true, and I have no reason to doubt it, who was the man I married?'

'At the time of Cleeve's death your future husband was calling himself John Larkin and I have no reason to think that was not his real name. The two men, Cleeve and Larkin, were journalists and they shared a flat in Exeter. Laura Wynn, the woman who makes jewellery, lived with her mother in another flat on the same floor.'

A tremor of distaste. 'That is unfortunate! Did this woman know that my husband was . . . that he was impersonating someone else?'

'No, she thought that her memories of the two men had become confused; she had not known them very well.'

'But she recognized him?'

'As one of the two – yes. At the time Cleeve was killed, she and her mother had already left Exeter.'

Another prolonged silence. One of the large casement windows was open and a cool breeze stirred the curtains. Patricia sat very still; obviously she was trying to grasp the implications of what she had heard.

'Was my husband a criminal?'

'He was never convicted of any crime but he must have had some compelling reason for taking on another man's identity.'

'To escape being caught?' Wycliffe did not answer, and after a pause she said, 'Will all this have to come out in the press?'

Cleeve's words came back to him: 'I don't have to tell you what the family of a murdered man has to go through if there is any mystery about the crime.' He felt sorry for the woman but there was no reassurance he could give. 'It must come out; the reason for your husband's change of identity is almost certainly connected with how he came to die.'

'Yes, I'm sorry.'

He changed the subject. 'Do you know if he had a gun?'

'A gun?'

'An automatic pistol; we found ammunition for an automatic in a locked drawer of his desk, but no pistol.'

She shook her head. 'If he had a gun, I knew nothing of it, but there was so much I didn't know.'

'In the same drawer – the only locked drawer – we also found these.' He drew out of his pocket the envelope containing the playing cards and laid the cards out in order on a small table close to her chair. Finally he added the little lapel badge.

'May I?' She picked up one of the cards, then another; when she had examined all five, she put them back on the table and picked up the lapel badge. 'I don't understand – what are these things?'

Wycliffe said, 'Each of the cards, as you see, is dated, and the dates run from September 4th to July 18th. Without going into detail, we think those dates refer to the years '54 and '55. There can be no doubt that these were the warnings which he spoke to me about.'

She looked from the cards to Wycliffe. 'They mean nothing whatever to me. It seems all the more strange because he hated card games and I doubt if there is a pack of cards in the house.'

Wycliffe said, 'We shall have to find out what they meant to your husband.'

She nodded. 'I suppose so, but I shall be sorry if what you discover about his past casts a shadow over his memory and over our children.'

He had no more questions and he stood up. She was apologetic. 'I really am sorry not to be more helpful but I know so little . . .'

'If anything occurs to you, however trivial it may seem . . .'

'I will let you know, of course.'

She came with him to the door. He had left his car down the drive by the white gates but instead of making in that direction he walked round the house to the rhododendron tunnel and on through the wicket gate to Henry's Field.

He felt vaguely depressed, for despite the news about Cleeve's true identity he could see no way ahead. He reminded himself that Celia Dawe's body had been found on Tuesday morning, Cleeve had gone missing on the night of Wednesday and it was now Friday afternoon. Not long for the investigation of a double

162

murder, but his case was by no means wide open. It was not what he called a computer exercise. A girl is found raped and strangled in a ditch by the motorway; a householder is stabbed to death in his burgled house – these are computer exercises – crimes without an obvious context. Thousands of scraps of information have to be matched against each other and correlated – or not. Finally, something like an answer may pop up on the screen if you are lucky enough to have fed in the vital facts and clever enough to have pressed the right keys. But this was definitely not such an exercise; there were clearly defined links between the murdered man and a small number of people.

He muttered to himself a list of names: Patricia, Geoffrey Tull, Laura Wynn, Roger Kitson, Gervaise Prout. . . . He might have added Borlase, the photographer, but he had ceased to take him seriously. Then there was a possible unknown who might have sent the card messages through the post but would need to have been on the spot on Monday night when Celia Dawe was murdered and again on Wednesday night when Cleeve died.

As he emerged from the garden on to the heath he was astonished to see men erecting a small marquee close to the dig; two of the girls were conducting parties round the site – probably made up of people more interested in homicide than archaeology; Gervaise Prout was supervising other students who were taking out a fresh trench near one of the excavated huts. Only a large, roped-off area round the site of the fire, and the presence of a bored policeman, remained as evidence of the tragedy. For the archaeologists it was business as usual. The press had been and gone.

Wycliffe followed a newly made path through the heather and was greeted by a lugubrious Prout.

'I suppose we are right to carry on, Mr Wycliffe. Patricia says that we should, though I have little heart for it at the moment.' After a pause he went on: 'We have come across a length of walling linking this hut with another, not yet excavated, and the interesting thing is that the wall seems to have been built from stones brought up from the seashore . . .'

Wycliffe said, 'I see you have a marquee going up.'

Prout sighed. 'Yes, we had to have something if we were to carry on and that will serve as long as we don't have any unseasonable gales.'

They stood for a while, watching the students clearing soil from either side of the newly excavated wall.

Prout said, 'I suppose you have just come from Patricia? I met her briefly yesterday evening in the lane on the way to the cottage. She is a remarkable woman.'

'The cottage?' Wycliffe playing dumb.

'Kitson's place.' Prout stooped to examine the loosened soil by the wall. 'You have something there, Donald . . . Let me see . . .' He came up with a piece of pottery which he rubbed free of soil with his thin fingers. It was part of a largish pot and it included a segment of the rim with an area decorated with a spiral motif. 'Glastonbury ware – rather later than most of our finds, perhaps first century . . . Go carefully, Donald, there is probably more.' He turned back to Wycliffe. 'What was I saying? Oh, yes – Patricia, a dear lady, so kind and generous. I dare say Kitson arouses her compassion.'

The reporters were back outside the Incident Room, though not in strength. Perhaps his proper course would have been to prepare a statement on the Cleeve/Larkin change of identity and issue it then and there but he decided not to be precipitate.

'No developments I'm afraid. Believe me, we're working on it.'

'The widow won't talk to us.'

'Can you blame her?'

'Is it true that Cleeve's life was threatened?'

'I've told you – no developments. I'll give you a statement when I've got something to say.'

Sunlight streamed in through the tall narrow windows of the old schoolroom and there were splashes of coloured light on his table, due to a bit of stained glass in one of them. He was in a strange mood, suddenly everything had become unreal: the bare schoolroom with its peeling green walls, the battered tables, the scratched filing cabinets, his colleagues bending over their reports . . . He had known such experiences since childhood when, quite suddenly, everything seemed remarkable, nothing was ordinary any more. His mother would say: 'Why aren't you playing with your toys, Charles?' Later, at school, it was 'Day-dreaming again, Wycliffe!' Now DS Lane was watching him and probably thinking, 'Why does he just *sit* there?'

He forced his thoughts back to the case, to his brief catalogue of names: Patricia, Geoffrey Tull, Laura Wynn, Roger Kitson, Gervaise Prout – one of them? Or two of them in collusion? Of the five, three were newcomers: Laura Wynn had lived in the village for just over two years, Kitson for less, and it was only eighteen months since Prout's first visit to talk about the dig. Cleeve's playing cards had started to arrive ten months ago. Laura Wynn and Kitson admitted to an acquaintance with Cleeve going back more than 20 years. Those were the facts.

And those cards; the five Jacks of Diamonds, their dates as enigmatic as the strangely stylized features of the two-headed knaves. Taken along with Cleeve's secrecy about them and the Larkin/Cleeve identity switch, they must surely mean that Larkin had been involved with others in some criminal act. Yet Records had no trace of him, so he had escaped the law. Had his accomplices been so lucky? If not, the threats and his reaction to them might be explained.

But after 28 years?

He brooded while the little splashes of coloured

light on his table crept nearer the edge.

Cleeve had employed a firm of Exeter inquiry agents to investigate Laura Wynn; had he thought it worth doing the same for others? Such firms were notoriously cagey but with a little pressure they could usually be induced to co-operate and it was a line worth following. It occurred to him too that whatever had prompted Larkin to adopt his flat-mate's identity must have happened while he was in Exeter. DS Mitchell was looking after enquiries at that end but a visit would do no harm and it would be a chance to look in at headquarters . . . He was talking himself into it. The truth was that he felt the need to look at the case from a different perspective.

He turned abruptly to Lucy Lane: 'I'm going home this evening; I shall be in Exeter tomorrow and I expect to be back either tomorrow evening or early on Sunday morning. I'll keep in touch.'

'Any special instructions, sir?'

'Yes, I want a round-the-clock watch on Kitson. Unobtrusive, so try not to use the foot-putters. I simply want to know his habits, his comings and goings and any visitors he may have.'

'Is he to be followed if he goes out?'

'No, that won't be necessary.'

At a little before five o'clock Wycliffe was on the quay, waiting for Helen to return from her trip.

'There she is now, Mister. That's Billy's boat jest rounding the point. I told 'ee Billy wouldn't be late tonight, 'ee got a fishing trip laid on for six an' no gear aboard yet.'

The tubby little man in a squashed sailor-cap was pointing to a beamy craft, low in the water, making her way up the creek.

'What's it been like today outside – rough?'

'No; sou' east by east, a bit o' breeze. They'd run into some chop going but they've 'ad wind an' tide be'ind 'em coming back. I reckon they'll be coming ashore direc'ly thinking they'm bloody Nelsons.'

'Wasn't he sick at the start of every voyage?'

A fat chuckle. 'So'll some o' they 've bin I reckon.'

Helen came ashore, flushed by sun and wind but there were a few pale faces.

'Had a good day?'

'Marvellous! I wish you could have come.'

'I thought of going home tonight; I want to look in at the office and there are one or two enquiries in Exeter . . . I shall be back Sunday morning if not before. Do you want to come?'

She hesitated. 'No, I don't think so, we might as well get what we can from the cottage, it seems silly to go home. You'll sleep at the house?'

'Where else?'

'Then I'll ring Nora and ask her to air the bed.'

Nora was a daily woman who had agreed to sleep at the house and look after the cat while they were away.

CHAPTER SEVEN

Friday evening

Wycliffe arrived home in the late evening. The Watch House, an old coastguard station, stood overlooking another estuary, another river. A mile upstream was the little village of St Juliot, and beyond that the naval base and the city sprawled over its creeks and hills like a grey lichen encrusting the landscape. But of this, nothing could be seen from the Watch House, here there was only the channel and the slopes and fields opposite. Now they were visible through a golden haze, the last rays of the setting sun.

'Why do we go away?'

Nora, a pragmatist, said, 'I suppose because you want to. I'll get you something to eat.'

He poured himself a drink and took it out into the garden. A tour of the demesne, taking stock, his every movement monitored by Macavity, green-eyed and stand-offish after days of having only Nora for company. Grass to be cut, weeding and dead-heading to be done, hedges to be trimmed, but no damage – no damage because no gales.

A makeshift supper, then bed.

Saturday

By eight o'clock next morning he was in his office but his personal assistant was already waiting for him. Diane, alias the Snow Queen, alias the Ice Maiden.

'Mr Scales intended to be here but there's been a big

robbery somewhere near Buckfast – silver and glass, a connoisseur's job, he said.'

She was blonde and exquisite, made up with resolute restraint, a hint of eye shadow, a touch of lipstick, a whiff of perfume – no more. She could have been of any age between twenty-two and thirty; the record said twenty-eight but she would hardly change for many years to come. 'Beauty in cold storage,' Scales said. With it all she was inexorably efficient.

'Your appointment with Sowest Security is for twelve o'clock, with a Mr Jim Harris. It will take you an hour to drive to Exeter (she always allowed for his sedate driving) which means you must leave by ten forty-five.

'Mr Scales asked me to remind you that DS Mitchell is in charge of the enquiries in Exeter and you can contact him at the Central nick there.'

He was fiddling with the things on his desk, the telephones, the clock calendar, the desk diary – putting them back where they *belonged*.

Diane said, 'I was sorry about your holiday; I hope Mrs Wycliffe wasn't too disappointed.'

He spent an hour dealing with the paper work she presented to him and left for Exeter on schedule.

He liked Exeter, it was his idea of the right size for a city and it was still a cathedral and market town not dominated by industry. Despite Hitler, post-war architects and developers, enough of the old town survived to preserve a sense of history. He parked off Fore Street and walked to Langdon Row where Sowest Security had their offices over a building society. He presented himself at the reception desk on the second floor at one minute to twelve. Diane had done it again! A pert brunette with a high and prominent bosom admitted that he had an appointment and he was shown into a rather seedy office where a little man with dark curly hair was feeding papers into a pocket file labelled with the name of a famous firm. Mr Harris had rehearsed the occasion.

'Ah, Mr Wycliffe! I'll be with you in one minute . . . Do sit down.'

Harris put the file in a drawer and extended a soft hand. 'Always a pleasure to assist the official arm – provided there is no betrayal of a client's confidence, eh?'

'This client is dead.'

Mr Harris had broad, squat features and his wide mouth had been extended in a toothy smile, now it contracted promptly. 'Dear me —'

'Murdered. David Paul Cleeve. of Roscrowgy-in-Roseland. He employed you just under a year ago to investigate a lady called Laura Wynn and, more recently, you may have been asked to supply a security guard for his property.'

'Indeed?' Harris spread his hands. 'At any one time, Mr Wycliffe, we have on our books —'

'I'm quite sure, Mr Harris, that you don't run your business by not remembering clients as celebrated as David Cleeve, or by not knowing that the report of his murder was spread over yesterday's papers.'

Harris was unperturbed. 'I don't concern myself with the day-to-day work of my operatives, but I do know that Cleeve was a client, as you say. I also saw the report of his tragic death in the paper yesterday. What, exactly, did you want to know?' The smile was back but less expansive.

'Whether Cleeve employed you to investigate other subjects and, if so, who they were and what you found out.'

A hoarse chuckle. 'It's a good job we don't stand on ceremony round here, Mr Wycliffe. Some of my acquaintances in the business would want an application in triplicate pinned to a court order before they would part with that much.'

'Does that mean that you did have other commissions from Cleeve?'

'One other.' A sly smile. 'But I really shall have to

refer to our records if you want details.' He shouted: 'Bring in the Cleeve file, Sue!'

A minute or two passed then the girl with the high-rise breasts teetered in and dropped a pocket file on her boss's desk; she went out again without a word spoken.

Harris riffled through the contents of the file and came up with a few pages of typescript clipped together. 'Here we are! The subject was male, Caucasian; name of Shirley – Jack Philip Shirley. Our client said the man had been released from Parkhurst in October 1960 after serving five-and-a-half years of an eight-year sentence for burglary. At that time Shirley was twenty-nine years old . . . six-foot-one in height, and weighed approximately two hundred pounds. We received our instructions last March . . .'

'What were you expected to do?'

'To find out what had happened to him in the last twenty-odd years.'

'And what did you find?'

Harris showed his yellowing teeth. 'I hope you'll remember this when the occasion arises, Mr Wycliffe . . . We had no trouble in picking him up after Park-hurst. He was an electrician by trade and he got a job with a firm near Southampton docks. Eighteen months later he was still there but then he was caught flogging material from the firm's store and sacked. They didn't prosecute and Shirley just faded out. We didn't pick up any trace of him again until a fortnight ago. I'd even asked Mr Cleeve if he wanted us to go on with it because these enquiries cost money –'

'What happened a fortnight ago?'

Harris turned the pages of the report. 'You can see for yourself. We had a report – largely by chance – that Shirley was dead. Not long after he left Southampton he was working for a fly-by-night firm in Brixton and it seems he contracted pneumonia and was taken to hospital where he died within forty-eight hours – a weak ticker. Here's a copy of the death certificate, dated August 15th 1962.'

'You reported this to Cleeve?'

'On the 15th of this month I sent him a copy of this.'

'Have you any idea why Cleeve was interested in this man?'

A grimace. 'We don't investigate our clients, Mr Wycliffe; we shouldn't keep 'em long if we did.'

'I would like a copy of that report; the department will pay reasonable clerical charges.'

'Really?' Harris was ironical. 'But I wouldn't like to milk the Law. I'll get Sue to run off a copy, it will stop her brooding on her boobs for ten minutes. As you go out, tell her where to send it.'

Wycliffe was beginning to like Harris and they parted with mutual regard.

He joined the Saturday-morning shoppers. One could still catch the atmosphere of a country market-town with the farmers and their wives coming in from the villages for a morning's shopping and a meal out. He promised himself a decent lunch later.

In March, probably at the time he received his second playing card warning, Cleeve had instructed this security firm to investigate Jack Philip Shirley, released in October 1960 after serving five-and-a-half years. That meant that Shirley had been tried and sentenced early in 1955 – the key year as Wycliffe saw it.

He made for the Central nick and received VIP treatment. He drafted a telex to CRO – 'Urgent and Immediate. Details of offence for which Jack Philip Shirley received eight years in 1955.' He directed that the reply should be sent to his headquarters. Criminal Records would have to dig in their card indexes for Shirley's offence ante-dated Big Brother's computer.

DS Mitchell arrived; he was responsible for trying to fill in the detail of Larkin/Cleeve's stay in Exeter. Mitchell was young, hard, and ambitious; a career cop with a very clear idea of where he thought he was going. Mr Polly would have recognized him instantly as a fully paid-up member of the Shoveacious Cult. At the moment he was bright-eyed and bushy-tailed.

'I've got something on the Mellor Street flats, sir.'

Perhaps Wycliffe looked vague, for Mitchell went on: 'Where Larkin shared a flat with the real Cleeve on the same floor as the Wynn woman when she lived there as a girl . . .'

Wycliffe re-orientated. 'Well?'

'There's an old man, living in a home out at Heavitree, who occupied the flat below the two men.'

'Good! You've talked to him?'

'This morning, sir. He's quite with it – I mean he's mentally alert.'

Wycliffe had a feeling that Mitchell might have been reluctant to say the same of him.

'He remembers Larkin and Cleeve and he says Larkin gave up the flat immediately after Cleeve's death which wasn't long after the Wynns went. As he put it, "It was all-change on that floor." '

'Anything else?'

'Yes. He says that about six months after Larkin went, the police came enquiring about him; they questioned everybody in the building, but he had no idea what it was all about.'

'You'd better see if you can find anything in our records.'

'I'll get right on to it, sir.'

When Mitchell had gone Wycliffe leafed through the telephone directory in search of Prouts. There were more of the clan than he had supposed, but only one Gervaise C. and his address was given as Bankside, St Germans. He wanted to see where Prout called home and it turned out to be not a great way from the Watch House; both were on the Cornish side of the river. He could drive over that evening or leave it until he was on his way back to Roseland in the morning.

Before leaving Exeter he ate fillet of sole with cream and onion sauce and drank a single glass of lager, sharing a table with an aged clergyman who must have slipped from between the pages of Trollope. He lectured Wycliffe on the relative merits of Bath, Portland and Caen stone for building churches. All this within sight of the great west front of the cathedral.

Afterwards, feeling philosophical, he walked to the car park, collected his car, and drove back to headquarters.

Saturday afternoon: the big, ugly building, a honeycomb of glass and concrete, was almost deserted and his footsteps echoed in the empty corridors. His own department was reduced to one detective sergeant and two constables.

He spoke to Mr Oldroyd, his chief, on the telephone, then drafted a statement for the press. Saturday afternoon was a good time to issue a press release as nobody would expect him to lay on a briefing until Monday morning. The statement confirmed that the murdered man had been threatened for some months before he was killed. It went on to say that the man known to the public as Peter Stride, and in private, as David Cleeve, was in fact, John Larkin. All this was as neatly wrapped up as a potato in its jacket and Wycliffe hoped that it would take the media a while to work out the implications.

There was a reply to his telex, succinct, but heart-warming in its promise: 'Jack Philip Shirley sentenced eight years Bristol assize 13th May 1955 for his part in burglary of Shotton House, Yeovil, Somerset 4th September 1954. Indicate further details.'

Wycliffe was pleased, and it was the dates which pleased him; they checked with those on the first and third of the playing cards sent to Cleeve; which must mean something. But Shirley was dead and had been for 20 years when the cards were sent. He certainly needed details but he preferred to get them from a less impersonal source than Criminal Records.

He telephoned Jim Clarke, his opposite number in the

Somerset police and a companion of various jaunts and jamborees.

'Yes, I know about the case, Charles, but it was before my time here. The papers called it The Shotton House Shooting —'

'Shooting?'

'Yes, a police constable was shot and killed by a man resisting arrest after a burglary. As far as I remember there were four men involved but only two were caught – one of them got the chop.'

Murder! And murder of a police officer, a crime which at that time was almost certain to incur a death sentence.

Clarke was saying: 'Officially I suppose the case is still open. What's this all about, Charles?'

Wycliffe explained and Clarke offered to turn up the files.

'I'd rather talk to someone who worked on the case; is there anyone still around?'

Clarke laughed. 'I'll say! Joe Enderby; it was Joe's hour of glory as a chief DI. He's retired now, of course – living with his daughter near Chard.'

'Do you think he would talk to one of my chaps or to me?'

'Joe would talk to a brass monkey about that case if he thought the creature was listening. I'll give you his number . . .'

But ex-Chief Detective Inspector Joe Enderby was at a cricket match and Wycliffe arranged to ring him later in the evening.

Scales arrived and for a couple of hours they discussed administrative matters and cases on hand, while in the real world outside the flow of traffic into the city, with people returning from the countryside and beaches, reached its peak. It was seven o'clock when he and Scales parted company in an almost empty car park. He could have driven straight back to Roseland but he had told Nora he would be home for a meal. He

175

decided to take a look at Prout's house, then go home as arranged.

Bankside was not the name of Prout's house, as he had thought, but of a road, lined with detached houses on one site; houses in the upper bracket, worth £80,000 to £100,000 out of anybody's piggy bank. They over-looked the river but the tide was out, leaving an expanse of mud which gave off a rank smell of decay. Trees were obviously encouraged, gardens were immaculate, and those houses which had names avoided the worst excesses – no Dunroamins or Beuna Vistas, and certainly no Teddimars or Patruths. The cars in the driveways were Rovers, BMWs, Audis and Jaguars. In one of the gardens a military-looking gentleman was shaving his hedge with an electric clipper.

'Gervaise Prout? Let me see . . .' He squinted into the evening sun. 'Two, three – four houses along, the one with an *Amanagowa* cherry sticking up like a blasted maypole in the middle of his lawn – quite absurd!'

No car in the drive and the grass around the *Amanagowa* in need of a trim; Wycliffe rang the doorbell. A short delay, then the door was opened by a plump little woman in a floral dress reminiscent of a seed packet. She looked very slightly dishevelled, as though disturbed during a nap.

He introduced himself. 'Is Dr Prout at home?'

A rich brogue and an obvious desire to please. 'I'm afraid not, sir. He's away at present, but I'm his house-keeper. Do come inside, sir, perhaps I can help . . . '

With plausible mendacity Wycliffe said, 'I thought I might catch him at home; I know he's working on a dig down west but it seemed likely that he might come home at the weekend.'

He was shown into a large room, nominally a drawing-room, with lounge chairs; actually a library where bookshelves were interspersed with display cases containing reconstituted pots, querns, spindle whorls, and tools and ornaments of bone, ceramic and metal

. . . Above the cases and shelves the walls were hung with framed photographs of archaeological occasions.

'Like a museum, isn't it? That's what I say to him; more like a museum than a sitting-room.' The house-keeper had obvious pride in her charge. Wycliffe looked in vain for a desk or table. 'Is this where he works?'

'Oh, no! His study is next door – here, I'll show you.'

She opened a communicating door into an adjoining room which looked out on a patio and the back garden. A large, square table, more shelves but this time they were loaded down with proceedings and transactions of learned societies. Above the mantelpiece there was a portrait in oils of a young girl, a compelling portrait conveying an impression of fragility, so vulnerable that one could scarcely imagine the subject cooking a meal, catching a bus, playing a game, or doing anything other than being her lovely self. But her eyes were strange – oddly blank.

'Isn't she beautiful?' The housekeeper, aware of his interest. 'She must have been his sweetheart when he was young – I suppose she could have been his wife. He never mentions her but there's a photograph of her on his dressing table.' She added, speaking in a lower voice: 'Some tragedy, I reckon. You've only got to look at her to see she wasn't the sort to make old bones.'

Wycliffe changed the subject. 'I should have thought Dr Prout would have been home fairly often, seeing his dig isn't all that far away.'

She shook her head. 'He came up last Wednesday for a meeting at the university, and he spent the night here on the way back – the first time I'd seen him for nearly a fortnight and then it wasn't for long. He was late home from the meeting and not in the best of tempers because he had trouble with his car. He'd left it in the garage down the road and he was afraid it might not be ready for him in the morning.'

'And was it?'

'Oh, yes. I told him it would be; Mr Trewin looks after his regulars.'

As she spoke she was constantly tidying this or straightening that, her hands were never still. 'I suppose you wanted to talk to him about those terrible murders?'

'Yes, I did, but I shall be down there tomorrow, so it's of no importance. I'll talk to him then.'

'He'll be so upset. If I got it right, this Mr Cleeve, apart from being a friend, was paying for the work down there.' She turned to him, shrewdly confiding: 'There's no money in archaeology, you know, sir. If the doctor wasn't well off he couldn't carry on. He's a director of a company – Fecundex – you've probably seen their adverts on the television.'

She came with him to the gate, after failing to persuade him to stay for a cup of tea.

At the corner, there was a garage on what was virtually an island site. 'Bankside Garage: Petrol and Repairs.' Wycliffe slowed down, hesitated, then pulled in on to the forecourt. Thirty years of experience had made him cautious. A dark, youngish man came out of the cave-like interior of the repair shop, wiping his hands on a rag.

'Mr Trewin?'

'He's not here. Can I help?'

Wycliffe produced his warrant card. 'A routine enquiry to eliminate one of your customers from a hit-and-run case.' A euphemism rather than a lie.

'Fire away.'

'Dr Gervaise Prout – his car is a dark-green Granada saloon?'

'You must know that it is.'

'Were you here on Wednesday evening?'

'I've been on every evening this week.'

'On Wednesday evening did Dr Prout bring his car in for attention and leave it with you?'

'He did; the engine was missing – a bit of trouble with the electrics. I told him I'd see to it right away. He said he wanted to drive down west in the early

178

morning and would I leave the car ready on the fore-court where he could pick it up before we opened.'

'You did that?'

'Yes, but Bert – that's Mr Trewin, told me he didn't pick her up until well on in the morning, then he was in a tearing hurry.'

'Thanks, that's all I wanted to know. It eliminates Dr Prout from our enquiry.'

So much for that.

He drove through a tortuous maze of lanes to the Watch House. Nora had a cold meal ready for him – sliced ham with potato salad.

'If you wanted something hot you should've said when you was coming.'

'This is fine.'

'There's beer and a bottle of white wine in the fridge if you want it.'

After the meal he put through a call to ex-Detective Inspector Enderby. A woman answered the telephone. 'I'll get father, it will take a minute or two because he's not as spry as he used to be – arthritis, you know.'

'I'm sorry.'

A few words of introduction and explanation then Enderby was launched.

'Yes, there were four of 'em involved – Jonathan Welsh, Jack Shirley, John Larkin, and Roger John Cross – all in their early twenties . . . At that time Shotton House was in the hands of the Wallis family and the old man collected boxes.'

'Boxes?'

'Snuff boxes, bonbonnières, patch boxes, rouge boxes – you name it, little things in silver and gold and porcelain; easy to carry, easy to fence – made for it. Lovely! Worth a bit, too.

'We'd had three or four of these robberies with the same MO in less than six months and nobody to put 'em down to. You couldn't use the motorway alibi in those days because there was no motorway.'

'How did the shooting come about?'

'It was as the four were leaving the house; one of our patrol cars came up the drive and they were spotted —'

'There was nobody in the house?'

'The family was on holiday abroad and the married couple who had charge of the place were in Wellington overnight for their son's wedding. Somebody who knew the house should have been empty, saw a light in one of the rooms and phoned the nick.'

'Go on.'

'Well, the plan was for the four of them to split up as soon as they left the house and, according to Shirley, that's what they did. Welsh had a different tale; he said that when they saw the patrol car, Shirley and Cross bolted, but he and Larkin stayed together. They hared off through the shrubbery in the direction of the boundary fence and the road. It was then that they ran into our young copper using his initiative.'

Enderby was shaken by a spasm of coughing. 'Sorry about that! It's these damned cigarettes – they'll be the death of me yet. Anyway, Welsh admitted threatening the PC with a pistol but he said he had no intention to shoot.'

'Did he admit that it was his pistol which killed the man?'

'He didn't have any choice because we were able to show that the bullets taken from the body had been fired from a gun of the same calibre and type as one purchased illegally by Welsh a fortnight earlier.'

'Wasn't the gun ever found?'

'Never.'

'Go on.'

'Welsh claimed that he merely threatened the PC to frighten him off but that Larkin grabbed the gun from his hand, slipped the safety catch, and fired three times at point-blank range. He said Larkin had panicked and would have gone on firing if the gun hadn't jammed.'

'It doesn't sound very likely.'

'No, and it didn't impress the judge or the jury. In his summing up the judge said, "You may think, members of the jury, that a man who carries a loaded weapon while perpetrating a crime, intends to use that weapon if the occasion arises." Anyway, Welsh got what was coming to him. Killing a copper in those days was a sure way to the big drop.'

'Did the others know that Welsh was armed?'

'Shirley swore that he didn't and he didn't think the others did either. I was inclined to believe him – Welsh was a wild man – a vicious streak there.

'As you know, it was six months later when we got two of them and, to be honest, we wouldn't have got them if Shirley hadn't tried to flog a couple of snuff boxes. He fingered Welsh but he'd lost touch with the others and didn't know where they were. We eventually traced Larkin to Exeter but the bird had flown long before . . . That was it – until now.'

'Presumably Welsh had a family?'

'Oh, yes. Very respectable people; his father owned a business in Newton – fertilizers and horticultural supplies – that kind of thing. Of course it was a great tragedy for them. There was a sister too; it seems she doted on her brother and I remember reading a long time after that she had committed suicide.'

'What was Shirley like?'

'Not very bright – that was my impression anyway, though he was supposed to have been a wizard with alarm systems. He learnt his trade as an electrician in a factory that made the things so I suppose he knew something about them. I don't know what happened to him when he came out of jail but it wouldn't surprise me if he got back in soon after.'

'I suppose there was a hue and cry after the other pair – Larkin and Cross?'

'You're telling me! More hours and overtime than I care to remember, and all for nothing. There was a rumour that Cross had tried his luck abroad and ended up as a mercenary in darkest Africa but I've no idea if it was true.'

'Presumably you had some background?'

'Yes, but they were both loners to some extent. Larkin had been brought up as an only child by his mother; they lived in Crewkerne and she made a small income painting and selling pictures. When Larkin left school he got a job on the local paper; mother died, the boy had to do his National Service and that's where he met the others . . .'

'And Cross?'

'Something of the same story except that mother was a former member of the *Ballets Russes* – Ukrainian by birth, and married to a British businessman who died young and left her fairly comfortably off. The boy went to Oxford and read languages, then he had to do his National Service and, like I said, that was where the four of them got together.'

Wycliffe's thanks were sincere; the kind of information Enderby had given him wasn't the sort one finds in the files.

'When I'm your way we'll have a jar together.'

Enderby said, 'No bother! It's nice to be taken down and dusted now and then.'

Early to bed.

On most fine Sunday mornings at some time between eight and nine he would be walking along the foreshore to St Juliot, the village nearest the Watch House, to collect his newspapers. But this Sunday, by half-past seven, he was already well on the way back to Roseland. The roads were quiet, hardly any traffic down the county and only a sprinkling of cars and caravans the other way. The bulk of the weekly emmet migration and counter-migration takes place on Saturdays, much of it under cover of darkness.

Wycliffe took stock. On the whole he was pleased with his weekend's work. He had identified the criminal act, 28 years ago, which seemed to be the source of Cleeve's fears and the motive for his murder. Four men: Jonathan Welsh, Jack Shirley, Roger John Cross and John Larkin – the Four Jacks? Was that too fanciful? Whether it was or not, three of them were dead. Welsh had been executed, Shirley had died a natural death, and Larkin/Cleeve had been murdered. That left Cross. . . . It occurred to Wycliffe that Cleeve had not, apparently, made any enquiry about Cross. Did this mean that he knew where Cross was or what had happened to him?

Progress. But was he any nearer finding out who had first threatened, then murdered Cleeve? Both he and Cross had escaped the law; they had that much in common . . . His thoughts chased each other in circles but he was beginning to feel optimistic. He even sang in a cracked voice:

'There'll be blue birds over the white cliffs of Dover...' and on a few open stretches of road his speedometer clocked an almost unprecedented 70.

'I'm high,' he told himself, 'it must be Nora's egg and bacon.'

He turned off the spine road which links the granite moors through the county and travelled south-westwards into china-clay country. A glimpse of sunlit sea as he approached St Austell entranced him and even the grim moonscape of the china-clay workings failed to depress. By half-past eight he was back in Roseland and entering the village, past the villas which bordered the creek. The pines and palms and a limpid quality of the light created a Mediterranean air, then he rounded a bend and the whole waterfront of the village was before him. It really was a toy-town village, the little houses painted in pastel colours, self-consciously neat, most of them with their tubs of flowers outside. There were few people about, only the boatmen getting their craft ready for the day, carrying cans of fuel and waterproof cushions across the quay and down iron ladders to their moored boats.

Wycliffe parked his car and let himself into the cottage. Helen had just got up and was making coffee.

A welcoming kiss and, 'Shall I get you some breakfast?'

'I've had the full treatment from Nora – bacon, egg and tomato – "A man needs a good breakfast inside him," Nora said.'

'I'll bear it in mind but what about a cup of coffee for now?'

He telephoned the Incident Room to say that he was back; and Division with instructions to send another telex to CRO – the full treatment on Welsh and Shirley.

Helen said, 'Any chance of meeting for lunch?'

He was tempted but decided against. 'No, I can't promise anything.'

A few minutes later he was turning off the waterfront up Zion Steps. The shops were closed. He wondered how Geoffrey Tull would be spending his Sunday. With his brother-in-law's money on the family horizon the future must look brighter. And Laura Wynn?

In The Vegetarian benches were stacked on the tables and a woman was on her knees washing the floor. As he approached the photographer's Borlase came out of his shop followed by the hideous yellow dog on a lead. The photographer was in his Sunday suit of mottled grey. He saw Wycliffe, pretended not to have done, and turned up the Steps, then he changed his mind and faced about with a nervous smile.

'Ah, Mr Wycliffe! I wasn't expecting to see you, they told me you were away.'

'Did you want to see me?'

Borlase looked paler, more pasty than ever; his eyes were bloodshot and his manner was timid. 'Only to tell you about the arrangements for Celia's funeral. I've got the coroner's certificate and I – we have arranged the funeral for two o'clock tomorrow. Celia is being taken into our chapel in the morning and we shall gather there for a short service at two o'clock before proceeding to the cemetery.'

'I shall try to be there.'

He walked along Chapel Street to the Incident Room and felt that he had been a long time away. DC Shaw was duty officer and DS Lane was sitting at her table; both were reading Sunday newspapers so crime did not press on the Lord's day.

'I thought you might want a word, sir.'

'I do.' He gave her an account of his progress. 'What news of Kitson?'

'He hasn't done anything exciting; he seems to have a regular routine –'

'Does he know that he's being watched?'

'It seems not. Weekes and Trembath have divided the daylight hours between them and they say he's never given the slightest sign. If he does know he must be playing some sort of game.'

'That wouldn't surprise me.'

Lucy referred to her reports. 'On Saturday morning he was up at half-past seven when he let the cat out, then there was music, apparently from a record player. Trembath, who has an ear, says it was Schumann. At a little before nine Kitson came out of the cottage leaving the door wide open and went off carrying a shopping bag. An hour and a half later he was back with a load of groceries and whatever.'

'And after lunch?'

'After lunch he was typing for a while then he had a visit from Mrs Cleeve who went in without knocking. She had her dog with her and the dog settled by the front door, very much at home. Mrs Cleeve stayed until four and after she'd gone, more typing, then music for the rest of the evening and bed at about half-past ten.'

'No other visitors?'

'No, sir.'

Wycliffe was restless, unsure of his next move. He ambled about the drab hall, stooping now and then to retrieve screwed-up bits of paper which had missed the waste bins, fiddling with the carousel, staring out of

185

the window at the drama of life in Chapel Street. From time to time he checked the wall clock against his watch. Finally, at twenty minutes to eleven, he came to a stop by Lucy Lane's table.

'I'm going to talk to Kitson; he's on the telephone so you can reach me there if you want me.'

'Good luck!'

For some reason he felt cheered.

CHAPTER EIGHT

Sunday July 24th
The single bell was clanging out its summons to
loyal members of the establishment, while dark-suited
men waited at the chapel door to welcome the non-
conforming elect. Exactly one week earlier Wycliffe had
been calling on Sergeant Pearce and was taken to The
Buckingham Arms for a drink. At that time Celia Dawe
would have been in one of the other bars and David
Cleeve was probably pottering about in his library-study
afflicted by that Sunday-morning lassitude which is the
fate of unbelievers. Now they were both dead, but
nothing seemed to have changed, the village went about
its business and its pleasures and the sun still shone.
Wycliffe recalled that someone had said, 'Living is like
making a hole in water.'

He was walking up the now familiar hill; the prolonged drought was taking its toll, the hedges were
dustier, the grass browner and the last of the foxgloves
had lost their petals. He passed the gates to Roscrowgy.
Somewhere across the river they were harvesting –
unthinkable on the Sabbath when he was a boy. At first
sight Henry's field seemed deserted but as he turned
off the road he saw a couple of the students, towels over
their shoulders, strolling from tents to wash-ups. He
crossed the field, passed the caravan, and glimpsed
Prout's white head bent over some task with the spec-
tacled Wrighton at his side. Neither of them looked up.
He reached the burned-out hut, turned down the
lane through the wood, and approached the clearing.

DC Trembath emerged from the trees like Uncas, the last of the Mohicans.

'He's working, sir; every now and then the typewriter clatters away for a bit, then it's quiet again.'

Trembath had been seconded from Division; a mountain of a man but light on his feet, and with the gentle features and manner which often go with great bulk.

'Have you seen him today?'

'Only when he put the cat out just after seven.'

Wycliffe said, 'I want you to come in with me.'

He opened the creaky gate and together they walked up the path to the front door. Kitson was at the table with the typewriter in front of him. In the middle of the table the cat was fast asleep.

Kitson looked up in mild surprise to see Trembath blocking the doorway. 'Ah! The spy has come in from the cold.'

Wycliffe said, 'Detective Constable Trembath.'

'Won't you both sit down? Bring up a chair from the corner there . . . Mr Trembath, make yourself comfortable if you can.'

Wycliffe said, 'One or two points . . .'

'I thought you people kept that for when you've been interrogating some poor devil for days on end – "One or two points . . ." '

Kitson's manner was light, bantering, but Wycliffe sensed that he was keyed-up, braced for a climax, and this would be the more understandable if he knew that he had been under observation for 36 hours.

In a conversational tone Wycliffe said, 'Jonathan Welsh, Jack Shirley, John Larkin, Roger John Cross.' A lengthy pause, then: 'All four were involved in a burglary at Shotton House near Yeovil on September 4th 1954.'

Wycliffe had settled as comfortably as he could on his hard chair and was filling his pipe. 'Do you mind?'

'No! Smoke by all means – you too, Mr Trembath.

I've noticed that during your vigil you favoured cigarettes; so do I, though Cleeve used to call them coffin nails.'

Poor Trembath looked like a naughty boy.

Wycliffe went on, 'In trying to avoid arrest, Jonathan Welsh shot and killed a policeman. Six months later he and Shirley were arrested. Welsh was hanged for murder and Shirley was sentenced to eight years for burglary . . .' Wycliffe's speech and actions were deliberate and slow, as though he was setting the tempo for a protracted session. He added, 'But I think you know all this.'

Kitson turned briefly to face Wycliffe. 'Why should I know anything of these people?'

Wycliffe said: 'Cleeve must have known them; he employed a private inquiry agent to find out all there was to be known about Shirley, and you were very well acquainted with Larkin.'

'Indeed?'

'Of course, you prefer to speak of him as Cleeve and I find it difficult not to but, as we both know, Cleeve was the name he adopted when he was wanted by the police after the Shotton House killing.'

Kitson tapped ash from his home-made cigarette. Trembath stared at a threadbare rug on which there was no trace of pattern remaining. A little clock wedged between books on a shelf became obtrusively audible in the silence.

Kitson said, 'Is this going on for much longer? If so I would like to do something about my lunch.'

Wycliffe shook his head. 'I shouldn't worry, Mr Kitson; if the only inconvenience one suffers from all this is a late lunch then it will be nothing to complain of.

'Returning to these four young men; they must have had romantic notions of crime. The Four Jacks – I wonder why they picked on jacks? The knaves in the pack, I suppose?'

189

The sun was shining through the little square panes of glass, directly on to the faded spines of rows of books. Another very hot day but small windows and thick walls kept the room pleasantly cool.

'I wonder which of the four was the Jack of Diamonds? The five playing cards sent to Cleeve were Jacks of Diamonds.' Wycliffe was speaking very quietly as though half to himself. 'Roger John Cross is the only one of the four not accounted for; the other three are dead.'

Trembath shifted his position and the strut-back Windsor creaked in protest.

With a sudden briskness of manner Wycliffe said: 'Do you have a birth certificate, Mr Kitson?'

'Not in my possession.'

'But you could get one?'

'I suppose so, if necessary.'

Wycliffe reverted to his former casual, rather sleepy manner. 'I wonder what it would tell us? That your name isn't Kitson but Cross? Of course, birth certificates are not to be relied upon; look at your friend Cleeve; I've no doubt he had a birth certificate – don't you have to in order to get married?'

Kitson was silent for a long time then he said, very quietly: 'All right, having got so far you are sure to find proof if you look for it.'

'You are Roger John Cross?'

'Yes.' He said it with a sigh which might have been of relief.

A plane flew low over the cottage, shattering the silence; the cat leapt off the table and padded about the floor bemused. Kitson lifted the creature on to his lap and made soothing sounds. Then, without any prompting, he began to talk:

'It was bound to come to this when David was murdered and perhaps I wouldn't have wanted it otherwise. . . . We met, the four of us, by chance or fate or whatever you like to call it – four beds in a row in a barrack

190

room when we were National Service rookies. For some reason we formed a natural group – at least it seemed natural in the circumstances. Shirley could scrounge anything anywhere; Welsh could talk his way round the recording angel, while Larkin and I were as green as grass and scared of the whole business – the cretinous NCOs, the military bull, and the stark reality of dossing down with twenty others in the same room. We were more than glad to latch on to a couple who seemed to know their way about. I'm not sure what we contributed but there were no complaints.' One side of Kitson's face twitched in a smile.

Aware of legal thin ice, Wycliffe warned him that he was under no obligation either to answer questions or talk about events which might incriminate him.

He responded with a laugh. 'What have I got to lose?'

Outside the long grass, the nettles, the docks and the brambles got on with the business of take-over in silence.

'The Korean war was going strong and, after training, we were drafted with the British contingent and largely owing to Welsh's wire-pulling we kept together.'

Kitson paused and began the lengthy process of rolling one of his cigarettes. He spoke, concentrating on the manipulations involved. 'Fifteen months out there strengthened the bonds between us, whatever they were. We became known as The Four Jacks – inseparable and slightly crazy.'

'Was that when you adopted the playing cards as symbols?'

'No, not then, it was just that we happened to have – all four of us – names that might be reasonably shortened to Jack.'

Wycliffe reminded himself that he was engaged in a police investigation; the atmosphere was more conducive to quiet nostalgic recollection.

'When we finally got back to this country, Welsh said

191

that we mustn't just separate and lose sight of each other so, at his suggestion, we agreed to meet every three months. As I said, Welsh was a persuasive talker, but I don't suppose any of us thought it would last long. Our first get-together was on a Saturday early in September '52, and it came as a surprise to three of us. We met at a pub we had frequented during training but after a drink or two we went to an hotel where Welsh had laid on a little dinner – very civilized. There were place cards, each one a jack from a deck of playing cards with our names on them – that was how the playing card business started. Typical Welsh, by the way, he had a strong element of fantasy in his make-up.'

'Who was which of the four jacks?'

'Shirley was the spade, Larkin the club, Welsh the diamond, and I was the heart.' A twisted grin. 'Don't ask me on what grounds the allocation was made. Anyway, in addition we were each given a little lapel badge in the shape of our suit with a 'J' in the middle.'

'These quarterly meetings continued?'

'They became a ritual.'

'Did you communicate with each other in between?'

'No, at each meeting we fixed up the next. It was Welsh's idea that they should be our only contact and as we settled back into civilian life and moved around we didn't even know each other's addresses.'

'What sort of man was Welsh?'

Kitson took time to consider his answer. 'Blond, with almost feminine good looks; slight of build but hard as they come.'

'I was thinking of his character.'

'I know, but that's more difficult. Have you read *Medicus*?'

'Yes.'

Kitson re-lit his cigarette. 'I've always thought that Aldo in *Medicus* was based on Welsh.'

'Wasn't he the chap who in some way or other muti-lated every girl he slept with?'

'Yes, but at other times he was a pleasant, enter-taining fellow, generous, affectionate, even sentimental. That was Welsh; I'm not saying that he mutilated girls but he certainly had a cruel streak which didn't show most of the time.'

It was odd, this concentration on Welsh, the man of the four who had been dead for 28 years; yet Wycliffe felt convinced that he was the key. Even the warning cards sent to Cleeve had been Jacks of Diamonds.

'Did you know anything of his family?'

'Only that they were in some sort of business. They must have been well off because Welsh was always in funds and he was sometimes absurdly generous – embarrassingly so. As to the family, I remember some mention of a sister – Barbara, I think she was called.'

'What about the burglaries?'

Kitson continued stroking the cat for a while without speaking then he said: 'If you mean how did they start, it was a casual conversation at one of our get-togethers – at least I thought it was casual at the time. When we met again we seemed to go on talking from where we'd left off; there was a lot of nonsense about a modern Raffles but I didn't think anyone took it seriously. By the second or third meeting after it was first mentioned, we were actually planning a robbery – just for an experiment. That was the way things went when you were with Welsh – he was a remarkable chap. He would float an idea, let it hang around for a bit, start a discussion leading to argument, then say, "Why not put it to the test? Just for the hell of it . . ."'

'The idea was to pick a smallish country house where the owners were away or just out for the evening, take only small, easily portable objects of moderate value, then separate – no get-away car or any of that nonsense; each to find his own way home with his share of the loot, to meet later at an agreed rendezvous. Welsh knew something that I didn't at the time – Shirley had worked in a factory where they made alarm systems.

'Well, it worked and, inevitably, we had to repeat the experiment. Welsh did all the planning; he selected the houses, decided on the timing and the kind of thing we should take. He seemed to know these houses from the inside and I suspect they were the houses of friends of his family.'

'What happened on the night of the killing? Did you know that Welsh was carrying a gun?'

Kitson paused long enough to collect his thoughts. 'No, I didn't know. As to what happened, we came out of the house and immediately saw a police car in the drive with two uniformed men getting out. We scattered and I saw no one after that but I did hear three shots which seemed to come from the other side of the drive.'

'Do you think it likely that Welsh and Larkin kept together?'

'According to what Larkin – strange to call him that now – told me, they did not, and I believed him.'

'When did you first meet Larkin again after the Shotton House affair?'

'It happened just as I told you, when we were both working in the museum. By that time, of course, he was calling himself Cleeve and I was Kitson. We stuck to our new names quite firmly, even when we were alone together.'

'What happened to you in the meantime?'

The cat was clawing at the tablecloth and Kitson lifted her down to the floor and straightened the cloth. 'A great deal, but nothing relevant to your case.'

'Your injuries?'

'Yes, but don't get any wrong ideas about them.' A grim smile. 'I spent some time abroad and this was the work of an unfriendly gentleman I met.'

'Did you kill Cleeve?'

Wycliffe's manner was relaxed, conversational, as though they were having an academic discussion rather than pursuing a police inquiry. 'There is the point that if you didn't kill him, who else could have had sufficient knowledge to do it in the way it was done – cards and all?'

Kitson turned to face him and his manner was grave. 'I did not kill him – why in God's name should I? As to who might have done it, don't you think I've racked my brains over that?'

'With any result?'

'None. When David received those cards I thought it was leading up to a blackmail attempt, and I said so. I could just about see Shirley in that role, but we know now that Shirley was dead and, in any case, the cards led not to blackmail but to murder.'

'What did Cleeve himself think?'

Kitson made a helpless gesture. 'I really never knew what he was thinking about anything, I sometimes wonder if he knew himself. He lived so much in that strange fantasy world of his books that he half believed in the reality of situations he had created. He pretended to believe that he was a guilty man – deserving of punishment – that was the image he presented.'

'And it was false?'

A frown. 'I'm not saying that it was false, but it was exaggerated.'

Wycliffe stood up. 'I shall leave DC Trembath to keep you under surveillance until the Somerset police take over responsibility.'

'What happens then?'

'I don't know; you may have to face a charge of burglary.'

'And?'

Wycliffe turned away and when it seemed that he

195

would not answer, he said: 'After twenty-eight years?'

As a small boy Wycliffe had played Snakes and Ladders with his sister. On their board an awesome snake writhed across from within a few squares of *Home* to somewhere quite near *Start*. He could still recall what it felt like to land on that repulsive head and have to slither down all the way under his sister's watchful eye. He felt much the same now, oppressed by a sense of anticlimax. The playing card nonsense had been unscrambled and that should have been the end of the case. But why would Cross want to kill Larkin or Kitson kill Cleeve? For his wife? Wycliffe had already decided that that kite wouldn't fly. He doubted if they were having a real affair and to imagine Kitson setting up that elaborate charade with the cards – for what? It would only point back to him in any case.

Lunchtime. Nora's breakfast at six-thirty was only a memory. He hesitated between a pub meal and The Vegetarian, but pub food on a Sunday was often below its best and he wanted something light. He was glad to find The Vegetarian still with several empty tables, then he saw Dr Hodge, but not before Dr Hodge had seen him.

'Come and join me!' Hodge was having soup with a crusty roll. 'My wife has gone to St Ives to see her mother; I'm on call. This soup is good if you like celery. What's the matter with you? You're taking all this too seriously – you look wisht about the gills, as the Cornish say . . . So our late lamented genius was hiding under yet another name – hiding from something pretty nasty I should say, reading between the lines.'

'Is there something in the papers?'

'Radio – I haven't seen a paper today, too busy. I heard it on the car radio.'

The waitress came.

'I'll have the same as Dr Hodge.' He was in a strange mood, weak and suggestible.

Hodge said, 'Now there's a rumour going round that Mrs C wasn't Caesar's wife after all. It's a wicked world, but surely a woman like her wouldn't fancy poor old Kitson?'

There were a few enterprising reporters outside the Incident Room but he got away after promising a Monday-morning briefing. Inside, most of the tables were occupied, the ponderous routine of the case churned on – most of it precautionary, in case things turned sour, then everybody could say: 'No avenue unexplored! No stone unturned!' Nobody with egg on his face. Well, he didn't make the rules of the game, thank God.

He sat at his desk and looked across at Lucy Lane feeling mildly guilty. The girl seemed to be there whether she was officially 'on' or 'off' and he wasn't bringing her into the conduct of the case as he would have done with her predecessors. He called her over and they talked for half an hour.

'So where do we go from here?'

She didn't answer at once, then she said, 'Do you think we know all we should about the Welsh family? I mean, if they really believed in the young man's innocence and in Cleeve's or Larkin's guilt, then there would be a powerful motive, even after this lapse of time.'

He was impressed because it was the conclusion he had reached himself. 'But it's not only a question of motive; there must be someone here and now —'

'There's a Miss Byrne wants to speak to you, sir; she won't say what it's about.' Dixon, the duty officer, in a low voice.

Wycliffe glanced across the room to the duty desk. Carrie Byrne, the housekeeper-cousin from Roscrowgy, looking anything but dowdy in a plain emerald-green frock. 'I'll talk to her.'

It was only as he got close to her that he saw her face was blotchy and the skin round her eyes was creased with tiredness. The woman was on the point of breakdown.

'You want to speak to me, Miss Byrne?'

'In private.' The words seemed to be jerked out of her and she looked round the room with apprehension.

'Of course!' He led the way between the tables to a little room at the back which was probably a store-cupboard when the place was a school. Now it had a little table and two bentwood chairs. Light came from a small window high up; like a cell.

She sat, holding her handbag with both hands. 'I haven't been able to sleep since that night . . . I feel so ashamed . . .'

Wycliffe, sitting opposite her, said nothing, but tried to look kindly and attentive.

'Patricia has always been good to me – more like a sister than a cousin, and I've everything to thank her for.'

'What do you want to tell me?'

'It's about the night David . . .'

'Wednesday night.'

'Yes, he had a telephone call saying something had happened to Roger.'

'Roger Kitson?'

'Yes. That was why he went out and if he hadn't gone he wouldn't have been killed.' She suppressed a sob which became a snort; she took out a handkerchief and held it to her nose and mouth.

Light dawned on Wycliffe.

'You were with Mr Cleeve at the time?'

She nodded, helplessly, like a child.

'You were upstairs in his part of the house?'

'We were in bed.' Words came in a rush now. 'I wasn't really being disloyal to Patricia; I mean, if it hadn't been me it would have been one of the others and he had to go out for them. David couldn't do without women . . .'

'Is there a telephone in his bedroom?'

'No, it rang in the library but the door was open.'

'You could hear what he said?'

She nodded again.

'Tell me.'

She wiped her nose and her eyes. 'He sounded irritable; he said: "Oh? What do you want at this time of night? . . . Of course I'm alone!" Then his voice changed and he was obviously worried. I can't remember his exact words but they were something like: "Is he hurt . . . Don't be a fool, you must know . . . No, don't do that, I'll be right over . . . tell him I'm on my way." I heard him drop the phone then he must have picked it up again because I could hear him dialling, but he couldn't have got through because he didn't speak to anybody. He came back into the bedroom and dressed very quickly.'

'Did he say anything?'

She hesitated. 'He just said, "It's about Roger. You'd better get back to your room." He went into the library again, I suppose to fetch something, then he was gone.'

It left a pathetic picture; Carrie gathering together her clothes with the shreds of her modesty and stealing back to her room.

'Did you get the impression that he was speaking to Kitson?'

'No, I didn't; I thought he was speaking about Roger to someone else.' Her lower lip trembled. 'I should have told you this before but I couldn't bear . . .'

'Never mind, you've told us now. I'm going to hand you over to Miss Lane and she will write out what you have said and ask you to sign it. We shan't use it unless it is absolutely necessary.'

He left the two women together in the glorified cupboard which had to serve as an interview room. The unassuming, unaspiring Carrie Byrne had solved one problem which had troubled him – how Cleeve had been lured out of his house late at night and induced to cross Henry's Field in the darkness. Now he knew how, but by whom?

He went back to his table. It was very hot and the atmosphere was somnolent. He was thinking about Welsh, the young man with whom it had all started. Jonathan Welsh, Jack of Diamonds; blond with almost feminine good looks, slight of build, but hard, a great talker, affectionate, sentimental, but with a cruel streak; sometimes absurdly generous, a strong element of fantasy – Kitson's assessment. Enderby had said ' . . . a real wild man – a vicious streak'.

Contradictory, mutually incompatible elements provide the mix for every one of us but this recipe must have added up to more than ordinary instability and on a July morning 28 years ago that young man had been led out from his cell to the scaffold.

'Welsh is dead!' Wycliffe muttered to himself.

Dixon came over from the duty desk. 'Somerset police are sending a detective sergeant and a constable to interview Kitson, sir.'

'Do they want to take him back with them?'

'No, sir. Their instructions are to take his statement, then all the papers will be sent to the DPP for an opinion.'

Which probably meant that Kitson and the police would be let off the hook.

He had thought about Welsh, now he was thinking about the crime, the crime of the Four Jacks. Four young men had set out to commit a particular type of crime – robbing country houses. It was a good recipe; there was something in it for everybody – profit, risk and for the squeamish it was all down to insurance. Shirley was dim and probably went along with the others because one way of avoiding slog was as good as another. Larkin and Cross probably needed the element of adventure, even of romance. If it wasn't robbing the rich to pay the poor it was the next best thing. And the playing-card Jacks were a symbol of their camaraderie; they even had badges.

All this planned and organized by Welsh who had thought up the scheme and skilfully sold it to the other three . . . And Welsh was the wild man.

Did it really add up? Wycliffe wasn't sure.

It was Sunday and he had been on the go since six-thirty. Suddenly he was very tired. 'I'm going home.'

The trippers were returning after a day in the sun. On the waterfront there was a general movement towards the car park; at the quay one ferry was loading and another waited for the berth. He had no idea how Helen had spent the day and he felt guilty.

She was waiting for him. 'I've had a lazy day. This morning I went to church at St Just; I had lunch in the wine bar and this afternoon I took a book and lay on the grass below the castle. I think I slept most of the time.'

'Do you want to go out for a meal?'

'If you like, but I've got a couple of veal cutlets in the fridge . . .'

'Suits me.'

They drank sherry in the kitchen while the meal was prepared. Afterwards they sat in the living-room with the window open to the waterfront. Helen was browsing through the Sunday supplements, Wycliffe was drifting between sleeping and waking, slumped in his chair. 'Do you think we know enough about the Welsh family?' Lucy Lane's question; the answer was an emphatic 'No!' It occurred to him that the Welshes had run their business in Newton and it was there that his former sergeant – Kersey – had been transferred as CID inspector. He got up from his chair.

'What are you going to do?'

'I'm going to ring Kersey.'

It took a little while speaking of this and that then they got to business. 'Do you know anything of a family called Welsh who run some sort of horticultural business in Newton?'

'Afraid not, sir. There's no horticultural firm trading under that name.'

Wycliffe explained what he was after. 'The son was executed in '55; I think there was a daughter who later committed suicide. I want to know what happened to the family after '55 and to their firm . . . Phone me at the Incident Room sometime tomorrow afternoon, you should have something by then.'

When he replaced the phone Helen said, 'Are they all right?'

'What?'

'The Kerseys – how are they getting on?'

'Oh, fine . . . fine!'

'Is Joan still having trouble with her back?'

'I forgot to ask.'

'Oh, Charles!'

CHAPTER NINE

Monday July 25th
The promised press briefing was held at sub-division,
partly because there were better facilities, partly to keep
the reporters out of the village. He had to drive to King
Harry, cross the river by the chain-ferry, then drive up
the hill past Trelissick to the Truro road. As a way to
work there was much to recommend it, especially on a
morning when the air was fresh and sweet as on the first
day of creation. Georgian Lemon Street was a pleasant
sight too, but the nick, though newish, was much like
any other when one was inside.

He gave a succinct account (he hoped) of the case so
far; a digression on the Four Jacks, and a brief résumé
of the Shotton House affair. Hard luck on the Cleeve
family but there was no way around that. A young man
was involved in several burglaries, in the last one a
policeman was shot and killed; one of the young man's
accomplices was hung for murder, but he adopted a false
identity and wrote himself into fame and fortune. Then,
nearly 30 years later, after a series of melodramatic
warnings, he was killed by a poisoned dart and his body
cremated . . . Plenty of column-inches there; not only
for the proverbial nine days but for a re-hash at each
stage of the legal grind if it ever came to that.

A little monkey-face reporter whom Wycliffe knew
of old, said, 'It's like The Ten Little Nigger Boys, Mr
Wycliffe, except that there are only four. One was
executed, one died a natural death, one was murdered
and then there was one – what happened to him?'

'The police are in touch with the fourth man.'

'Is he in custody?'

'No, we have no case against him and the Shotton House burglary is the concern of another force.'

'May we know the fourth man's name?'

'The Jack of Hearts.'

Guffaws. They were in a good humour, with more than enough to be going on with.

When they had gone the DI was waiting for him. 'There's a package from CRO and another from the Somerset Police – I was going to send them on by messenger but –'

In the DI's office he unpacked his parcels and laid out their contents. He spent an hour working through the material and ended up with three mug-shots of Welsh, a copy of his official record, and a series of notes taken from statements made at the time. He had also constructed a little table which pleased him:

Dates on the playing cards	Events which they recorded
Saturday September 4th	The Shotton House killing
Tuesday March 8th	Arrest of Welsh and Shirley
Friday May 13th	Trial verdicts
Thursday June 16th	Rejection of Welsh's appeal
Monday July 18th	Welsh executed

(The card symbolically torn across)

A riddle finally solved.

A uniformed copper brought coffee on a tray, a whole pot with a cup and saucer instead of a mug; rich tea biscuits – luxury.

Wycliffe studied the photographs while he nibbled his biscuits. Despite the white-sheet background and the front lighting the man came through. There was certainly something immature as well as feminine about the features, and his mouth had that curious delicacy which one associates with cruelty. But it was the eyes which compelled Wycliffe's attention; they were empty of expression, looking out with a disturbing blankness at the camera and the world. Wycliffe was reminded of young, blond, brainwashed Nazis in their field-grey uniforms with swastikas on their arms. Perhaps that was why this man's face seemed familiar . . .

Then he remembered the girl in the painting.

It was not an experience comparable with Saul's on the Damascus road, not even with that of Archimedes in his bath, but from that moment Wycliffe knew that he was at last pointed in the right direction.

Enderby had said that the Welsh family ran some sort of horticultural business in Newton, way back in 1955; Prout's housekeeper had told him with pride that her employer was a director of Fecundex – a firm in the same line of business. Coincidence? Perhaps, but add to that the fact that Welsh had a sister and that his mug-shots, despite the unsubtle techniques of HM prison photographer, vividly recalled the painting of the girl which hung in Prout's study . . .

He picked up the telephone and spoke to the switch-board operator: 'I want to know if Fecundex Limited are listed in the Exeter district directory – I'll hold on . . .'

It took only a moment. 'They're listed as Fecundex Horticultural Products —'

'And the address?'

'Tanner's Lane, Newton, sir.'

That seemed to clinch it, but there would be news from Kersey later.

Another telephone call, this time to the Incident Room; he spoke to Lucy Lane: 'I want a couple of DCs to keep an eye on Prout – as discreetly as possible but he mustn't be allowed to give us the slip.'

As he approached the village on his way back he turned off the road and up the drive to Roscrowgy. He parked in front of the house and caught sight of Patricia dead-heading a rhododendron bush not far off. He was mildly shocked. Would Helen go on with her gardening routine if he were lying dead? Why not? He had to admit that she probably would; the sensible thing to do . . . He walked over.

'I wonder if you will spare me a few minutes?'

She dropped a couple of browning heads into a plastic sack. Her features were drawn and she looked tired, but she seemed pleased rather than otherwise to see him.

'I was just thinking that I'd earned a cold drink and I'm sure you could do with one. Let me take you to the courtyard then I'll see about something long and iced.'

They sat on the white metal chairs in the shade of an umbrella maple. The drinks turned out to be lager in tall glasses, misted over. Very refreshing.

He said: 'You may have heard from Kitson how the case has developed?'

'Yes; Roger telephoned.' She was silent for a while, sipping her drink, then she said: 'It is an humiliating experience to discover that for twenty years one has been . . .' She hesitated for a word then went on: 'one has been totally ineffective.'

'Ineffective?'

Her face was turned away from him but her voice betrayed her emotion. 'When I married David I saw it as my job to make it easier for him to do the work I so much admired. Yet in twenty years I never succeeded in winning his confidence sufficiently to help him in the one way which might have meant something.'

Wycliffe said, 'I think you are very hard on yourself.'

'That is kind.' She turned to him, suddenly brisk. 'Forgive me! I am being morbid. What did you want to ask me?'

'About the dig in Henry's Field: I wonder if you know how it came about that Gervaise Prout undertook the work?'

She was clearly surprised and diverted by the question. 'You mean how it all started?'

'Did the initiative come from your husband?'

'No, David was interested in the remains and he spoke of the possibility of a dig and Christie was keen, but it was a letter from Gervaise which set it going.'

'They knew each other?'

'No, the letter came out of the blue. It simply said that the sight was an interesting one and might be important for Iron-Age studies in the south-west. He wondered if David would consider the possibility of a dig if funds could be raised.'

'What happened?'

She placed her empty glass with Wycliffe's on a tray. 'I think David made some enquiries about Prout's academic standing then he invited him down. He was impressed by Prout's enthusiasm and not only agreed to the dig but offered to finance it.' She smiled. 'Something must have impressed him.'

'Didn't it strike you odd that, avoiding all forms of publicity as he did, he should invite a stranger down and be willing to co-operate in a venture like that?'

She nodded. 'I suppose I did, but I was very pleased; it came at a time when he was beginning to . . . to loosen up, to go out more and to be more responsive to contacts. I see now that he was beginning to feel more secure.'

It was an idyllic spot; the sunshine and shade, the patterns of shadows, the fragrance of flowers and the sound of water trickling into the pool . . . Wycliffe thought that it might be hard not to feel secure in these surroundings.

'What was your husband's opinion of Dr Prout?'

Such a direct question jarred on her sense of propriety but she responded. 'I think he was amused by him – by his single-mindedness, but also a little irritated. He said once that Gervaise was like an iceberg, only one-seventh above water. Although David was so secretive himself he couldn't stand that characteristic in others.'

'And you – what do you think of Dr Prout?'

A frown and a moment to consider. 'He is an agreeable man with enthusiasm for his subject which he can communicate to others.'

'But?'

She laughed despite herself. 'There are no buts – or only a little one. I have to confess that at first I was irritated by his curiosity. I was a victim, so was Christie.'

'About what was he curious?'

'About us as a family. At one point I wondered if he was trying to steal a march on David's would-be biographers. When he found that we had nothing to tell he stopped asking questions.' She smiled. 'It was only a small thing, mildly irritating.'

Wycliffe got up. 'Thank you for the drink and for being patient with my questions. Do you mind if I go through the tunnel to the dig and leave my car where it is?'

'Please do whatever is convenient.'

She walked with him back to the spot where she had broken off her work and he continued through the tunnel and through the wicket gate into Henry's Field. As he crossed the field he saw that Prout's caravan had been shifted to a position near the marquee and the site of the wooden hut. Nearby a man was working on the telephone pole which carried the wires to Kitson's cottage. Wycliffe went over and found Prout, standing in the shade of his van, watching the man at work.

'I'm having our communications restored, Mr Wycliffe.' Prout being rather self-consciously jovial. 'The phone was previously in the wooden hut and as they are not willing to connect it to a marquee I'm having it in the van.'

'I suppose you need the telephone?'

A quick glance. 'Without it one feels cut off on these digs, and the students like to be able to ring home. I had to go into the village this morning to phone my housekeeper; one doesn't like to disturb Patricia at this time.'

'I expect your housekeeper told you that I called on her on Saturday?'

A frown. 'Yes, she did. I suppose one must get used to having one's every statement checked in these circumstances.'

'I'm afraid so.'

Wycliffe was no longer watching the telephone engineer, but Prout. 'Odd that Kitson's line should have been cut on the night of the fire, don't you think? His wire came nowhere near the hut.'

'These things happen.' Prout met his gaze, blue eyes unflinching.

With a casual parting word Wycliffe made his way across the site. After a month of almost unbroken sunshine the students were as brown as Indians. Christie, wearing shorts and a bra, her auburn hair caught in a pony-tail, was trowelling away soil from a trench, occasionally dropping sherds of pottery into a plastic bowl. She looked up as Wycliffe's shadow fell across the trench.

He said something fatuous: 'Everything under control?'

She smiled. 'Yes, I think so, thanks.'

He returned to his car and drove back to Chapel Street and the Incident Room. A few minutes with Lucy Lane, then it was lunchtime. He went down the Steps. How long was it since he first set eyes on Zion Steps? Nine days; yet the Steps had taken their place in his daily routine. Now the episode was almost over; in a day or two all that had happened in those nine days would be condensed into just another case-file and the people he had met would either be forgotten or they would be remembered as witnesses who would wait their turn to enter the box at any trial there might be . . .

At any trial there might be . . . a trial in which the innocent would suffer more than the guilty.

Borlase was in his favourite position, just behind the glass door of his shop, looking out. Laura Wynn had customers, he could see her standing behind the counter, serenely detached, while they examined her wares. Farther down, Geoffrey Tull was on his doorstep, talking to a pin-stripe suit with a brief-case. In The Vegetarian all the tables seemed to be occupied.

Wycliffe would have found it hard to say what was in his mind. Was he conning the field? Hardly, because he was no longer in doubt of the outcome. Scarcely aware of any intention he ended up at The Buckingham Arms. Business was good but he was immediately signalled from behind the bar. Polmear's heavy features were flushed and covered with little beads of sweat.

'If this weather goes on I shall just melt away and trickle down the nearest drain.'

'Leaving a fortune behind.'

Polmear grinned. 'You should be here for the other nine months of the year.' He called a waitress. 'Here, Judy, lay-up for Mr Wycliffe in the cubby.'

'Are you going to the funeral this afternoon?'

'Of course! She worked here, didn't she? And she was damned good at her job. I miss her. Life isn't all about bed, Mr Wycliffe – only mostly.'

Wycliffe meditated on this observation while he ate a very tasty quiche with a green salad and drank a carafe of Liebfraumilch.

The graveyard was on the slope above the village; the air was filled with the resinous scent of pines. The mourners gathered at the graveside and they could look down on the houses, descending in steps to the creek. Wycliffe was surprised by their number, most of whom were unknown to him. Borlase was much in evidence in a black suit which must have survived many funerals and now was turning green with age. His sisters had not come. Polmear had squeezed him-self into a grey suit which was too small for him and sported a black tie. Wycliffe spotted Dr Hodge and, next to him, Andrew Cleeve, wrapped about with a dark raincoat several inches too short, probably a relic of his schooldays and looking ludicrous in the sunshine.

The words of the burial service, rendered with all the elocutory skill of an auctioneer in a cattle market, still came through as solemn and moving. Celia Dawe's coffin was lowered into the grave and the party was over. People moved away, murmuring platitudes. Wycliffe lingered and so did Andrew Cleeve. The boy looked across at him, tentative, anxious.

Wycliffe walked over to join him. 'A lot of people.'

'Yes, but not many bothered with her when she was alive.'

They walked down the steep slope together. Andrew slipped off his coat and rolled it under his arm. As they reached the gate he said: 'There's something I have to tell you . . . Mother agrees that I should.'

Wycliffe waited.

'We were talking about what you said to mother this morning when Christie mentioned something I hadn't heard before – that Gervaise Prout was in Exeter on Wednesday and that he didn't come back until Thursday lunchtime.'

'He went to the University for a symposium. Didn't you know?'

'No, I didn't, but his car was in its usual place on Wednesday night. He keeps it in the lane to Roger Kitson's cottage, just off the road. When I was coming back from Truro and saw the fire I got out of the car and ran down the lane far enough to see where it was before haring off home to raise the alarm. Prout's car was there then but I thought nothing of it. Of course when I got home I found that one of your chaps had already called the brigade.'

Wycliffe walked back to the Incident Room, feeling lucky; he had not dared to hope for such direct evidence. Andrew's evidence would clinch a possibility which had been in his mind since he had seen the relatively isolated garage where Prout's car was supposed to have spent the night on the forecourt. An hour's trip either way, the job done, and back before anyone was about. Very cool.

Prout had called Cleeve on the telephone from the wooden hut and Wycliffe thought he could make a good guess at providing the other half of the conversation overheard by Carrie Byrne:

'This is Gervaise.'

'Oh? What do you want at this time of night?' Irritated.

'Are you alone?'

'Of course I'm alone.'

'I'm speaking from the wooden hut; Kitson is here, there's something very wrong with him —'

'Is he hurt?' Anxious.

'I don't know, he —'

'Don't be a fool, man, you *must* know —'

'No, I don't; he was talking wildly and he kept asking for someone called Larkin. Now he's gone quiet and I can't rouse him. Do you think I should call a doctor?'

'No, don't do that, I'll be right over . . . Tell him I'm on my way.'

That or something like it would have lured Cleeve out of his house into the open. Even so he had tried to check. Carrie Byrne had heard him dial a number to which there was no reply – no reply because Kitson's telephone had been cut beforehand. And Cleeve had gone back into the library – to fetch his pistol?

In the Incident Room Potter was duty officer.

'Anything from Mr Kersey?'

'No, sir.'

But Kersey came through a few minutes later.

Wycliffe said, 'I think I know something of what you've got for me – that the Welsh family business is now Fecundex Horticultural Products.'

'That's right. They changed their name way back in

'56 after all the notoriety over the murder case. I've just been talking to the managing director – a chap called Bannister. I know him slightly, we use the same local, and he's been with the firm since the flood.'

'Is the family still involved?'

'There's none of 'em left. They had only the one son, and a daughter, the daughter was a couple of years older and she married – guess who?'

'Gervaise Prout?'

'Ah, you knew. Anyway, he was a research student without twopence to his name but it seems to have been a real love match and Papa Welsh approved. He even persuaded Prout to come into the firm.'

'Did it work?'

'Very well, apparently. Prout was soon in charge of sales and he also showed a flair for gadgetry. He patented several bits and pieces for crop spraying, for greenhouse control systems and that sort of thing. His patents made a nice fat profit for the firm.

'The Shotton House affair came three years after Prout had married into the family and it was the beginning of the end of the Welshes. The parents were devastated, and the sister devoted herself first to proving her brother's innocence then, when that failed, she went all out for a reprieve. It seems she spent her time chasing lawyers, gathering what she imagined to be fresh evidence, and God knows what else. She took a room near the prison and visited her brother as often as the authorities allowed – right up to the last.

'Of course, she didn't stand a chance, it was an open and shut case, and it broke her. Eighteen months after the execution she was put in a mental home and spent a year there, then she was sent home, supposed to be cured. Within a fortnight of coming home she went out into the garden, soaked her clothes in paraffin and set herself alight . . . Poor old Prout found her while there was still life in her body.'

213

Wycliffe said: 'And afterwards?'

'Prout stayed with the firm and in 1962 Papa Welsh died; his wife had died three years before. In his will the old man left all his personal estate and a two-thirds' interest in the firm to Prout – the other third went to Bannister.'

'Was that when Prout felt the call back to archaeology?'

'No, it seems he kept up his interest all through but it wasn't until the 'seventies that he began to spend most of his time away from the factory; now he's only there two or three days a month.'

'Did Bannister query your interest in all this?'

'No, he'd read about Cleeve's involvement in the Shotton House business and he seemed to think it natural that we should come asking questions about the Welshes – God knows why.'

'Do you think he'll pass on news of your visit to Prout?'

'I shall be surprised if he doesn't. Is that bad?'

'It doesn't matter at all. In fact, there's something else I want you to see him about, and you can make this official. We need to know whether his firm manufactures or stocks any compounds containing nicotine. If so, we want to know the nature of the preparation, its nicotine content and its availability to anyone with access to the factory. We shall also want a sample for analysis.'

Wycliffe remembered Joan Kersey's back just in time.

'Oh, she's found an osteopath who seems to have a winning way with backs – at least I hope that's what it is.'

Wycliffe's feelings were oddly ambivalent. The three Wise Monkeys must be satisfied at last: Motive, Means and Opportunity, but if it hadn't been for the luckless Celia Dawe . . .

One more gap: he spoke to John Scales on the telephone. 'I want you to send someone to Prout's house at St Germans with a warrant. There's a house-

214

keeper. We want to know whether Prout has a work-shop – any sort of DIY set-up: once upon a time he patented gadgets for horticultural equipment . . . If there is such a place, put seals on it until we can arrange a proper examination by Forensic.'

Four o'clock and the weather seemed even hotter. Wycliffe's shirt stuck to his back and he was conscious of damp patches under his arms; he was tempted to go back to the cottage for a shower and a change of clothes but decided against; he was inventing ways of putting off the inevitable. Perambulating around the room he came to a stop by Lucy Lane's table. 'I'm going up to the site and I want you to come with me.'

She brought his car to the door; they drove up the hill past the entrance to Roscrowgy, and turned down the lane to the dig. They parked behind Prout's Granada, left the car, and walked down the dry rutted track as far as the burned-out hut.

Henry's Field seemed deserted, the caravan, the tents and the marquee were still there but there were no students to be seen, only the hairy, bespectacled Wrighton, a pathetic figure trailing a plastic sack and stooping now and then to pick up a sweet paper or cigarette packet left by litter-bugs. DC Curnow emerged from behind the marquee. 'He's in the caravan, sir; been there since just after one.'

Wycliffe approached Wrighton: 'All on your own?'

The young man looked at Wycliffe through his big round lenses. 'It was too hot to work out of doors so Dr Prout gave them the afternoon off and they've all gone swimming. Dr Prout is in his caravan and doesn't want to be disturbed.' Wrighton seemed to feel excluded from both camps.

Wycliffe knocked on the door of the caravan; no response, so he knocked again. Wrighton had stopped work to watch. Still no answer.

'You wait outside for the moment.' To Lucy Lane.

215

He turned the handle, opened the door, and found himself in the kitchen section. To his left he was vaguely aware of the sleeping compartment but to his right there was a more roomy area resembling the saloon of a yacht: a table, bench seats, shelves and cupboards, all built in. Prout was sitting at the table and open in front of him was a bulky ring-file of the kind used by students.

He raised his eyes from the file in the manner of one who suffers an unwelcome though anticipated intrusion. 'Ah, you've come.'

Prout had changed, he looked older, but more than that it was as though a mask had been discarded and it seemed to Wycliffe that he was seeing the real man for the first time. Gone the defensive bonhomie; gone, too, the high-pitched voice which had seemed always to tremble on the edge of a nervous little laugh. The face of the man at the table was grave, introspective, and closed.

Speaking very slowly, Prout said: 'There is no point in prolonging this; I am very tired. Of course I realized from the start how it might end and I have no doubt that your case against me is a strong one. I shall make no attempt to defend myself in law.' He paused, resting a slender hand on the open pages of his file. 'For the rest, my justification is here. Nothing of this is mine, it is my wife's work, a record of her fight to establish her brother's innocence and of her efforts to secure a reprieve.'

The door of the caravan had remained open and Wycliffe could see Lucy Lane waiting only a few feet away. He should have yielded to protocol and called her in but he wanted to gauge the temper of the situation first.

Prout had gone back to his file; he was turning the pages with deliberation, almost with reverence, as a monk might turn the pages of a holy book. Wycliffe waited. Only when he reached the end of the file did Prout look up:

'See what she wrote on the last page.'

The page was blank except for three words, written in a schoolgirlish hand: 'I failed him.' Melodramatic but, in the context, moving.

Prout's voice became harsh. 'It destroyed our life together and in the end it destroyed her. She spent a year in a nursing-home under treatment . . . They said she was cured but within weeks of her coming back to me . . .'

A long pause, then he went on, 'I made him suffer – though not as much as I would have wished.' He closed the file. 'I've no regrets.'

'And the girl? What about Celia Dawe?'

Prout passed a hand across his face. 'That girl . . .' He shook his head. 'Isn't it always the innocent who suffer most?'

'You believe in your brother-in-law's innocence?'

For the first time Prout showed signs of anger, his pale features flushed. 'Would I have done what I have done otherwise?'

'You could have been wrong, you may still be wrong.'

A faint smile. 'Oh, no! I can't deny moments of weakness – of doubt, but now, thank God, I'm sure.' He turned in his seat to open a little cupboard. 'This is my proof.' He laid an automatic pistol on the table. 'Your experts will tell you that this is the pistol which killed that young policeman at Shotton House, twenty-eight years ago – the crime for which my wife's brother was hanged. It is of the same calibre and make. I took it from Larkin's body on Wednesday night and you will find his prints on it as well as my own.'

Wycliffe reached across for the gun and Prout made no attempt to stop him, then Wycliffe signalled to Lucy Lane to join him. Prout glanced up as she entered but made no comment.

'Gervaise Adam Prout, I am taking you into custody

in connection with the murder of John Larkin, alias
David Cleeve. You are not obliged to say anything but
anything you do say may be taken down in writing and
used in evidence.'

Tuesday July 26th
In the Incident Room Wycliffe was turning the pages
of the ring-file. On the first page was a single word:
'Jonathan'. The file was a detailed record of everything Welsh's sister had done, over a period of four
months, to save her brother. It included correspondence with lawyers, Welsh's own letters from prison,
correspondence with Members of Parliament, with
the Home Office, and even a petition to the Queen.
There were detailed accounts of visits and interviews;
of rebuffs and, more rarely, of encouragements.
There was nothing of sentiment or bitterness in this
stark record which spoke for itself, and Wycliffe was
moved. Only in two places did emotion break through:
a photograph of four young men in battledress was
labelled with their names: John Cross, Jack Shirley,
John Larkin and Jonathan Welsh. The figure of Larkin
was ringed about in pencil so heavily that the point
of the pencil had cut into the print; the other instance
came at the end where the girl had written, 'I failed
him.'

On an adjoining table the contents of Prout's
pockets were laid out: a ring of keys, a few coins, a
handkerchief, a notebook and pencil, and a wallet of
tooled leather. The wallet contained a few pounds
in notes, a couple of credit cards, and four photographs – one protected by a polythene envelope. This
was the girl in the painting, his wife. The other
three had been 'taken off' and enlarged from a group
– Shirley, Cross and Larkin; the prints were faded
and creased.

Had Prout arrived at Roscrowgy in all innocence
and found his quarry by chance? Or had he tracked

the man down and made a plausible approach? That was what the photographs seemed to suggest. At any rate, within eight months of his first visit, on the precise anniversary of the Shotton House killing, Cleeve had received the first of the five playing cards.

The atmosphere in the Incident Room was lethargic, deflated; the process of winding down had started. In a day or two they would be moving out and their precious files would be transferred to headquarters, there to provide the ingredients on which lawyers would go to work. The mass of paper would continue to grow and the personalities and events of the case concerned would be slowly digested into a legal soup.

Wycliffe, brooding, shifted irritably in his chair and muttered: 'Adolescent games!'

'Sir?' Lucy Lane at the next table, preoccupied with filing reports.

'Adolescent games and attitudes. That's what this case has been about – people who have never grown up.'

'I'm sorry; I don't understand.'

'I'm not surprised. But didn't all this start with four young men in the throes of a retarded adolescence? They dressed up their crimes in romantic trappings – all the nonsense of reunions, and badges, and calling themselves by the names of cards – like kids playing cops and robbers, or star wars . . . Then we have the ineffable Prout, married to and deeply in love with a beautiful though fundamentally unbalanced young woman. When she was overwhelmed by the terrible consequences of her brother's wildness and killed herself, he turned real tragedy into melodrama with his absurd vendetta; working out his fantasy at the cost of two more lives – one of them certainly innocent.' He spread his hands in a gesture of helplessness. 'Don't you agree that such people corrupt themselves through a sort of juvenile naïvety?' Then he broke off, slightly embarrassed. 'End of sermon!'

'You believe that the Welsh boy was guilty?'

'He was convicted and sentenced after what seemed to be a fair trial.'

She persisted with diffidence. 'But?'

A vague gesture. 'I've talked to Cleeve and read his books; you've made a study of his work: what impressed you most about the man who wrote them?'

She smiled. 'Write your answer using one side of the paper only; do not write in margins . . . I suppose it was his obsession with evil and with our apparent helplessness to control or contain it.'

Wycliffe nodded. 'Perhaps he was one of the Four Jacks who finally grew up and realized his responsibilities.'

'For responsibilities, read guilt.'

'Perhaps.'

The mills continued to grind. Kersey reported that Fecundex held a small stock of an outmoded pesticide containing 40 per cent nicotine; a sample had been sent for analysis. Scales telephoned to say that a garden shed in Prout's back yard was fitted up with the usual home-handyman's equipment and it had been sealed pending the arrival of the man from Forensic.

The message from Ballistics did not arrive until late afternoon. Wycliffe spoke briefly on the telephone then turned to Lucy Lane. 'It seems the gun Prout handed to us is the one purchased illegally by Welsh a fortnight before the Shotton House killing. They are carrying out further tests but they've no real doubt that it fired the bullets which killed the policeman.'

It was the last day of his official holiday and the Wycliffes decided they would have one more excursion to look back on. They would drive to Pendower, walk along the coast to Portloe, and return to the car by way of Veryan.

'Have we got the map?'

'It's in the car.'

'The binoculars?'

'They're on the window seat.'

'We're ready then . . .'

Instinctively they both turned to look at the telephone, but it did not ring.

THE END

WYCLIFFE AND THE SCHOOLGIRLS
by W. J. Burley

First Debbie Joyce, a cabaret singer, was found strangled. A week later, in the same city, Nurse Elaine Bennett was murdered in the same way and the alarm went out – a psychopathic killer is on the loose.

But Wycliffe was not convinced. Slowly he dug into the past of the murdered girls – a past that took him back to a school holiday and the persecution of one particular child by 'the group'. Was someone working off an old revenge – and how many more women would die because of a cruel schoolgirl joke?

0 552 12805 8

RECOIL
by Jim Thompson

'My favourite crime novelist – often imitated but never duplicated – is Jim Thompson'
Stephen King

After fifteen years in the State Pen for armed robbery and kidnapping, Patrick M Cosgrove needs a job to get parole: but only one man is willing to give him one, the sinister Doctor Roland Luther. Soon Lila, Luther's beautiful ash-blonde wife makes it clear that she comes as part of the package as well. Things couldn't look better for him, apart for one thing. If the jealous Doc finds out that he has laid one finger on Lila, Cosgrove could end up back at the Pen. Or in the morgue . . .

'A blisteringly imaginative crime novelist . . . mesmeric abilities as a story teller . . . he outwrote James M Cain at his most violent, amoral, terse and fast-moving . . . a classic American writer'
Kirkus Reviews

'Dashiell Hammett, Horace McCoy and Raymond Chandler . . . none of these men ever wrote a book within miles of Thompson's'
R V Cassill

'If Raymond Chandler, Dashiell Hammett, and Cornell Woolrich could have joined together in some ungodly union and produced a literary offspring. Jim Thompson would be it'
Washington Post

'Master of the American groin-kick novel'
Vanity Fair

'Read Jim Thompson and take a tour of hell'
The New Republic

0 552 13242 X

A SELECTED LIST OF CRIME TITLES FROM CORGI BOOKS

☐	12792 2	THE COMPLETE STEEL	Catherine Aird	£2.50
☐	12794 9	A LATE PHOENIX	Catherine Aird	£1.95
☐	12804 X	WYCLIFFE AND THE PEA GREEN BOAT	W J Burley	£1.95
☐	12805 8	WYCLIFFE AND THE SCHOOLGIRLS	W J Burley	£1.95
☐	12806 6	WYCLIFFE AND THE SCAPEGOAT	W J Burley	£1.95
☐	13232 2	WYCLIFFE AND THE BEALES	W J Burley	£1.95
☐	11042 6	CONSIDER YOURSELF DEAD	James Hadley Chase	£1.75
☐	11096 5	THE DEAD STAY DUMB	James Hadley Chase	£1.95
☐	09648 2	HAVE A CHANGE OF SCENE	James Hadley Chase	£1.75
☐	11309 3	HAVE THIS ONE ON ME	James Hadley Chase	£1.75
☐	10715 8	I HOLD THE FOUR ACES	James Hadley Chase	£1.95
☐	10765 4	MALLORY	James Hadley Chase	£1.75
☐	11457 X	YOU HAVE YOURSELF A DEAL	James Hadley Chase	£1.95
☐	11308 5	YOU MUST BE KIDDING	James Hadley Chase	£1.95
☐	12021 9	RUMPELSTILTSKIN	Ed McBain	£1.50
☐	13242 X	RECOIL	Jim Thompson	£2.50
